IN HIS
GRANDFATHER'S
SHADOW

RICHARD
STAINER

PROLOGUE

Stay Out Of The Shadows

Not light, not dark; not warm, not cold. The source of all that is begins to penetrate our world and brings with it all that we need to survive in this barren wilderness that we call life. We are on a journey that ends where it begins. It is a cycle of death and rebirth. In the centre of a field at the base of an incline stands a tree, not just any tree, but an English oak. It is spring, the eve of Beltane. New life can be seen everywhere if only you would look. The light touches the branches, kissing them lightly yet enfolding itself firmly around them. The old oak knows its purpose in this life and all that it stands for. Its ancestors have played their part in the history of this land and they are proud.

There is a relationship that cannot be seen: the relationship between the oak standing in the early morning rays, casting a shadow across the land, a shadow that dances in relationship with the sun; a relationship that does not depend upon anyone, just the two of them. Standing at the foot of the oak, I offer a prayer to the creator of all that is, seen and unseen. The oak's shadow moves, blocking the direct light from the crops reaching out for life. The crops know that with a little patience the shadow will move further and they can once again have their own relationship with the sun. I contemplate the relationship

3

that we each have with the sun, and the Son. Why do some people rely on others to say what kind of relationship anyone should have with the Divine? Each relationship is unique, in the same way as it is with all life.

I turn to see a tree that once stood reaching out in the same manner as the oak; it too enjoyed an intimate connection with the light, but is now being choked, the very life that is its by right is slowly being drained from its centre. Appearing to be full of life, everything beginning to wake up with signs of new birth, the ivy wrapped around the old tree gives a much fuller picture; birds are even still nesting and singing from within. But a closer look shows it is a picture of death. The tree is dying from the ivy now entwined around it.

I walk on deep in thought, my mind beginning to return to the story of a young man I once met, one of many lost souls who had forgotten, or never found, their purpose in the world; their true sense of being, the meaning to all life, all that is. I have walked with many, as I did with Josh. His is the story I have decided to write down. My time left in this world is but a few summers, my home now a seventy-foot traditional narrowboat, Harvester. *I took the name from the Biblical letter of James, chapter 3, verse 18: 'And a harvest of righteousness is sown in peace for those who make peace.' In my life, all I ever search for is peace and all I wish to share is peace. People are like trees; they cast shadows in which others decide to walk, or wrap their teaching and ideas around others until they are living in the other person, making them their prisoner.*

The words and ideas that I use in telling Josh's tale are not just my own but come from the many nights I have sat round an open fire with lost souls and other seekers of the Eternal Flame. In what follows, I will endeavour only to be true to how others have experienced this same tale. There is always a personal risk in telling another's story since how we see ourselves and how others perceive us can be like two sides of a coin, opposite yet inseparable.

Believe only that with which you feel comfortable.

CHAPTER 1

The Shadow

"Just a cash flow problem, nothing to worry about." It was the answer he always received. Throwing his keys at what was once his manager's office door, he had turned on his heels not waiting to see if the glass had broken. At twenty-eight, Josh now had no job, no income and no faith. He had been in a serious relationship for six years, but Megan couldn't take his moping around the house all day any longer. And he was in debt, a concept with which Megan could never come to terms.

"Find a job or somewhere else to live," she screamed at him on more than one occasion. This time, he had had enough and walked out of the house.

If Josh were asked which roads he had travelled that day, or even through life, he would never have been able to answer. At that moment, to his way of thinking, he was at sea without a rudder, battling the worst storms he could ever have imagined. Spiritually, he was staggering round in circles in the desert, seeing mirages in every direction. *If only I could find an oasis, a wise man sitting by a pool from which I could drink. If only.*

◆ ◆ ◆

Iona is one of those thin places in this world where lives can be transformed. For some, it is an oasis in the wilderness of life, for others just a tourist stop to be crossed off the list of places to visit while in Scotland. Which it would be for Josh was yet to be determined.

The sun was bright, surprisingly warm for early spring, and well past its summit. He stood on a small, sandy beach as the last ferry took the day trippers back to Mull, restoring a certain, somehow reassuring, stillness to this small piece of heaven. The bag he carried was only half full and blue in colour (or had been when it was new). Borrowed from a friend, it had clearly seen better days – just a light grey now – with a small reminder of its past glory when you opened one of the side pockets. The lodgings were not hard to find, just as the email had said: right off the boat, walk halfway along the path adjacent to the coast and it was on the left. The door, like Josh's bag, had seen better days: once white with a chrome handle, it was now distinctly off-white (nearly yellow) and the handle was worn down to its grey knob. The bell above the door rang to announce his arrival to all.

As soon as he entered the room to which he had been directed, he found it claustrophobic. Leaving his bag next to the small window with its view across to Mull stretching out over a spring lawn, sandy beach and clear blue water, he immediately walked back out, locked the door behind him and headed for some open space in the direction marked 'St Columba's Bay'. The sea air was cool and, as his foot sank for the first time into the boggy earth, he wished he had put his boots on instead of sandals. Sitting with his back to a large stone, Josh looked out across a calm sea. In the distance lay the shore of Ireland, while all around were cairns left by other pilgrims who had visited this sacred place before him. Picking up a stone that fitted snugly into the palm of his hand, he climbed carefully so as not to disturb the others already left there. Placing it on the very top he then sat back down just a short distance away.

"You came."

Josh turned, rather startled, to see who had spoken. The voice was calm and gentle. He saw no one; he was quite alone. He even stood up from his resting place to see better who it might have been, knocking the sand from his jeans in the process. As the clouds began to part, the warm and gentle sun settled upon his face. He continued to stand for a while and still sensed that he was not on his own. Even though he could not see anyone, he could definitely feel a presence. It was as real as the oxygen around him; even though it is not seen by the naked eye it is still there. Josh's lungs would have been crying out in burning pain were it not true, telling every other organ in his whole body of its non-existence.

The words that he'd heard, or thought he had heard, stayed in his mind all through dinner. Josh had come to the table a little after seven, ordered one of the two vegetarian meals on the menu and then waited for well over an hour to be served. He was convinced that they had forgotten about him, sitting quietly in the corner looking out over the bay towards the ferry, which was now safely moored on Mull for the night. It was hard to believe that even at this hour, the sun was still shining brightly outside, forming a golden path that linked the two islands, a path that only a soul could travel. After finishing his meal finally, Josh turned towards the bar across the other side of the inhospitably dark room. He looked over the shoulder of a rather large lady in a faded green dress to see which ales they had on draught. Once more disappointment set in; he could only see what some might call beer, still others lager, but to Josh it would only ever be 'fizzy pop'.

"You came." Josh sat up sharply in bed. Had he dreamed those words or was someone in the room? Trying to find the switch on the bedside lamp he knocked cold tea over the small wooden table. The lamp, too, ended up on the floor after it. The room was evidently empty, but that feeling was there again. Josh found it hard to relax, even harder to go back to sleep, sensing he was not alone. The light stayed on.

The following morning, setting out just after dawn so he could be by himself, a tired Josh climbed to the top of the island. It was only when Josh stood at the very top that he first laid eyes on the figure, standing a short distance from where he had climbed, with his back to Josh, staring down the hill to where lambs were taking it in turns jumping on and off a small mound while their mothers just lay nonchalantly looking on. The man was wearing a pale brown, sandy jumper and dungarees. Josh stood for a few moments before turning to make his way down, saddened that he was not going be able to sit there on his own after all.

"You climbed all this way, while everyone else is still tucked up in bed, just to turn round and climb down again?" The voice was instantly familiar and those first words made him stop in his tracks for a few seconds, before he even dared to turn towards that strange presence, which he felt was with him yet again. The state Josh's mind was in he could have imagined anything, so he began once more to descend. "You came all this way and now you're leaving."

Josh stopped and just gazed ahead at the old Augustinian nunnery; it stood but a hundred paces from the abbey where the community now lived. It was in those old ruins that Josh had found himself the day he came ashore, just standing in what was once the sanctuary, feeling a great need to pray. But he had just turned and walked away. What was the point in praying if no one was going to listen? Anyhow, the large group on a guided pilgrimage of the island made it easier to move on. *Why do tourists and religious misfits dress so freakily?* Josh had thought to himself.

The lone figure was now standing beside a single cairn that could be seen from most of the island. He was no taller than Josh and must have been in his late sixties. His features were just plain, his white beard neatly trimmed and his light grey hair blowing ever so slightly in the morning breeze, but something about his face could only be described as being full of peace.

"What did you say?" Josh asked in a rather nervous voice.

"I just said that you had come all this way and now you were leaving."

"Do I know you?"

As it turned out, the man never did answer Josh's question but at that moment in time and for some strange reason that Josh could not explain, he did not realise or care. Instead, the man responded with a question of his own.

"Have you found what you were looking for; is that why you are leaving?"

"Who said I was looking for anything?" As Josh spoke he found himself looking over the man's shoulder, staring beyond where the man stood, out over the Atlantic. He found himself not wanting to look him in the eyes while his privacy was being invaded. It felt uncomfortable being asked questions to which he did not know the answers. Josh did not lie to him; he just needed to think through how to reply.

"That is why you came here, is it not?" His voice was low, peaceful. For a moment it appeared to Josh that he was hearing the voice in his head alone and not with his ears, but that was a silly thought, so he shook his head and once again looked into the old man's soulful, blue eyes. It was like looking into the ocean, deep, very deep and full of the mystery of life.

For the first time in his entire life Josh found himself being totally open and honest with a complete stranger. But then again, was this man a stranger? Something deep within him, from a place he had never been before, came like a raging torrent with the power of Niagara Falls filling every single cell in his body. He experienced a profound sense that he knew this person intimately and, what was more, that this person knew him.

"I don't really know why I came here, or what I'm looking for." Josh paused, yet again looking out over the Atlantic, searching for words to describe his thoughts and feelings. He couldn't bring himself to look at the man even once more that morning, for his eyes were full of emerging emotions, filling up like pools in a storm.

"You came because I invited you here." Josh could have sworn that his lips hardly moved.

Have you ever been lost within your thoughts, staring into infinity, listening to words being spoken to you? You know they make no sense at all but you understand, at a deeper level within your consciousness, their real meaning. They strike some secret chord that only you understand. If you were to try and explain it to a friend, where would you start? This is exactly how Josh felt.

"Why?" Josh asked without thinking.

"You are lost and in unfathomable pain." He paused and turned round to see what Josh was staring at; or was he being polite, not wanting to add to Josh's embarrassment? The pools had now turned into streams making their way down his face.

"Why here?"

"This is where it all started, many years ago."

"Where what started?" Where were all these emotions coming from Josh thought to himself, emotions that could clearly be heard now within the words that he spoke?

"The answers to all your questions, questions that will continue to engulf you like a darkness surrounding your innermost being, will wrap themselves more and more tightly until you cannot breathe." He ceased talking for a while as if to let the words sink in, like rain on to dry land, before he continued. "The darkness will then become your prison, the light inside you slowly fading before finally going out. I have seen it happen in so many… Too many."

"Tell me," Josh asked as the old man took his arm and led him down the hill, "did you speak to me on the beach yesterday?"

"Yes."

"Then why did you not show yourself then when I spoke to you?"

"I was sitting next to you all the time."

"I did not see you."

"Did you not feel my presence beside you?"

"And last night in my room?"

"Sitting on the chair near the window watching you sleep."

"Why did I not see you?"

The man did not answer that last question, but just shrugged his shoulders as if he didn't know, even though Josh sensed he did. They walked for a while in silence; Josh noticed what looked like gardening gloves tucked in the back pocket of his dungarees. Questions were flying around Josh's head like bees trapped in a honey jar. When he was about to ask one that sat on the tip of his tongue, another got stuck at the bottom of his throat.

On the far side of the island near St Columba's Bay, just a hundred and fifty feet from the shingle beach where Josh had sat the day before, stood a small circular hut. How Josh had failed to see it then he didn't know.

"You can come inside and sit down if you wish." The man's voice was gentle and reassuring, putting Josh at ease.

Once inside, it was plain to see that he lived alone. It was basic but clean: a mattress on the floor, two chairs either side of an old, worn table. His host made tea on a small, open fire, setting two mugs, a milk jug and teapot on the table in front of where Josh was sitting. All of them had the same decorative pattern, a single green spiral.

"How do you find the island?"

Josh wanted to make a wise remark, something a bit witty, like "By ferry", but despite understanding so little of what was happening to him, he did know that this was not the right place for sarcasm. So Josh just said the words many have used before: "It is a special place, a thin place."

"Thin? What do you mean?"

Josh stared out of the small window across the shingle beach, trying to find the right words to use so as not to feel dense.

"Many come to the island and never experience what you are experiencing, and then, on the other hand, many do." The old man spoke softly.

"What happens to them?"

"A small number leave having had their lives transformed and go on to live the life they were meant to." He paused long enough to pour the water into the pot, replace the lid and return the kettle to its stand next to the fire. "Others have their lives changed for just long enough to return home and go back to their busy lives but slowly forget what they experienced here. I have even known pilgrims come here looking for a miracle and receive one, only to reason it away later, as if it never happened."

"What about the others, who never experience anything?" Josh enquired.

The young guest hadn't noticed the two soup bowls sitting next to the fire, which his host now placed gently on the table. "Tomato alright?"

"Please." Josh looked at his watch and was surprised that it was already past lunchtime. When he looked back, soup was spilling out of the bowl and on to the table, but still the old man tried to pour more into it.

"Er, I believe the bowl is full." Josh paused for a short moment. "You can't get any more soup in."

"It is the same with many who come to these shores looking for spiritual nourishment. They are so filled with themselves, their own concerns, needs and desires, that there is no room for anything else. Everyone these days is an expert, read all the right books, knows the right answers; the one thing they don't know is themselves." The old man hesitated, giving enough time to clean the table and to allow

Josh to mull over the events that had just taken place, together with the words that had been spoken, before continuing. "Many people search for the meaning of life only to be able to control it; by doing that they hope to master their own destiny and that of those around them. Controlling others gives people the sense of power. *True* power, though, comes from knowing yourself and controlling your own emotions and mind, and not letting others control them for you."

"I know myself, I control my own mind." Josh was a little too quick to reply.

"That's good to hear. It's the first lesson to master if you want to walk a spiritual path."

"It feels like I have known you forever," Josh had said earlier, while he was clearing the table. The old man hadn't answered straight away, but when the answer came it was in the form of a kind of meditation, an instruction. Josh was to spend the next day alone, searching his past to see if they had met before. It seemed to Josh to be a strange thing to do; he thought that surely he would have remembered if they had met, but then, if that was the case, why had he himself asked the question in the first place?

It was nearly dark when Josh stepped out on to the beach. He had spent the day just staring out over the ocean, going through the day's conversation in his mind, while his host had sat silently watching every move he had made.

"Just be and it will come to you. Trust..."

Josh felt that the old man was about to finish the sentence but instead he just stopped, smiled and closed the door, leaving Josh alone once again.

CHAPTER 2

Time Past

Sleep evaded Josh; there are only so many times you can turn in bed. Eleven thirty and it was still light outside. The curtains could have done with being made of a thicker fabric, Josh thought to himself. He lay there, staring at them for a while, brown with an orange and gold pattern. It made no sense; who would choose to buy such curtains; but then, who in their right mind would conceive the idea to produce something so ugly in the first place? Josh sat up on the side of the bed with his head resting in his hands. He was cross with himself for criticising the motives of people he didn't know. He never used to but that was another life, not this one.

Throwing on a dirty T-shirt that had been screwed up and discarded on the floor of the bathroom the night before, and jeans that had been hanging on the back of the door, he went in search of something to read. He had left the home that he had once shared with Megan in such a rush, almost being pulled out of the house by an invisible force and dragged up the motorway, that he had forgotten to bring anything to read, except an old journal that was still tucked safely into his bag.

The hotel lounge was dimly lit so he fumbled around looking for the switch on a rather unattractive table lamp, the light revealing bookshelves filling the whole wall adjacent to the door.

He whispered to himself, "Why the bloody hell did I not just stay in bed!"

Josh was never one to use those kinds of words normally, but these last few weeks they had started to come out, and worse, they now came as freely as water out of a tap. There before him was book after book on the Gospels, Celtic spirituality, pilgrimage and all matters of faith.

Josh laughed and muttered to himself, "I once read those kinds of books, even studied them, but now it is bloody useless when you have little, or no real, faith at all." That is what his degree was in – theology – for all the good it had done him. The book he eventually chose, knowing he needed something to read else it was going to be a long night, was T.S. Eliot's *Four Quartets*, a familiar book, like an old friend. Old friends can bring back so many memories. He had received his first copy when he was only eight years old, a gift from his grandfather.

Returning with the book to his room, Josh once again lay upon his bed staring at the curtains, remembering the first time he had seen the book that he now held in his hands. The cover was identical; it could have been the very same one. Josh did not even have to turn on the light or open the book to search its pages for one of his favourite lines, a line that always reminded him of his grandfather. He could hear it in his head spoken with his grandfather's voice: sweet; rough, but never stumbling; always word-perfect; always spoken with a warm gentle smile on his face, his eyes bursting with love, full of grace: '*If you came at night like a broken king...*' That night, it was as if his grandfather came to him; he was once like a king to Josh.

The book had always looked small resting in his grandfather's hands, which were big and rough from his manual work at the local factory. He had started there at the age of fourteen, the very same week he left school, following in the footsteps of his father, uncle and brother. He was never asked if he wanted to work there or what he wanted to do with his life; it was just assumed, taken for granted. After all, that is what the working-class men in that part of the city did. One day he picked up his lunch box with his sugar sandwiches and made his own way to school; the next, he joined what looked to him like a massive army walking to the large gates. Behind those gates stood the ominous buildings, which, when he was growing up, he had once believed were on fire. At just three years old, he had ventured out on to the street alone; his older brother had left the gate unlatched, being more interested in the young girls across the road. Little Arthur, for that was his grandfather's name, had come running in, tripping over the uneven doorstep, worn away by the years. It sent him flying head first across the floor, smashing into the kitchen table leg. Through his tears and gasps for air he screamed that the factory was on fire, sending everyone rushing from the house in a panic, knowing that if it were true they would all be in for difficult times ahead. His grandfather told Josh, then not much older than he himself had been, how he remembered standing there, watching them all laughing at the smoke coming out of the large chimneys. Very often his grandfather had stood waiting at the gate for his own father to finish work so he could ride on his shoulders. Now he walked through the large, white gates that towered over him, a passage that had been forbidden to him all his life; little did he know this would now be his life, trapped at such a young age.

The years were not good to Arthur. He lost a son, Josh's uncle, Paul, to a rare blood disorder when he was only five. Paul spent months in hospital, only being allowed home in the few days before he died. Josh's mother was the youngest of three children, the one boy, Paul, who died and two girls, Sheila and then his mother, Mary. Josh remembered being told how his grandfather showed no emotion whatsoever at that moment, the moment when his only son was taken from this world. He just stood for hours looking out of the large bay window in his bedroom, which overlooked his vegetables in the back garden. Mother and son remained motionless on the bed. Josh's grandmother sat cradling Paul, wrapped in his favourite muddy yellow blanket, with tears like raging rivers racing down her cheeks. The sound coming from her mother was like nothing Mary had heard before; the young girl lay nearby in the room she shared with her sister, pulling her pillow tightly over her head with her tiny hands to block out the heart-wrenching sound.

They moved the swing Paul so loved to play on a week to the day after the funeral. It had been Paul's favourite place in the entire garden. "Higher, higher," he would scream through his laughter as his parents took it in turns to push him. In its place, they planted a tree in his memory. On the day he planted it, Arthur looked at his wife with her two daughters gathered around her; she had not stopped weeping for days. He said in a low and broken voice:

"From this day on there will be no more tears; the only weeping will be done by this tree." The willow grew alone.

Josh didn't turn the light on in the bathroom as he got up, not that he was afraid that anyone would see the tears rolling down his face, but because somehow he could feel the darkness wrapping itself around him, safe as if in the arms of a comforting mother. He washed his face in cold water and after a few seconds of searching on the floor for a towel, he returned to the dimly lit room. He read for a while until his eyes became heavy. Then, turning off the bedside light, he once again lay staring up at the ceiling, resting his head on the palm of his hand.

When Josh was a small child, four, maybe five, he would spend his summer holidays playing on a white, sandy beach on the north coast of Cornwall. He loved to play by a small, ever-changing stream, building sandy walls like dams to keep the water in the private pool he had dug for himself. Once the sun had warmed up the water, it was like sitting in a bath. All would go well for a time; Josh was happy in his own little world playing with his imaginary friends. They were the best ones to have; they never argued and they were always there for him, ministering to his every whim. His brother, Paul, named after his uncle, was five years older than Josh, and his sister, Sally, a year younger than Paul; the two of them would go off exploring the shoreline leaving Josh to find his own amusement. Josh was never allowed to accompany them.

"He ruins everything," they would cry at their mother.

Josh never learned. Whenever they returned, without fail they would leap into the pool so carefully constructed, sending the water rushing against the sandy banks. Just like a real dam, once it was breached and the walls began to collapse, no matter how hard Josh worked, and even if his father came to his rescue, they could not stop the warm water from coursing out. The wall could be rebuilt but it was never the same. It is like that with the walls of the mind, as Josh was soon to discover afresh. Memories can lay hidden, dormant, behind our inner walls for years and then just one little tap and the cracks appear, small at first, then larger holes where you remember small events of the past, breaking in until the whole bloody thing comes tumbling down and the past becomes the present.

There was never very much money while Josh grew up; times were hard. His father worked long hours as a farmhand so his children rarely saw him. His mother had a part-time job at the local bakery to help make ends meet. Sometimes she would bring home food that should have been thrown into the bin but to Paul, Sally and Josh it was a feast. When they saw those white bags full of goodies it felt like Christmas. It was very rare for all of them to be sitting at the table waiting for the food to be placed upon it. While his mother worked, Josh spent time with his grandfather. When she dropped him off at his grandfather's house she would tell her father quite categorically that Josh was not to eat sweets or play with the fire. Yet, the door had scarcely closed behind her when Josh was allowed to toast bread on the fire or have a sugar sandwich. Josh's favourite treat was a layer of cheese on top of home-made marmalade on freshly baked bread that grandfather made. The days were short, time passed, hours like minutes. They played in the park. Sometimes, on market day, they would walk the two miles into town to look at the pigs, sheep, chickens and cattle. Josh's grandfather would lift him up so he could rest his feet on one of the pen's bars and look down on the strange-looking creatures. Josh loved the smell of the market above all. Grandfather could not drive so they walked everywhere. They would walk for miles with Josh's little hand resting in complete trust within his grandfather's larger one, pausing to look in the shop windows as they made their way home. Josh would sit on his knee where he would tell the young boy stories about his life and the wider world. Some were true and, Josh now knew, some were not, or certainly not as true as he had believed at the time.

His grandfather was not a religious man in the traditional sense; he had stopped going to church with his wife many years ago. The last time he stood in St Mary's, the church in which they were married, and where all three of his children had been baptised, was the day of Paul's funeral. He stood between the great stone Norman arches, shook the rector's hand, no words passing his lips. Then and only then did his eyes fill with emotion. The rector nodded as if he understood the pain welling up inside him. Father Tom watched on as this proud man walked down the church path with his arms around his wife, comforting her, supporting her, each one trembling in the other's arms.

Those close to Arthur, however, knew that even though he never did return to the church, he was a spiritual man and a man of very deep faith. He shared it with very few, and Josh might never have known how privileged he was to learn from Arthur during those early years of his own spiritual journey.

It was from his grandfather that Josh learnt about the great prophets, Elijah, Elisha and Solomon, and the kings of the Old Testament; he made the story of David and Goliath seem so real. Then there was the story of Columba and the isle of Iona. Several months after Paul's death, Josh's grandmother had taken her children to visit an old aunt in the north, her husband travelling with them as far as Newcastle. He kissed each of his children on the forehead and then wrapped his arms round his wife, not bringing his eyes to meet hers. He hustled them out of the station to where his sister-in-law was waiting.

"See you soon," he said gently.

"Please stay. Come with us, Father," Josh's mother had pleaded.

Mary stood holding her mother's hand while they all watched him make his way back into the station.

"He will come back, won't he?" Mary sobbed.

"Of course, he will. He just needs time alone."

He had caught a train to Oban, missing the last ferry to Mull by minutes, so he spent the night staring across the sea. The next day he walked the whole way to Fionnphort and that night, he sat on a small beach eating the last of the sandwiches that his wife had made for his trip. Wrapping up two apples and a half-empty bottle of water in an old plastic bag with his clothes, he waded out into the water and swam the short distance to the isle of Iona. What happened during his time there he shared with no one, though he had clearly met someone who changed his life.

Josh learnt about Jesus and his teaching from his grandfather; he was the only one who made it seem that he knew Jesus personally, knew him in his heart. When Josh accompanied his mother to church, the preacher spoke as if he was talking about a completely different person called Jesus. The story that Josh knew was of a teacher full of love, kindness and grace. The preacher made him sound scary; if Josh did not carry out the teachings of the church he was going to be punished.

Just before spring, on a cold, icy February morning, after making toast, Josh's grandfather started to teach him about preparing the ground so it was ready for planting. Wrapped up in the warmest clothes Josh owned, the early morning frost still bit into his tender skin. The old man turned the soil with such care as if the very earth could feel the fork penetrating its depths. Most of his teaching, though, went over the young Josh's head. It was only in time that Josh came to realise that his old companion was not just talking about the soil for planting seeds that would grow into plants, but the soil in which a man's faith is planted, how one's spiritual heart needs just as much care and preparation. While Arthur knelt down on one knee to remove a stone tightly wedged between the tines of the fork he told his young grandson an ancient story.

Wherever the master went, many would follow. Just as the sun was reaching its summit he sat with his back to the water, his friends, disciples, sat on the ground around him. Thaddeus stretched out, with his head resting on his hands, eyes gently closed; a cool breeze stirring from the lake made it bearable to lay there. This strange behaviour was in keeping with his character. Those around him never paid Thaddeus much attention; they knew he was listening, taking it all in. He would mull it over for hours, days sometimes, without a word and then, without any notice, start unpacking the teaching with whomever walked beside him. Sometimes, if he didn't quite grasp what the master was saying, he would walk beside him for hours in deep discussion. Thaddeus needed to know the very essence of every word that was spoken. There were times when the master just smiled and patted him on the shoulder before moving away to walk alone for a while. On this occasion, the master began another of his stories:

'During planting season, a young farmer rose early, just before first light, and went out to sow his seed. While scattering his seed, some of it fell on a nearby path where the birds came and ate their breakfast. As the farmer walked on, some of the seed fell on rocky ground where there was not very much soil. Though it started to grow, because the soil was far too shallow the sun came out and burnt the roots. Then seed fell among the thorns, which choked the plants while they tried to grow.'

Josh's grandfather took up the story as his own: "Other seed fell on very good soil, just like this that I have worked upon for years, turning and feeding it, caring about what goes into it. There is never a weed to be found in my soil," he would boast. "The seed that fell on to soil like this bore lots of fruit, fruit that would last. Your heart is the soil the master was referring to. Thaddeus had a good heart." It was evident that his grandfather held that young disciple high in his affections.

Looking at his grandson standing there in the cold, arms straight by his side, the old man smiled. "Always think through very deeply the teaching and stories that you hear; always ask questions no matter how silly they might sound and never take what anyone tells you to be the truth until you having looked it up for yourself." The smile dropped from his face, somehow signalling to Josh the importance of the words he was about to say, as the old man turned back to working on the ground while continuing with the story.

"Never believe or take on someone else's faith, only your own; never, no matter how believable it is. Always question, always think things through and look them up before you allow them into your head, into your heart. Always." The last word was sharp, seemingly hanging in the frozen air. "The mind is like this fork, a tool for turning over the soil of the heart, to prepare it for where the seed of life is planted. Use your own fork; not someone else's."

◆ ◆ ◆

In the late spring of that year they had visited the parks and local woods together. Josh learnt so much from his grandfather about the seasons and their importance. To Josh's young mind, the old man seemed to know everything about the earth; whatever he touched grew and blossomed; there was not one single plant in his garden or in the woods that he did not know, not only the common name but also the Latin. He knew about herbs and how to use them for cooking or healing. On their days out in the woods, the two of them would sit down on the grass, usually under the canopy of an old oak, and enjoy sampling the different kinds of food that they had gathered on their exploration of the area.

◆ ◆ ◆

The summer of eighty-nine was the most enlightening, a time when Josh grew, not only physically and mentally but also spiritually. It started in the spring. It was three weeks since Josh had seen his grandfather, who had been confined to his bed. He had collapsed on the anniversary of Paul's death, the one day in the year he never spoke or ate anything.

Early that morning, Josh's mother called to drop off some sewing, socks she had darned for Josh's grandmother. Arthritis in her fingers now limited the kind of work Mary's mother could do, so Mary would help out whenever she could. As they walked through the gate, Josh looked up to see his grandfather at the bedroom window. Josh smiled and waved. The young boy could not understand why he didn't acknowledge him, why his grandfather was not as happy as he was. Josh could not comprehend why he was not allowed to run up the stairs; he was stopped halfway through the living room. The tone in his grandmother's voice froze his Doc Marten boots to the bare wooden floor just short of the rustic red rug that covered half the room, the rug on which he had spent many afternoons lying with his grandfather, playing with his cars. His favourite one was an old Ford, red in colour, a gift from one of their outings to the market, a treasure he would keep all his life.

"You are not to go upstairs, you hear me."

He turned, stunned. "I want to see Grandfather; he doesn't know I am here," Josh shouted.

"He wants to be left alone."

"But..." As he spoke that one word, her face changed as if she had seen a ghost. It was a split second before she smiled, forced, but a smile nonetheless, and pointed to the

27

back door from which Josh had entered, her voice now more calm and soft.

"Please play outside in the sun for a while," Grandmother said with half a smile.

Josh raised his voice and stamped his feet. "I want to see Grandfather." As he spoke, his mother knelt down in front of him, resting her kind hands on his shoulders, her face was distraught but at the same time trying to smile.

"He wants to be on his own today. Please try and respect his wishes."

Josh stood under the weeping willow with his back leaning on the trunk, hands tucked in his pockets, a favourite cover when he played hide-and-seek. It did not matter how many times he ran to the sanctuary of its shade, his grandfather never found him; he never looked beneath its canopy, at times so obviously avoiding it like the plague.

Josh stared at the upper window, not blinking once; the window was open to let in a warm spring breeze, the only movement the old brown curtains.

Did he see me? Josh wondered to himself, as he raised his small hand to his waist to give a little wave, lowering it again when he had no response.

It was just after they left that his grandfather collapsed. On his way to the hospital the medics heard him talking, whispering. At first they thought he was trying to talk to them, but then they realised that he was hallucinating. Their names were Alan and Henry, not Paul, and they did not understand the relevance of the willow tree, but still he mumbled.

Those three weeks felt like an eternity. His mother was fed up with the same questions over and over again, but always assured Josh that it was nothing he had done.

At last, it was time to visit once more and Josh could not hide his excitement as he skipped up the path; he was about to erupt like a volcano. It had started building just after breakfast, when he was told about coming to visit to his grandparents later that day, and now nothing could contain his impatience.

But everything was changed.

All that summer, Grandfather never left his wheelchair; he sat in the garden when it was not raining, with the same muddy yellow blanket over his legs. His mother, Mary, gave up work; how they as a family survived Josh never knew. He could remember lying in bed listening to his parents arguing about money, the bills piling up. He hated hearing the doors slam, then hearing his mother sitting on the stairs sobbing. He didn't think his father ever hit her, but he was never absolutely sure. Some nights Josh would venture from his room and peep through the banister rails, wanting to creep down and put his small arms around her neck to comfort her, but he was too afraid. So he would sit and cry too, at times biting his finger so as not to make a sound. Sometimes, his brother, Paul, would open his bedroom door just far enough to throw whatever was in his hands in Josh's direction, trying to make the younger boy go back to his room. Sally, if she dared, would lift her sobbing brother up in her arms and carry him back to his bed. Then, lying down beside him, she would stroke his blonde, matted, curly hair and sing lullabies until Josh would finally fall asleep.

At that time, the two of them, mother and son, practically lived at Josh's grandparents' house. His father took on a second job and Josh didn't see him for months. Sally and Paul stayed with their dad; in Josh's eyes they were always his favourites.

Once, during one of his parents' blazing rows, Josh heard his father state quite clearly: "I never wanted any more kids! Two, a pigeon pair, is what we agreed. I don't want three mouths to feed; we can't afford them."

A very distraught Josh told his grandfather then what he had heard, but never about the fights. His grandfather smiled, put his arms around Josh's tiny waist and lifted him up on his knee.

"He didn't mean it; he really loves you." Not even the warm smile that melted across the old man's face, trying to hide the pain, the grief, the memories of a loved but lost child that was ripping his heart in two, could convince Josh.

Over that summer, it was obvious the deep love Josh's mother had for her father and the love he showed in return. On the surface she was happy, but deep within her soul, in that place which is so hard to describe, there was a pain Josh would not know until later in his life; watching a loved one die is the hardest thing in this world you can ever experience. They never went to the market again. Josh would sit beside his grandfather's wheelchair, listening to stories of Jesus or stories that he told only his closest friends. Even though his physical strength was waning, he could still speak with real conviction and a warmth in his voice that brought the stories alive in the young boy's imagination. Some mornings, when the old man was too weak to rise from his bed, Josh would sneak into his room when no one was watching and lay beside his grandfather, who would simply smile and snuggle up closer beside him.

Then, on the twenty-first of September, the autumn equinox, even before Josh had time to clean his teeth, his mother led him to the far end of the garden where they sat down on the damp grass; it had been uncut for weeks. The tears in her eyes told him something was terribly wrong.

"What is it?"

"It's Dad." She paused and looked down the garden to the house where Josh could see his grandmother staring from the small circular landing window, which always reminded him of a cobweb. Until that moment in time it had been his favourite part of any house he had ever seen, yet even years later, Josh would not look consciously or subconsciously in that direction because of what happened that day. He tried to get to his feet but Mary stopped him.

"Father?" The small, bewildered child sat watching his mother, mesmerised by the tears breaking over her eyelashes and making their way down her soft, distorted face.

She took in a deep breath, bit her lip, and then said with a broken voice, "No, not your father." She paused again, as if she did not want to speak aloud the distressing news consuming her within. Then finally, she spoke. "Your grandfather died in his sleep."

Josh's eyes too began to fill like little pools of water. He looked in his grandmother's direction, and then at the ground. "Did Jesus take him to his house to be with Paul?"

Mary bit her lip hard this time, looking towards the willow tree. It must have hurt, as a trickle of blood appeared; she nodded as her body began to tremble.

The day before the funeral Josh crept into his grandfather's room. It never dawned on his young, pure mind that his grandfather's body would still be in there. Grandfather lay in a light oak coffin in his favourite brown suit, his hair combed back. He looked so peaceful, almost as if he was asleep. As Josh leaned over to kiss him, his red eyes noticed his grandfather's tie was not done up as the old man liked it; it was crooked. So, with his little hands he reached out and straightened it. Josh had seen it many times but somehow this was the only time he took any notice of the orange and gold pattern on the brown tie.

The whole family took the death hard, Mary more than most. The following June, Paul, Sally and Josh were joined by Helen; Josh was now no longer the baby of the family. The more his young mind thought about it, the more it felt as if he had not only lost his grandfather, teacher and friend but that his mother had lost interest in him as well. Also, with the further mouth to feed, they hardly ever saw their father and then, on the rare occasion that they did, he was always asleep in his favourite armchair. Their mother returned to work too so that Father did not have to work such long hours but instead of helping, so that they might have more time together, it drove them apart.

"I can support my family!" he would scream when he thought the children were asleep. But how he ever thought that they could sleep through all the shouting and banging, as the door would shut hard behind him as he went outside for a smoke (the one thing he was banned from doing in the house), was beyond them. Josh's bedroom overlooked the small garden; from his window he could see the small red dot in the darkness, like a lighthouse flashing to warn seafarers of the dangers that lay ahead. The red light grew brighter as his father inhaled for that last time, then it hit the ground and was extinguished by the sole of his father's boot as he twisted it. Josh had visions of his father doing this to his own head. As his father made his way up the path, Josh knew that the silence he had been enjoying would be broken again.

Grandmother was not up to looking after herself, let alone anyone else, after her husband died; she seemed to just give up, as if her reason for living had been extinguished as well, which in some senses it had. Josh did not know then, but had grown to understand since, how much she loved her husband; but then, everyone who really knew him loved him, everyone except Josh's father.

Josh's sister Sally, resented being made to look after her young brother whenever her mother was at work and she was not at school. Josh came to believe deep in his soul that his mother always had something better to do around the house than spend time with him. Overnight, it seemed as if Sally took the express route to adulthood well before her time. Brother and sister walked to school most days together. Poor Josh was always the first through the gates, standing alone in an empty playground hoping his friends would arrive before the older children came and questioned him, searching his pockets, confiscating whatever caught their eye. Sally's school was a good twenty-five minutes further on from Josh's; so it was that he stood alone in the morning and was the last child to leave each evening. He would hide so that Mr Dawkins, the head teacher, did not see him. On the one occasion that he caught Josh lurking in the bike shed, the young boy was marched by his ear into the darkness of the corridor outside Mr Dawkins' study, only to overhear the head teacher's part in what was clearly a sharp conversation with Josh's father. It took what seemed like an eternity for Father to pick up after being called to the phone; of course, he was always working some distance from the main farmhouse.

Scared beyond what he would ever admit, Josh sat there looking at the graze on his knee that he had acquired while trying to evade detection. *If only I had not fallen and made the noise of an invading army, I might never have been discovered,* he thought to himself. At that moment, Josh saw through the window that his sister was coming up the street, oblivious of what lay ahead for her and her young charge. Seeing Sally's approach, and without a thought, he leapt to his feet, grabbing his worn-out school bag – which was no more than an old Co-op carrier bag – and ran out of the door, shouting back over his shoulder to the head's secretary, "She is here; see you tomorrow."

Before the startled woman had time to come to her senses, Josh was out of the door and through the school gate thinking how he would stay out of her way till she forgot all about him. Josh kept silent on the way home, never once looking at his sister or daring to tell her what had happened. She never paid much attention to Josh anyway. Sally had her own friends to talk to and they were much more interesting in her eyes.

The first thing Mother and Sally knew about Mr Dawkins' phone call was when Father came home. Josh had felt sick to the pit of his stomach ever since he'd heard the head's part of the conversation, shouting on the phone at how irresponsible his father was. Josh had gone to bed early, before supper; he did not want anything to eat in case he brought it back up. He didn't want the light left on either, which surprised his mother. He tried to convince himself that if he lay still in the dark when his father came home, the old man would open the door, see that he was sick and asleep and leave him alone. Josh had always hated the dark and the sense of fearful anticipation of his father's return made it seem as if, that night especially, the darkness wrapped around him like a coffin. When the shouting finally stopped, his father went outside for a smoke; there was no mistaking the mood he was in as he closed the door behind him.

In the silence that followed, Josh heard his bedroom door open very slightly and then close. The first thing he knew about someone being in his room was their knuckles meeting his face, then stomach, before he was dragged from his bed, hitting the floor hard, and kicked repeatedly in the stomach. Josh could not see in the darkness who was attacking him, nor could he cry out; the wind had been knocked right out of him. Josh could hear feet running up the stairs and then the breath of his assailant warm on his face.

"You little bastard. Tell anyone I am in here and I will do it to you again on the way to school." Then Sally slipped silently under the bed, just moments before their father came breaking through the door; even when the light came on he was not prepared for what followed.

"You poor little bugger, you do look sick," he said as he lifted him back up on to the bed. Josh was pale and shaking, not from any illness, of course, but the terror of the attack that had just taken place and the thought of what was to follow. But instead of chastising him, his father tucked Josh in under the cotton sheets before gently stroking his hair. He sat for a while on the side of the bed, just staring – Josh could feel his eyes tracing every feature on his face – before kissing him as he rose to leave the room. "You little bugger, I thought you were pulling a fast one, pretending to be sick." Josh smiled from the heart, making a wish under his breath while crossing his fingers that his father would come and sit with him more often. It was only much later on in his life Josh found out that his father would indeed sit for hours at the end of his bed and just watch him sleep. That night, just as his father was leaving, Josh called out to him through the pain:

"I don't like the dark." The old man turned and smiled and for the first time Josh saw the deep love he had for him, but also a great sorrow. Josh would only come to know after his father's death how much he hated his work, hated his boss and the very thought of going to work each day. He worked long hours under appalling conditions and was not always paid what he was owed. He would find out how his mother had told her father what was going on, how his grandfather had tried to get alternative work for his son-in-law at the factory but to no avail; and all the time, his father was convinced that grandfather did not approve of him.

On one occasion, in one of their many rows, Josh heard his father proclaim, "Your father loathes the day you met me." He was convinced too that her father had not really asked about the job, however many times she said otherwise.

But this night, the other side of his father smiled at the boy he loved and, just as he pulled the door shut, Josh thought he heard him say, "I will leave the light on till I come to bed." But then, he could have misheard those words as his mind quickly moved back to the danger still lurking beneath him.

Sally slid from under the bed; he could see she had been crying as it made her face look dirty.

"So you have a bad stomach, do you?" As she spoke, she pulled back the bed sheets and thumped her brother between the legs. Before he could scream her hand was over his mouth and through a forced grin and eyes like a demon, she added, "I think that has taken your mind off the pain. Get me into trouble again and I will remove them." With her hand still tight over his mouth, she leant over him as if she was going to kiss him, but instead she pulled a large amount of hair out with her teeth before spitting it back in his face. She too smiled as she left but her eyes were not full of love. As Sally shut the door her hand reached back to the light switch, plunging Josh once again into darkness. He regretted the light switch being so close to the door.

Josh remembered turning over in the blackness of that night in total despair, alone and frightened. He pulled his knees up under him and cried out to the one person he needed the most.

CHAPTER 3

The Voice

Josh was weary no longer, his mind jolted into full consciousness. Sitting up in bed staring into the past, he knew where he had heard that voice. It was many years ago, at a time when he had felt abandoned by those he loved and trusted. The reason it had been eluding him all day could only be because the last time he had heard it, it was not with his ears. The voice had spoken deep within his soul. Yet now he knew for sure that it was the same voice that he had been hearing over the last couple of days.

When Josh reached the beach it was a little after 4 a.m.; it was already light enough to see clearly. He sat for a while some distance from the small cottage where he had spent most of the day before. Its white walls sat nestled among the soft green, rolling hills, deep enough within the contours of the land that he could see neither the door nor windows. He was tempted to march up to the front door and knock until he got an answer. But what answer did he want, or was he looking for? He was confused. While he was walking from his hotel everything had seemed clear. He had heard that voice before. He knew who this man was, if indeed he were a man; he knew what he was going to say and the answer he would receive. But now, the fog was descending fast upon him; visibility was suddenly very poor. When the fog lifted once again, Josh looked across the bay, to his left, and over the sea to Ireland. The early sun was beginning to make its presence felt upon his face. With his eyes he could see for miles; with his mind even his own thoughts were obscured; the fog had engulfed him and nothing was clear. Now he was no longer sure of what he had heard, dreamed, even questioning if yesterday had happened at all. He decided to walk to clear his head.

"It is early and I'm not sure which door to knock on, or if he is up; I'll walk for a bit then call back later to see him," he spoke out loud as he tried to convince himself.

Breakfast was still being served when he returned to his hotel. German tourists were arguing in the main hall, complaining that their window was draughty and that it was unthinkable in this day and age that there was no cable television in their room. "Get a life", Josh felt like saying as he tried to squeeze by. Neither one of the guests made any gesture to move. Three elderly couples were still enjoying their obviously congenial breakfast, one just finishing his coffee, another scraping what looked like blood from his shirt. Josh concluded it must have been jam as no one came rushing to his aid, his wife just shaking her head in disgust. Sitting next to the window looking out to Mull, Josh picked at his toast, leaving more on the tablecloth than his plate, and drank three mugs of black coffee. His thoughts were not on the present moment, but the events of the previous day. Who *was* the old man with whom he had spent most of the day? It dawned on him that he hadn't even asked his name; it never entered his head to do so. The voice, the way he communed with him, was so familiar. He seemed to know him so well, felt so whole, at peace in his company, and so alive. The waitress came and cleared the table; he shook his head at the offer of another coffee. She had worked on the island long enough to recognise a troubled soul in torment. She offered him a gentle smile trying to show she sympathised with him. When the waitress later finished clearing the rest of the tables, she glanced back over to him, nodding to herself before turning off the lights as she closed the door behind her on the way through to the kitchen. Josh was so preoccupied with the darkness within him he didn't even notice the lights going out. In silence, he sat alone.

His mind continued to wander over the last few months. His job was the one thing that defined him, gave him money in his back pocket, a purpose to get up in the morning, status, a place in the world, a reason for being alive. He would dread meeting a friend, or even a stranger, at a party in case they asked what he did for a living just so that he could be put into a category; in Josh's mind (and only in his self-critical state) being unemployed meant trash, a dosser or loser.

"What you doing with yourself these days, Josh?" an old school friend had once asked simply, while resting his hand on his shoulder, as if to steady himself from the too many drinks consumed that night. Seeing the gold dripping from his wrist, catching the rich light, felt like a nail in Josh's coffin. Josh lied, and regretted it the very instant the words passed his lips; he then made an excuse to leave and, without even looking his friend in the face, he left the party altogether, not even telling Megan he was going.

He heard the front door open, then voices coming from the hall. "You're sure he's home?" Josh had recognised

Janet's accent immediately, even though she spoke very softly as if not to draw any attention to her presence in the house.

"His car is in the garage; his keys are on the table." Megan didn't try and hide her entrance into her own home nor, for that matter, her displeasure at being abandoned at a party and having to fall on the mercy of Janet to bring her home.

"See you Monday, and thanks again for saving my life!" Megan called from the porch just before Janet closed her car door.

"Don't mention it." Josh heard the door close. You can always tell the quality of a car by the sound the door makes as it closes, Josh thought.

"They have more money than sense," he whispered, just loud enough for himself to hear.

It took Megan thirty-five minutes before she came up the stairs. Josh listened for her movements, as she used the guest bathroom to shower in; then the door to the spare bedroom closed just loudly enough for him to hear. He thought about going to see her, his heart telling him to, but his pride would not allow him to get out of bed. He closed the private journal that he was reading. He could not remember how many times he had studied its pages since he had lost his job. Tucked neatly away with his childhood belongings, stored in boxes in the loft, he had recently come across the red leather book that he had not read since he was ten. To be honest, he had completely forgotten he even possessed it, let alone read it before. His mother had taken it from him when, she had said, he had become obsessed with it. On rediscovering it, he had sat in the loft with a dim light behind him and opened the front cover. His grandfather had bound it himself and inscribed on the inside front page, written in his own hand, were the words:

*In loving memory of a lost life and tormented soul.
A man's journey through this world, searching for meaning and understanding to life, is not over until he is laid to rest in the ground from which he came. Even then I am not sure his soul will not be tormented still in the grave.*

What Josh read in his grandfather's private journal, the torment his hero's soul must have gone through, only deepened his depression. Once again, they were kindred spirits travelling the dark night of the soul; once again, his grandfather was leading him. Once again he walked in his shadow, as he had done so many years ago. Hand in hand. The sun on his grandfather's face, and his grandfather's shadow upon his.

Sitting alone in Saint Michael's, my eyes are caught by two figures side by side within the stained-glass window: one holding keys, the other a sword. Both knew the torment I am now feeling, both souls knew the darkness that now fills my very being. Losing my son, Paul, is more than I can bear; more than anyone can bear. I truly wish it were me that the Lord had taken. On more than a dozen occasions, I have knelt before the altar and offered myself in the place of my dear, sweet son, but there was never any answer. The priest never had an answer and still Paul died. What is the point to this existence, what is the point to anything? Whatever faith I had is now dead, buried with Paul.

Josh flicked through the many entries that had been made over the months as his grandfather wrote, stopping to read more deeply the ones that resonated with his own emotions.

I was called into the office as soon as work started. Mr Hughes sat behind his light oak, kneehole desk, and I remember when his father and his father before him had sat there. A mouse of a man, not a patch on his father; never once looked in my direction while he spoke. After giving over twenty years of my life to his family, he had the nerve to say he did not think I was what the company needed at this time, they were expanding and needed new blood. He passed me a letter without giving any eye contact. I never opened it 'til I was sitting under the willow tree in the garden. "I knew your granddaddy and your father. They built this company. I was good enough then, good enough to be promoted, trusted to run a department without anyone looking over my shoulder!" My tone and words made him squirm, until he could bear only to look at the bloody wall. I was so mad I threw my locker key at his window. "It's because I took time off to mourn the death of my son, isn't it, you cowardly, little man! Where will I find work now?" Hughes never once looked in my direction. After reading the letter explaining once again their reason for dismissing me, I walked into town and posted it through old Mr Hughes's door. I wrote on the back of the letter, just simply saying thank you for standing by those that put food on his table and clothes on the backs of his children. I was cross to the point I wanted someone else to feel the pain I was feeling. I saw the curtains move

43

as I closed the gate on my way out of his drive. Later that day, around five, there was a knock at the door. Old Mr Hughes stood there with his mouse of a son, who could still not look me in the eye. Old Mr Hughes told me how sorry he was that I had been treated badly and hoped I would return to work in the morning. I sensed in that moment that he saw the pain within my eyes, as he nodded and said that I would receive a proposal in the next couple of days offering me a settlement and pension; if I was not happy with it to call and see him. He bade me good day, turned and walked away down the street.

He was as good as his word and the proposal was more than generous. I found out on the day I visited the solicitor, to sign the documents, that he too had lost a child and that was why he retired early, a secret he had kept very quiet. The child lived only twenty-four hours but had affected both him and his wife very deeply, even to the point Mrs Hughes was institutionalised for a few weeks.

Josh flicked to the last couple of pages that had entries, still leaving more than a third of the book blank. There was one sentence that he knew off by heart that was begging to feed his thoughts.

I will travel north in the morning to an island that haunts my dreams. Maybe there I will find answers, some solace.

This last sentence floated around his mind before he lost consciousness.

Megan had just placed her breakfast dish in the sink and finished her Earl Grey tea, leaving the mug on the granite worktop next to it. Not once did she look across at Josh when he entered the well-appointed kitchen; antique oak, white marble floor, no table, just an island with breakfast bar in the centre. Josh wanted to say how sorry he was but the words would just not leave his mouth; his breath would not have carried a feather one inch past his nose. Silent tears slowly weaved their way down his face. Megan picked up her black briefcase from beside the breakfast bar and headed for her car, still avoiding looking in his direction. It was as if he didn't exist. Josh, on the other hand, watched every step she made as if his life depended upon it, almost holding his breath until the door closed behind her. For a very brief moment, his mind wandered back to the time his parents had argued over money. Then he pondered how, in contrast, he had never heard of his grandparents ever arguing about money, even when his grandfather was made redundant. At times the mind can be very selective in the information it uses in its thought processes.

So it was that another long, drawn-out, lonely day began again. It was two thirty before he closed the red journal. Josh studied every page, every line, in the same way he had done for weeks. It never crossed Josh's mind that what he read bore no resemblance to what Arthur had taught him in his youth; a mind engulfed in darkness rarely sees past its own imprisonment. When Megan's blue Renault Clio turned on to the drive, Josh moved more quickly than he had all day; his dizziness lasted just until he reached the kitchen. He had been sitting in the bay window overlooking the drive since he closed the red book some time earlier, doing nothing but stare into the distance.

CHAPTER 4

Even In The Darkness The Light Will Find You

The service finished a little after 9.30 p.m. in the abbey. Josh headed for the bar before retiring for the night. He wanted to make sure he could sleep; he was hoping a couple of whiskies would do the trick, a trick he had mastered quite well over the last few months. Sitting at the bar, he toyed with the idea of knocking on the strange door before it got too late. But each time he convinced himself it was time to go, he ordered another drink. Darkness was falling fast, filling his heart with fear, by the time he headed for the beach. He stood once again some distance from the small cottage which looked to Josh to be empty, deserted. The moon slipped behind one of the few slow-moving clouds crossing the otherwise clear night sky. When the silver moon returned to her place amongst the orchestra of stars, Josh had his back to the cottage with his head hanging from his shoulders. Hands in his pockets, he walked without thinking, if it is possible for someone to stop thinking, but when the heart stops beating the mind becomes a shadow of its former self. Once back in his room Josh cursed the shower as it ran from cold to ridiculously hot, nearly burning the skin from his back. Sleep evaded him yet again. Long before it was time for breakfast, Josh had decided that he was losing control of rational thought; maybe Megan had been correct when she suggested he was on the verge of a breakdown. Why did he feel so sick inside? He walked to the far side of the island, the rising sun resting gently upon his shoulders, the hands of his grandfather guiding him once more. He would never visit the old hermit (as he now thought of the strange man who had greeted him on his arrival). God – or however he understood the Divine power in that moment – would never come and be with him, even less talk with him; that only happened in the Old Testament or in the lives of the holy saints, not to him; they were just stories, not real life. He felt in his heart that his life with Megan had come to its final breath too, even though he had so much to say to her, confessions of his deepest heart to share with the one with whom he had shared so much of his recent life.

Josh had his lunch – leek and potato soup with a soft bread roll – in a small café not far from the ferry. Tourists came and went all the time so there was nothing unusual, except for one man, mid fifties, salt-and-pepper hair tied neatly in a ponytail, his beard white. It seemed to Josh as if he almost had something of an ancient religious figure about him. He carried two red rucksacks, one obviously full with a large staff attached to it, the other empty. And he had a striking self-confidence as he walked from the ferry. Josh smiled to himself while considering if this saintlike person needed to use such a thing as a ferry to cross the water. His lunch soon gone and the next ferry seemingly bringing nothing of any interest, Josh headed not for the first time to climb Dun I, the highest point on the island, from where he sat through the afternoon staring out to sea. Josh returned to his room a little after seven, showered, then took his table in the restaurant. While looking through the menu he was startled by a soft, angelic voice and the sound of the chair opposite where he sat being drawn away from the table.

"May I join you for dinner? I do dislike eating alone."

Before Josh could answer, the uninvited guest had sat himself down.

"Boy I'm hungry; can you suggest anything from the menu?"

Josh didn't answer, just passed across the menu he was holding.

"Sorry, no specs. Left them in my room." The man smiled at Josh as he laid the menu down. At that moment, the waiter arrived to take their order. Josh ordered the only vegetarian item on the menu and "I will have the same", the visitor added, without a moment's hesitation. "Do you want to share a bottle of wine with me?" Once again Josh was not given time to answer. "Bottle of the house red, please."

"Gawain." He held out his hand. "My mother called me Garth but most people call me Gawain." He looked at Josh with eyes that were inviting him to speak his own name.

"Josh."

"Hi, Joshua."

"Just Josh."

"So, Josh, what brings you to this remote isle?" Gawain's smile was like hot coals sitting on snow as, that night, the hardness of Josh's heart began to melt. For some strange reason Josh could not comprehend, it felt like his very soul was being spoken to. While they talked through dinner and during their stroll to the abbey, and then finishing the evening in the pub, it crossed Josh's mind more than once that he was hallucinating again; that Gawain was just another incarnation of the person he had met on Dun I. Before he realised what was happening, Josh had told Gawain his life story, of grandfather and his journal, Megan, even losing his job. It was the reference to the journal that removed Gawain's warm smile just for a moment so brief that Josh hadn't noticed. It was at the time they called last orders behind the bar that Josh finally told Gawain about losing his faith.

"How can anyone believe these days?"

Gawain leaned back in the buff-coloured chair, which was nearing the end of its life, a life spent witnessing the stories told next to the fire for many years, though the fire was left unlit at this time of year. Logs rested there still, just waiting for a single spark to ignite them into roaring flames, light that would dance around a dark room bringing illumination and warmth, tender to the human skin coming in from the cold, dark air. The fire held within it the promise of a light that could save but also a light that could consume an individual if he or she did not know how to respect its power, its spirit. Gawain knew that he needed to choose his words very carefully; he had listened diligently to the words Josh had spoken that evening, the pain rising from the very depths of his being and threatening to erupt like a volcano at any moment. Such an eruption at this point could destroy the very precious, vulnerable soul he had travelled so far to save. He sensed that the logs that had caught his visual attention represented Josh's faith; it was not by chance that he had been directed to that place by the fire. Gawain decided he needed to rest before he engaged Josh on the subject of his faith, or lack of it. He knew from past experience that one wrong word, a phrase misunderstood, could inject poison into a person's soul. It could be instant or a slow, painful death, the malignant force of words carelessly spoken weaving its way ever more deeply, seeping into the very essence of his being, over a number of years. It would all account to the same thing: death to a beautiful soul. Faith is temperamental; at times emotional, never rational or definite, always struggling for survival in a world that requires certainty, proof and answers. Gawain was tired from his journey; he had travelled at a moment's notice, grabbing two rucksacks, filling one with the unironed clothes that were sitting on his dining table. Breakfast dishes still lay on the draining board as the door latch clicked behind him. During his meditation that morning, his spirit had been stirred, as he heard a familiar voice telling him it was time to fulfil a promise. In his mind's eye, he was sitting on Dun I on Iona, a place where he had sat as young man looking for answers, for peace in his soul and rest from the battering waves of life. A man came and sat beside him, turned after a couple of minutes, without saying a single word, and smiled as tears rolled down their faces. They held hands, not as lovers, but as souls sharing the same pain that only the Divine could heal.

The sun didn't show itself the next day; the wind was bracing, coming from the east. Josh skipped breakfast and was already sitting in the abbey when Gawain arrived. There was a place next to him but Gawain chose to sit opposite. Gawain closed his eyes, sat erect, and placed his hands opened towards the ceiling, resting them upon his legs. Josh watched very closely and even though Gawain's eyes were closed he could feel him watching him.

"Do you want to walk?" Gawain asked softly as they left the abbey.

"Sure, you have a place in mind?"

"Actually, I do." Gawain spoke with a warm face, eyes full of love and deep with wisdom reaching back to the beginning of time, to the first days of creation itself. Josh looked into them for only a few moments, long enough for their souls to converse. Josh felt like diving right into the vastness, the healing presence, the pure energy for which his soul ached. He followed Gawain's steps without another word.

While they walked Josh watched Gawain closely. He could not tell his age; he knew he was entering his autumn years but by how far, he just shrugged his shoulders to himself, as if confirming his own thoughts. Gawain stood five eleven, slightly overweight by twenty pounds or so; he walked lightly upon the ground, gliding with each step.

This can't be real, thought Josh, *I must have lost it completely. I am following a stranger out into the wilderness. God, if you are real, help me, restore my mind. But then you can't; it is beyond your power. You're not real.*

Josh continued to walk, trying not to think, and yet thoughts just kept flooding through the cracks of his will. He felt like he was drowning, gulping for air, for meaning to life. It took twenty-five minutes to reach a large circle of stones set at the edge of a fern-covered valley. One solitary cow watched them descend. Gawain continued to walk around the outside of the circle heading for what must once have been the door. He turned just in time to see Josh about to step across the small stone wall.

"No, Josh, use the door," the tone in Gawain's voice making Josh change direction and continue round in the footsteps of his guide. "Always enter by the door; never take a shortcut, that's how you get lost."

51

Josh had no idea what Gawain was talking about but before he could challenge him, Gawain had sat down with his back to the wall facing the entrance they had both come through. He was motioning for him to sit down beside him, which Josh did.

"What is this place?" Josh enquired.

"An old hermitage."

"Why did we come here?"

"Shh. Before we talk, let's pray awhile."

"Why?" Josh allowed a puzzled frown to form slowly upon his face.

"Contemplate what has brought you here in this time, to this place."

When Gawain had finished his own prayers, they sat for a while in silence. Gawain had assumed the same position as earlier in the abbey; for forty minutes neither one moved. Josh sat watching the cow wander, stop to chew before moving on to a new piece of ground and starting the whole process again. A group of walkers passed by, paused as if to enter but then had a change of heart and moved on without as much as a mutter.

"You started to tell me about your faith last night."

"I did."

"If I can remember your words correctly, you asked me 'how can anyone believe these days?' I think that's what you said."

Josh stared for some time into the sky before his eyes settled upon a lone walker tracing a path some way away. From a distance he would have sworn this was the very person he had met when he first came to the isle. At one point, the walker seemed to pause, lean upon his large staff like an old shepherd and stare in their direction. Was he smiling, even? Josh looked away, only for a moment, but when his eyes tried to trace back to where the old man stood, the hillside was empty, as if he had never been there. Josh smiled to himself.

"You're smiling; your face is radiant." Gawain sat looking at Josh for a while. "This place has this effect on people who are open to its spirit."

"I see things that are not there." Josh's eyes were still tracing the skyline.

"What kind of things, in particular?"

Josh described aloud for the first time the person his mind had imagined when he arrived just a few days before. As he spoke, Gawain could not take his eyes from Josh's radiant face. When Josh finally stopped reliving his story, they both sat for a spell in untainted silence. Neither one heard the birds circling in the air, three doves, pure white.

"Megan is a Catholic." Gawain didn't reply to Josh's comment, which came as if from nowhere. Silence continued.

"I was brought up an Anglican," Josh whispered. Still, Gawain remained silent.

"If God exists, why have a divided church?" Josh looked to see if Gawain was listening but he was sat as if in prayerful meditation again.

"Megan married when she was sixteen, divorced at twenty. We spent time at one point, talking to her priest about getting married in his church. He was not very helpful. We talked about getting married in my parish church; he was not happy about that either." Silence fell again, like a soft blanket covering the interior of the stones. Silence can be infectious, intoxicating. In the stillness, Josh felt his heart begin to stir and he prayed for his once soulmate; was it true that he could feel her pain or was it just that love has a unique pain of its own? A single tear fell to the ground.

"We never went to church together for a long time. Her mother disapproved of my faith, said I did not belong to the true church. Megan could not take the constant criticism, dripping like a broken tap. It either drives you crazy or wears you out. She stopped coming with me. She stopped going anywhere." Josh rambled on while Gawain sat motionless. "We went to a prayer day for the local ecumenical group once. There were Baptists, Methodists, Anglicans and Catholics participating; we had such a great time, meeting and praying together. When we talked about having a communion at the next meeting, the Catholic priest pointed out in a very malevolent tone that the church, I think he meant his, did not consent to, or teach cross-communion, that it was quite clear that such a service should not happen. Therefore, if communion were to take place, he explained, the Catholics would all have to leave early. I looked around the room. It was quite clear he was making the other Catholics very uneasy, even embarrassed. Their eyes were fixed on the floor as if waiting for a hole to appear for them to descend into. That was the last time Megan and I ever prayed together. With her mother and priest always going on at her, she simply lost interest. Last time I went to church was Good Friday."

Josh stopped and looked around him for a while; he stood up and walked to the entrance of the small circle before turning to face Gawain.

"Tell me what the bloody cross is all about, God sending his Son to die, he just stood by and watched it happen! Men and women were spitting on him shouting and cursing him. Payment for sin. Whose? Mine! How come if I was not born then? Payment for whom? God? God paying himself? How does that work? Being paid for love, they say. But the only people I know, well not personally, are prostitutes! Being paid to forgive, to love? It just makes no sense." Josh turned, walked out by the gap in the stones through which they had entered, and, not once looking back as he walked away, shouted into the wind: "Why does God want payment to love us and receive us back, anyway? Bloody callous idea to me and I want nothing to do with it! Original sin is more like bloody slavery, if you ask me. I am looking for a God who will love me for who I am, sins and all."

Gawain finally caught up with Josh again on a small beach at the other side of the island. He stood for a while, watching Josh struggle with his emotions, sitting then standing, sitting again. Several times Josh wiped his eyes. Gawain descended to the beach along a single track. At the edge of the beach he picked up a handful of small, flat round pebbles and joined Josh, who was now skimming his own collection of stones across the water.

"Four is impressive." Gawain didn't look in Josh's direction as he spoke.

"Why are you following me?"

"If it's any help, I stopped believing in original sin and the payment made on the cross a long time ago."

Josh turned to walk along the beach, dropping the remaining stones; his shoulders were stooped. "You have no idea; no one does."

"Try me, maybe I can help."

Josh turned, looking Gawain straight in the face. "Why do you care? Who the bloody hell are you? For all I know, you might not really exist. I could be standing here on this beach talking to myself, but then that is nothing new, is it! I've been talking to myself since I arrived. Good job I am leaving in the morning."

Sometime later, Josh skipped lunch. He watched the ferry come and go for some time, returned to his room, picked up the journal and then sought sanctuary in the abbey for a while, sitting alone to peruse its pages once more while he waited for the rain to stop.

June 3rd

It has been a period of time since Paul was taken from Linda and myself, snatched before he'd even reached his prime. It is a cruel world that we are born into, a world of lies and deceit. Nothing is as it seems. Even our own reflection in the mirror is false, a lie. I once had a deep faith but now I see that was false too, a lie that was fabricated to make us fall in line and do as we were told. I see the church now only as the remains of a once powerful empire, an empire that ruled by physically enslaving its captives. It has now found an even better way of taking over people's lives, by enslaving/controlling them, not by the sword as they once did, but by false doctrine.

June 4th

Since I have been out of work I have spent many hours in the library reading, mainly books on faith at first. I was trying to come to terms with the loss of my dear, sweet son. I have spoken to priests and fellow Christians but still I cannot accept their reasoning, of why a god would let a young, pure soul die. Linda and I have been dedicated Christians all our lives, so why should we be punished in this way? I look at the cross and it makes no sense. How any father could subject his child to suffer on a cross, to watch him being mocked, spat at, beaten, is beyond me. Being a father, I would do anything to protect and save my children. If I could have taken Paul's place I would have done so in the blink of an eye. During the time I have been reading in the library, I have become acquainted with a rather strange young fellow, probably in his late twenties. At first, he would look over in my direction as if he was trying to work out if he knew me at all. After a few weeks, he came and sat in the chair opposite. 'Dear sir, I feel you are distressed and in need of assistance.' At first I was not sure how to answer this strange-looking man, or even how to address him. I sat like a fool just staring into his deep brown, earth-coloured eyes. He wore a dark suit, waistcoat and bow tie. His dress made him stand out, or at least he did to me. When I asked others after he'd left if they knew him, it was as if he never existed. 'Dear sir, you look like a soul that is in torment and looking for answers.' I told this complete stranger all that had happened since Paul had first become ill, right to the point where he came to sit down at my table. He thanked me and said he was terribly sorry and hoped I didn't think that he was rude in any way but he had to leave for an appointment – he assured me it was not anything I had said. As he stood up, he took a calling card out of his waistcoat pocket, placed it on the table and pushed it in my direction. 'Please call tomorrow morning around 10.30 a.m. for tea. I have a library that I think you might find has the answers you are looking for. 10.30, mind. Please don't be late.' With those last few words he was gone, as if he had never been there.

Josh's grandfather's words were becoming very familiar to him, filling his thoughts as if they were his own. The rain now past, upon leaving the abbey he climbed Dun I. By the time he reached the top the sun had finally broken through the clouds. Sitting on his coat and facing west, he continued to read of the pain and torment his grandfather went through. More than once he whispered, "Grandfather, I know the feeling."

June 5th

I arrived at Jonathan's home just before the allotted time, having spent the last twenty minutes leaning against the wall just out of sight of the large bay window on the first floor. The bell echoed through the house announcing my arrival. I was rather taken aback as the door opened like a curtain on Broadway, revealing a rather mature, well-presented butler. With a deftness of touch, he took my jacket, which had kept the chill of the morning from my bones. Even though it was June and all around me were enjoying the warmth of spring, I was still feeling the cold. The butler led me to what I was soon to discover as the library on the first floor. Jonathan rose from his chair, where he had been warming himself by the log fire. I learnt later that the fire was for me, but how did he know I was feeling the cold? Jonathan walked towards me, holding out his hand. Knowing he did not know my name and not wanting him to feel uncomfortable, I held my hand out grasping his own firmly. "Arthur." At the sound of my name he was quite at ease, it seemed, even though he was not the kind of person I supposed to be easily intimidated. Tea arrived only moments after I had been shown to my seat on the opposite side by the fire. Jonathan shared with me his stories of his travels, mainly in the Middle East. He had spent time in Egypt studying Egyptology. Five years at the expense of his late father. Jonathan explained how he grew up going to Sunday Mass each week with his entire family. How he had served at the Lord's Table, even thinking of training for the priesthood. During his time studying for a PhD in archaeology at Oxford, he never missed Mass, or so he said. But after his time in Egypt and the esoteric writings that he had studied, he no longer had any faith, in a living god; just the evolution of humankind.

I sat for a few moments looking around the well-lit room. I was surprised that there were so many statues, some even as tall as my own height at over six foot. Two hours soon passed and lunch was brought to the library and placed on a small table in the corner near the bay window overlooking the street. I was alarmed to realise that the place I had stood while hesitating to approach the house hours earlier was fully in sight. Had Jonathan seen my reluctance, I wonder?

I left just after 2 p.m. with the offer that I could call at any time to use the library. As the door closed behind me, that same reluctance took hold of me once more and I was not sure if I would ever take up the offer to return.

June 7th

I spent my time in the garden today. There was lots to do. I have neglected it for too long. As I tended to the vegetable patch, my thoughts were of my meeting with Jonathan. The beans had come loose from the wall and had to be reattached. I hoed through the entire vegetable area. I tied the roses, then rested beneath the willow tree. I sat in its shade for a while sheltering from the midday sun. All the time, over and over, I pondered that visit and all that it held. It was well before dinner when I decided never to return to the library, resolving not to take Jonathan up on his offer. The story he shared about Horus had deeply disturbed me, as if stalking my innermost thoughts as would a skilled hunter. I had little faith before I met that man and now I am questioning even that. I looked up the word 'esoteric': that which is known only by a few.

June 8th

The question that keeps bouncing round my mind is: if I have placed my trust in a story that is not real but just a myth, where does that leave me? What was the point of Paul's short life? I spent the day sitting under the willow tree, going over it in my mind. There were moments when it felt like Paul was sitting there holding my hand. Linda kept coming to the window to see what I was doing. At one point I thought I saw the local priest standing next to Linda staring at me too. The question I keep asking myself is WHAT IS THE POINT? I so wish I were no longer here, that I had never been born.

June 15th

For the last few days, I have sat in the comfort and protection of the willow; determined not to study/read/explore faith any more. But then I found myself standing on the other side of the street from Jonathan's house looking up at the bay window. How long I had stood there before he saw me I have no idea. My heart nearly stopped when he opened the door, walked down the steps and crossed the street. He put his arm around my waist, and led me in. We sat for a while in his library once more. Silence filled the room as we took tea together. It was evident that he had been expecting my return. Books had been placed on a desk near the window. An empty notebook sat together with a black fountain pen awaiting me to take them up. I was startled by Jonathan's soft voice as his words cut through the silence, like a hot knife through wax. 'The path of knowledge is a disturbing one, while at times enticing. For some it is a path that they cannot help but walk, every atom in their body or universe will drive them forward to seek knowledge of the truth that will lead them into the light. Others are happy to sit in the darkness of their own ignorance.' Jonathan insisted that I sat at the desk and study the books placed upon it. The books were antiques and obviously rare. Collected from the four corners of the world, some in a language I could not read, but I was assured that the handwritten accompanying notebook was a true translation of the original text, translated by Jonathan's late father. It was clear that Jonathan shared his father's knowledge of the ancient tongue. 'Unless you study for yourself and work out the answers that your heart desires you will never be free; you will never grow to your full potential.' I explained that I already had a journal that I was keeping and, for some reason that I still don't know, I took it from my inside pocket and passed it to him. He opened it and flicked through it, without reading it in detail – I think he recognised it from our

61

first meeting in the library. He placed it on the desk and removed the new notebook. I am disturbed still by the fact that he spoke no words, no comment at all; he just returned to his seat by the fire. He retrieved a book from the table beside him that he had been reading; reopening it at his page marker he sat in silence and spoke not a single word until it was time for me to leave. As I turned into my road this evening, I was a little troubled to see the local doctor closing the door to my house behind him and slipping quickly into his car. This is not the first time I have seen him sneak from my house.

Josh placed the journal on the ground, closing his eyes as he rested for a moment. Gawain parked himself down beside him without speaking. Josh still had his eyes closed and for a second it crossed Gawain's mind that he was asleep, but his body was too tense for that. When Josh opened his eyes, he snatched his journal out of Gawain's hands.

"What, what do you think you are doing?" Josh launched himself on to his feet as he spoke.

"I knew your grandfather, you know."

"Sorry?" replied a startled Josh.

"I met him here, many years ago."

"On Iona?"

"Right here, in this very spot."

"When?" Josh turned his whole body to face Gawain, the tone in his voice scarcely concealing a certain belligerence rising within him. Gawain was calm, composed, as if he was waiting for an onslaught; his voice was full of compassion.

"You lie! You never met him. I tell you what is troubling me, you read a few words in a book and now you are going to play games with my head." Josh walked towards the path he had climbed to get there.

"Please hear me out, Josh."

"No, you are not real."

"I was young, disturbed about my faith. I had made promises I could not keep; my soul, like yours, was breaking, dying. I wanted to die. I sat here and your grandfather came and sat with me. He held my hand and wept with me; he then took me to the hermitage where we sat this morning to talk."

"He never mentions you." Josh waved the journal at him.

"It was after he wrote that."

"He only came here once."

"Sorry, you are mistaken. He came many times."

"No, you're wrong. Why would he? Like me he lost his faith and any interest in these kind of places." Josh flicked through the pages of the journal to near the end, and read aloud.

July 30th

I came to this place and found no peace. How can there be? God does not exist; if he did then he would take away my pain. Paul would not have died. A priest once said to me my son died because of a sin I committed. My soul died when Paul died. The church is a joke; it does not care about people; the only thing they care for is their beloved institution. I will never return to this place or any like it, nor will I darken the doors of a church again.

Josh looked at Gawain, the older man's face distraught, full to overflowing with pain from the centre of his being. There were no tears, just sheer pain. His face showed the complete opposite side to the morning in the hermitage; the radiance had gone, darkness had arrived. There is nothing worse than seeing a soul in torment.

"I met him a long time after he wrote that; he had changed. He told me he spent a lot of time with you. Does your experience, your memories of your grandfather reflect what is written between those pages? He changed when he left these shores."

"He never went to church. That part is true."

"He believed, and in a way that is hard for some to understand, he still belonged to the church."

"You don't know what you are saying." Joshed waved the journal again. "He had no faith; *no* faith."

"You were never meant to see that journal. Arthur, your grandfather, wanted me to collect it from him before he died."

"You lie! Why would he want you to have it? He left it for me, ME!" The last word Josh shouted loudly, not caring who heard him.

"Believe me; he loved you more than most, which is why he would never have wanted you to read it."

"No, he left it for me. Why would he not want me to read about his life?"

"Arthur called that the 'dark journal'; he gave it to me to look after. I held it for years but in his last few months he asked to read it one more time before he died. I visited him and left it, promising to return at the end of the month. He died before I could fulfil that promise."

"You failed him."

"No. I did call, days before he died, but your grandmother would not let me in to see him."

"Why not, if you were such a good friend?"

"She'd never met me; she didn't know I existed. Arthur never mentioned my name to anyone."

"Why?"

"Different world."

"'Different world'? What does that bloody mean, 'different world'?"

"Josh, I cannot tell you. It's nothing I can explain; you have to experience it for yourself."

"The journal was left for me by my grandfather; he wanted me to read it, to share his pain. That is obvious."

"No, Josh." Gawain's voice was almost a whisper. "Your grandfather would never want that for you; that was his pain and his alone and he learnt how to let go of it, he found peace in his heart."

"You called this the dark journal. What did you mean by that?"

"Arthur wrote two."

Josh first looked at Gawain searching for signs that he was lying, then he allowed his eyes to float out to sea – for a moment he thought he saw a whale – he exhaled slowly. His mind returned to the weeping willow in his grandfather's garden; through the branches he could see his hero holding the journal in his hands; he was smiling, gently shaking his head.

"Where is the other one?"

"Safe."

"Where, please? I need to read it."

"I am not sure Arthur would agree to that."

Josh finally sat down, remaining motionless for a time, and then asked simply, "Why?"

Gawain sat beside him. "Your grandfather was a great man, he was special. He only saw good in other people; he turned many lives around, he had a gift that allowed him to take away others' pain." Gawain looked out to sea. "He could heal, you know, heal another's broken soul. You only knew him in his later years."

"I need to read it. I need to know, please."

Gawain shook his head gently. "Your grandfather gave me a bit of advice when we first met: never live or follow another person's life; live only the one you were given. Find your own way; make your own choices in life. Stay out of the shadows of others."

"Please." Josh's voice began to waver.

"Spend some time with me, let me walk with you, as your grandfather walked with me. When you are ready, I might, *might* let you hold it for a brief moment."

CHAPTER 5

If You Came This Way

Megan sat in traffic, exhausted from the last couple of days. Josh had not returned home for two nights running, his mobile was still sitting on the kitchen table, and none of his friends had heard a word from him in weeks.

One of his closest friends, Alex, had said in a very concerned tone when she called him: "He has not answered any of my texts or phone calls and I have left many messages. Lost count of the emails I've sent from the office and home – I've heard nothing from him. I called by the other week; I'm sure I saw someone move from the window when I pulled on to the drive."

"He never said you'd called."

"I didn't see him. I rang the bell, knocked on the door, even called through your letter box."

"When was that?"

"Last Monday, around 11 a.m., could have been 11.20 but no later."

"He *was* here."

"I didn't see him."

"Maybe he was in the garden; he sometimes sits under the willow tree he planted when we moved here; more so since he lost his job."

"No, I looked round the back and under the tree, even looked through the windows."

Megan did not respond; although Alex could not see her face he knew from the other end of the phone that she had started to cry.

"What's going on, Megan?"

"Don't know. I really don't know. Since he lost his job, he's been clearing out his old belongings, looking for anything that will sell on eBay."

"Why, are you short of funds? Can I help?"

"No, we are OK. I earn enough and more to pay the bills, but thank you anyway. But Josh thinks he must contribute to the pot. He even sold his Spiderman collection the other week."

"All his comics? They took him years to collect; didn't he start collecting them with his grandfather? He gave him his first copy, taught him how to look after them; it was him who started him off putting them in separate plastic bags. I can't believe he'd sell them."

"That is the only one he kept. The first one."

"Why now?"

"Sorry?"

"Why is he selling his stuff now? You have joked for years that he should be selling all that 'rubbish', as you called it, so why now?"

"I told him that he needed to start earning some money, get a job, or we would eventually have to get out of the house. I was trying to get his life focused again, instead of him moping around the house. It wasn't about selling stuff."

"What did he say to that?"

"Nothing. I think he only heard 'get out of the house', because apparently he said to one of the neighbours that I was thinking of throwing him out."

Alex took a few moments to respond. "Have you checked to see if he is at the abbey?"

Josh had for many years visited a Benedictine abbey nestling deep in the Derbyshire countryside. He had become friends with some of the monks many years ago, in fact, just after Alex was himself ordained to the priesthood in the Church of England. When Alex had suggested that Josh join him there for a short stay, he had jumped at the idea. Josh remembered his grandfather talking about the same order that he visited around the time his son became ill.

"I called, but all I get is the damn answerphone and they never return my calls."

"Why not just drive over there, it's only a little over ninety minutes from where you are."

"I will. Yes. I am going to go right now." Megan could no longer hide the emotional state she was in as her voice began to break. With a sob she said, "Sorry, I have to go."

"Call me. When you get there." There was silence on the other end of the phone. "Megan," Alex said quite sternly.

"Yes."

"You promise?" The only reply he heard was the phone line click dead.

◆ ◆ ◆

Megan turned on to the long, twisting drive, parking some distance from the main house. She sat for a few moments, simply staring at the old house that was once a farm and had been extended over the years, with the new refectory and behind the main building, an oak oratory. She sat contemplating what she would say to Josh once inside the house. In her imagination she slapped him, shouted at him and threw her arms around him. Megan's heart missed a beat when Dom Luke tapped on the window. She looked out at the old monk, maybe late sixties, or even early seventies or more, his hair cut close to his head, so close you could see his scalp, wearing jeans that didn't fit and a shirt he had obviously worn for many years. Megan counted two buttons that were missing; the cuffs were scuffed, as was the collar.

"Are you in trouble, my dear?" he enquired, showing that a good number of teeth were in need of some serious attention.

"I'm OK, thank you," she said, trying not to look at his teeth.

"I have been into town; we get Wednesday afternoon free. You passed me ten minutes ago on the road. Are you coming in?"

Megan explained to Dom Luke, as they slowly made their way to the main entrance, what had occurred over the last few months. She had not intended to mention any of her business to anyone but, like a broken tap, for some reason she could not stop herself. By the time they sat down in the refectory and Dom Luke had made a pot of tea he knew everything that had happened.

"I have not seen him for months; the last time he was here, he was with…" The old monk paused as he tried to recall the priest's name who had first introduced Josh to the community. "Father Alex," he said softly, with a smile that showed he was pleased with himself for remembering the name.

"I am not sure if this is any use to you, but he did write to the abbot asking if anyone remembered his grandfather and whether he could talk to them about him. One or two of us remember him, but it was so long ago we could not help him. He stopped coming, you see, just at the time I entered the community. The last time, if I remember rightly, was when a previous brother, on the night before his life profession, packed his bags and without any explanation to the abbot – or that is what we were led to believe at the time – just walked out of the door. Josh's grandfather left the same day, just a few hours after. The two had been close for a number of years."

Megan could sense that Dom Luke knew a different truth of what had happened but when she pressed him he paused, smiled and then carried on with what he was going to say.

"Nice man, that abbot was. He was the abbot when I came, the brother who just got up and left joined about the same time if I remember rightly." Dom Luke shook his head as he tried to remember yet another name. Tapping his head with his knuckles said, "The name is in here somewhere. Look, why don't you stay for prayers and by then I will have had the chance to speak with the other brothers and the abbot to see if they can shed any light on where Josh might be." Her mouth was full of tea and without giving Megan time to respond, or swallow even, when she opened her mouth all she saw was the tail of his black cassock as the door closed behind him. Megan sat alone with her thoughts as the time dragged by. Twice she ventured out into the main part of the house, which seemed deserted. Maybe they are watching me through some hidden camera, she thought. She smiled to herself for being silly, paranoid, and returned to the refectory.

She made herself a mug of coffee, found some biscuits stashed behind a pile of tea towels that she had used when she had first washed up her intended mug, not quite trusting the brothers' hygiene standards. Must be the brothers' late night snack, she laughed to herself.

Megan declined the offer to stay the night at the abbey until she came to realise that, in her haste to leave the house, she had left her purse on the dining room table. The fuel light came on as soon as she turned the key in the ignition. Moments later, Dom Luke opened the rather newly stained oak door with a warm, touching smile and a cup of hot chocolate, which Megan tried to decline. She sat on the single bed in a whitewashed room. Directly above the headboard hung a beautiful, simple wooden cross; in front of the small window to her left was a small desk with an icon of St Scholastica, the twin sister of St Benedict, resting upon it. Megan began ever so slightly to shake as tears made their way down her pale cheeks. The first hung on her chin, paused for a moment as it was joined by another and together they made a leap of faith into her steaming chocolate. Her thoughts were on the last words of a conversation she had overheard from Dom Luke on the phone moments before he replaced the receiver.

"You really cannot help her?" Just those words.

Megan stepped ever so lightly into the kitchen across the corridor, found three light green hand towels and returned to her room. On her knees as she mopped up the chocolate she had dropped, she wept. And she didn't care who heard.

When she awoke the next morning she remembered her dream. White sandy beaches, blue sea. Who can say how but she now knew deep within her very being where her soulmate would be – on the small, Scottish island of Iona. Josh had mentioned the name so many times. It was so obvious, so clear to her now. Before she left, she thanked Dom Luke and promised to put a cheque in the post as soon as she returned home.

The blue colour scheme of the embarkation lounge reflected her mood. The mid-morning sun was beating through the main window demonstrating quite loudly that summer had arrived. A party of Germans sat down in front of her; to the left a group of loud Americans talked about the state they came from. From where she sat, she watched the arrival of the ferry that was to take her to Craignure on the isle of Mull, from where she would catch the service bus to Fionnphort. It seemed to take forever for the passengers to disembark before the attendant would open the door for them to board. She wished she hadn't sat over the far side of the waiting room, either; she may have been first in but now she stood last but one in line. Why was everyone so happy, so full of life, while her spirit lay in shreds? Why were their hearts so full of wine, while hers was so empty, drained of life?

The sun was warm on her face through the smeared glass as the service bus wound its way down a single-track road to yet another ferry. Two trains, a ten-minute walk across Glasgow, two ferries and a bus ride; Megan had never felt so alone without Josh in her life. She felt there was no reason for breathing and at times even that seemed a struggle with her chest feeling so compacted. She hadn't eaten anything for perhaps thirty-six hours, but that wasn't the reason she was feeling sick. What would she say to him? How would he react? Would he shout, scream, turn and walk away or even run? She hoped he would walk gently up to her, place his warm, soft hands on her cheeks while their breath became one, their lips joining softly as they came together, the uniting of two halves of the same soul. As the bus turned the last bend in the road, her eyes came to rest upon her final destination, the place where she would find the answers to her heart, her journey's end. Her eyes filled. The bus stopped at the edge of the small village and a young girl in her early twenties got off, her arms full of presents. An old man, maybe her father, greeted her with a single kiss on her cheek and, taking the presents from her arms, he guided her up some concrete steps to an open door where, Megan could see through the living room window, an elderly woman was waiting. The bus pulled away before Megan could see the reception the young girl received inside.

Josh was nowhere to be seen. She checked the abbey, the MacLeod Centre. Her heart sank, her stomach twisted, her lungs suffocated. Out of desperation she tried the hotel on the seafront. Josh had been staying there but they had left that morning to catch the 3.15 ferry to Oban. The young man behind the counter seemed reluctant to give out any more information and was looking uncomfortable with what he had already divulged.

"Who was he with?" she asked.

"An older gentleman. Sorry, I cannot tell you his name."

So she had been right. He was here, but she was too late. At this hour, Megan had no choice but to stay on the island for the night since the last ferry had sailed for the evening. She asked if the room Josh had stayed in was available; the young man smiled, nodded his head and passed her the key to room 12. Dropping the small bag that she had grabbed to stuff clothes in for a few days as she left her home that morning, she too dropped, landing on the small bed and looking across the room at the strange-looking curtains.

CHAPTER 6

A New Chapter

Leaving the ferry behind them, Gawain drove to a small village on the Scottish border, down the main street with its houses dotted between trees of oak, ash and holly. At the end of the road they turned on to a rather narrow lane, which twisted and turned into an even narrower track. What looked to be a two or three-bedroom cottage stood at the end, yet was completely invisible from the road. Gawain pulled up in front of the main door; Josh presumed nothing, waiting to be invited in.

"Staying in the car?" Gawain enquired, with a warm smile.

As he walked into the cottage, Josh noticed that even though the furnishings were dated, it looked normal; not what he had been expecting somehow as they approached. The stairs creaked at every step as Gawain carried Josh's bag to the room he was to use. It was a large, light room, a double bed sitting in the middle. Next to the window, which overlooked a small wooded area, sat a small writing table with paper and pen, calling out to be used.

"The bathroom is down the hall – there is only one so we need to share."

"Fine. Thank you." Gawain smiled, nodded and closed the door behind him as he left, knowing that he had just been thanked for more than simply a comfortable room. Josh sat for a while looking out of the window. His thoughts were of his lost soulmate.

"People come and people go," he whispered as he stretched out on the bed. *Quilt and not blankets,* he thought, *Megan would approve.* He smiled as he closed his eyes.

Josh stirred at the sound of a tap on the door and Gawain's soft voice telling him that he had twenty minutes before dinner was going to be on the table. He remembered something about roast vegetables from the garden. Yawning, he swung his legs over the side of the bed. The shower soon refreshed him and he followed his nose to the kitchen, where he found Gawain sitting just outside on the porch, drinking a glass of deep red wine.

"Come, join me." Gawain poured wine in the spare glass on the table next to him. "Thought we might eat out here tonight. I know it is a bit chilly, might rain even, but it is good to be outside in creation, don't you think?"

Josh could not recall a time he had enjoyed just a plate of roasted vegetables more in his life.

"Do you want to call her? You can use my phone."

"Who?"

Gawain smiled gently and hardly parted his lips as he softly spoke her name. "Megan."

"Why do you ask?" Thinking, slowly swilling his wine round his glass, Josh managed to check himself just in time to catch a small tear about to make a run for it from his left eye. He let out a deep sigh. "She does not want me back."

"You don't know that."

"What's the point?"

"Josh, if you love her then there is always a point; just take the phone upstairs to your room and call. Please."

Josh helped clear the table and dry the dishes before he picked up the phone and walked slowly up the stairs. He stood looking out of the window while he dialled several times but each time hanging up before it could ring. Josh's heart raced as he finally dared to let it ring. The sound of her voice brought colour to his face – what was he going to say? Sorry, hi, it's Josh, how have you been? He didn't need to worry. *"Hello, you have reached the home of Megan and Josh. I am sorry we are not here at the moment but please leave a message and we will get back to you as soon as we can; bye for now."* The three pips came and went, but still Josh listened to the silence without speaking.

He then tried her mobile. That didn't ring at all but just went straight to her voicemail.

He stayed in his room for the remainder of the night. He could hear Gawain locking the doors around ten, then the slightest knock on the door. When Josh opened it, Gawain's hand came in; Josh took the cup of tea offered and the door closed again.

Josh's room faced east. Megan never closed the curtains at home and always insisted that the window stayed open. So it was that Josh went to sleep looking out at the stars wondering where his lost soul friend was, who she was with, wondering whether she still loved him. He woke early with the warm kiss of the sun on his face. Looking out of the window Josh could just make out the silhouette of Gawain sitting among the trees, just as he had that day in the hermitage. *Was it the morning sun or was Gawain radiating his own light?* Josh had thought to himself. He watched again now for a while before taking a shower.

"May I read the journal?" Josh asked while he was helping clear the breakfast table.

"No, not yet."

"What harm will it do?"

"There are lessons that you need to learn for yourself before you read what your grandfather wrote."

"I would like to be the judge of that."

"So be it. I will swap you one journal for the other."

"OK, I will fetch mine." Josh was already heading up to his room to retrieve the red leather-bound journal as he spoke. On his return, Gawain was sitting at the kitchen table; in front of him lay a white journal the same size as the one in Josh's hands.

"Josh, please sit." Gawain motioned with his hand to a chair opposite him, his face serious, focused yet calm. Josh sat with his eyes fixed on the white journal. "Josh, look at me," said Gawain, as Josh complied unhesitatingly. The two men gazed into each other's eyes. Gawain looked deep into Josh's soul. "If we swap, there is no swapping back. It is forever; you will never be able to read those words written by your grandfather again."

"No."

"If you want to read these words, you must let go of the past."

"No, my grandfather left these for me," asserted Josh once more, holding the red journal to him.

"I told you. I was to fetch them back before Arthur died; you were never meant to read them; no one was."

"I can't swap. I need what is written within these pages. I get my strength from within them. I feel him speaking to me, guiding me. No, I will never let it go. Please just let me read the other one. I will not move, I promise."

"Sorry, that wouldn't be right."

"I *could* just take it."

"You mean steal."

"Don't be dramatic; I only want to read it."

Gawain rose from his chair leaving the journal where it rested, gazing out of the window, his back to Josh. "You only see a small glimpse of who your grandfather was. You're allowing your mind to become obsessed with what you have read and the personal situation you are experiencing in your life at this time."

Josh quietly lifted the white journal, being careful to make no sound as he stretched across the table. Gawain didn't move as he said clearly:

"You dishonour your grandfather by taking what is not yours."

"He was my grandfather, not yours."

"Maybe so, but you're not the only person in the entire universe who knew him, who cared for him, or he you."

Josh sat with the white journal resting upon his lap, heart racing, his mind focused only on what lay within its cover: answers to his burning questions, medicine for the pain that was tormenting his soul. He didn't respond to Gawain's last assertion.

"If Arthur were here standing in front of you, ask yourself what would he be thinking, what *he* would say about your behaviour."

Josh remembered one time when he was six, reading a personal letter, or trying to – in truth, he did not understand most of the words or the contents. But he could remember his grandfather coming into the room and reprimanding him. Just as it was being pulled from his little hands he could now remember seeing the words, *'Yours in the spirit, Gawain'*.

"You never read what is not yours; you never touch what does not belong to you, no matter how much you desire to, or believe your life depends on it." His grandfather had spoken so very sternly to the young Josh.

Silently, Josh now got up and left the room by the side door into the garden, the bright sun in his eyes making him squint. Gawain retrieved the white journal from where Josh had left it back on the table and returned it to its resting place in the sanctuary of his own room. Gawain did not see Josh for the remainder of the day, nor did he look for him. Gawain knew that his charge needed time alone, but he could also feel that he was not far from the house.

Gawain sat still, erect, his seat an old beech tree brought down in the autumn winds several years back – a favourite place for him to meditate – hands resting on his thighs, palms facing the sky. Eyes gently closed, breathing regulated. Gawain could sense Josh watching him through the trees.

"You want to eat?"

A startled Josh spurted out, "What? No, yes. Whatever."

Gawain tenderly opened his eyes and smiled. "I am going to the pub for a light supper; you can join me if you can make your mind up."

The bar was empty when they arrived. They quickly ordered the vegetable bake, took their drinks and sat in the corner at a small, round table. Before the meal came Josh fetched two more drinks from the bar. While he was waiting, a rather thin man, pleasant looking, came and leaned on the bar next to him. Josh had noticed him enter the pub just after they had taken their seats.

"First time here?"

"Yes." Josh tried to sound like he did not want to carry on the conversation.

"You friends with Gawain?"

"Why do you ask?"

"Strange man," the customer replied. "Keeps himself away from the village, doesn't mix with the rest of us round here."

Josh picked up the two pints of ale and started to move towards his seat. "You a pagan as well, then?" Josh froze and turned on the rather annoying man.

"Come again?"

"Are you a pagan? Simple question."

"Do I look like one?"

"No," the odd man shook his head.

"Then why ask?"

"Because he is." The stranger looked in Gawain's direction.

"Sure, I am." Josh's sarcasm was hard to miss.

As he returned to the table, Josh didn't mention the rather odd conversation but later, when he laid down that night to sleep, he wrestled with his thoughts and the notion of Gawain being a pagan.

Next morning, after breakfast, Josh set out in search of answers. The day was warm but cloudy, and Josh wished he had left his coat indoors. Instead he carried it under his arm while he walked. The stranger had looked too old still to be working and, there not being too many people living in the few buildings making up this rural community, he believed that he would not be too hard to find. But even Josh was surprised how little time had passed before he saw the person in question walking up the church path ahead of him, open the door and walk in. Close on his tail, it did not matter how hard Josh tried to open the door quietly, its creaks echoed throughout the ancient building.

Three elderly people sat at the front, all turned to see who the intruder was, so Josh made to close the door on his way out. He heard footsteps make their way to where he stood.

"Do come in and join us, young man," a voice called out after him.

Josh looked to see who was talking to him and saw an elderly lady coming in his direction. She grasped his arm, would not take no for an answer and before he knew it, he was sitting next to the gentleman he had been searching for.

Morning prayer seemed to take forever but when it finally finished, the man leaned over and spoke quietly in Josh's ear, "Maybe you are not a pagan after all."

"Why did you say that Gawain is a pagan?"

"Come, I will make you a cup of tea; prayer always make me thirsty and we don't want the vicar to overhear us," he replied. As he did so, he nodded in the direction of the elderly lady who had dragged him to his seat.

"She's the priest?"

"Yes."

Josh watched her enter the vestry only to return carrying papers she wanted to place on the noticeboard.

"Ian."

"Sorry?" replied Josh, returning his thoughts from the priest to the man beside him.

"My name is Ian and yours is?" Ian extended his hand out to shake Josh's.

"Josh," he responded, taking Ian's hand.

Ian lived only a short distant from the church. A gravel path led to the front door, which was unlocked. The kitchen was covered everywhere he looked with icons and crucifixes; even the mug Josh was given a few moments later had written on the side JESUS LOVES YOU. Josh smiled inwardly, hoping it was true, but then he admonished himself for thinking such things.

"I was wrong, then. You are a Christian."

"Why do you say that?" Josh sipped his tea, burned his lips but without showing the discomfort he now felt.

"Morning prayer. Only committed Christians come during the week."

While Ian went on speaking for some time about commitment to the Christian life, Josh's mind wandered to the conversations he had with Megan, and the arguments that always followed in the later part of their relationship. Josh wished Megan's mother would keep out of their relationship, but instead she kept interfering, putting ideas into her daughter's mind. Josh was convinced that it was his future mother-in-law who had stopped Megan from marrying him when he had asked and who put her off going to church with him – or going at all for that matter. When Josh's mind came back to the room, Ian had stopped talking and was just sitting, looking at him with a rather annoyed look painted across his face.

"Do I bore you?"

"Sorry, it's just that some of the things you said reminded me of my partner."

"Your wife?"

"No, we are not married."

"You don't live with her then?"

"For six years I did."

"'Did'. You're not with her now then?"

"She kicked me out."

Ian's look changed like sand in the wind, from annoyance to horror; but before he could say anything Josh spoke again. Yet again during Josh's travels, he was telling a complete stranger his life story and for the life of him he could not think why.

"I lost my job so she kicked me out of my house, our house."

"Fornication."

"Come again!" Josh knew what the word meant and why Ian was using it but he was still surprised. Quite startled, in fact. At this point, Ian couldn't hold back:

"Fornication is a sin and God has punished you for being a sinner."

"No."

"John eight, verse forty-one. Ephesians five, verse three."

"I know my Bible," Josh protested.

"But you don't live it."

"Times have changed."

No more words were spoken as Josh rose from what had become a very uncomfortable seat. Angry and not a little confused, Josh didn't dare to look back as the door closed behind him. His was a soul departing in total chaos.

He sat in his room reading from his grandfather's journal and pondering all the various exchanges he had had with Ian over the past twenty-four hours. Could it be that Ian was right about Gawain? And if Gawain, might his grandfather have been a pagan too?

June 21st

When I arrived at Jonathan's home, I was surprised to hear that he was away down south at a religious festival. I was surprised because he had not mentioned that he held any religious beliefs. Yet upon the desk sat the books that I had been studying, exactly as I had left them, undisturbed. I read until the clock struck 4 p.m.

June 25th

Whatever faith I had, it died this day. What I had learnt from the cradle about Christ is only a copy of the ancient Egyptian myth of Horus – the similarity is just too close: "The rise of a star in the east, baptised in a river called Eridanus." Like Jesus, there is no record of his life between the ages 12-30. There are countless stories of him healing the sick, casting out demons; he even walked on water. Titles like The Word. Good Shepherd. The Lamb of God. Son of man. Even his death had the same feel to it. On a certain day, Horus, along with two thieves, one on either side of him, were crucified, placed in a tomb and then resurrected. Horus was known as The Way, Truth and Life. If that was not enough, Mithras too was described as the Way, he too was born in a cave of a virgin birth, just after the winter solstice. Unconquered Sun.

As if that wasn't enough to deal with, to round off the day I walked in on Linda and her doctor friend, drinking tea at my table.

July 27th

The loss of Paul haunts not only my dreams, but every waking minute of the day. I feel his tiny hand resting in mine, I smell his hair on the breeze. That moment when I felt his flesh – our flesh – in my arms, limp, cold. Lifeless. No one should have to watch their child suffer in that way. Watching Paul's mother, my beloved wife, cradle his lifeless body in her arms is too much, a vision that is burnt into the back of my mind forever. Once, I could imagine seeing the virgin Mary cradling her lost son, but I now know that such a vision is just a dream that someone once dreamt up. When I hear the sound of children running through the house, I am halfway through my study door when the train of emotions hit me, taking the wind from my sails, sending me into the spiral of darkness within which I am increasingly finding it hard to know in which direction I should be going. I have very little of worth in this life. No Paul. No job. Even though Linda never mentions me not working, she is embarrassed of me, she dislikes me being under her feet all the time. The physical side of our relationship was buried with our son. Some mornings, I find it hard to find a reason to rise from the safety of my bed. Having no work, I am a failure. If it were not for the little faith that I had at that time, I would have followed Paul. Now, even that is gone. So can anyone tell me what is the point of going on in this barren, infertile life?

July 29th

Now that Paul has gone, I am unemployable. What little faith I had is now dead. I know everyone is talking about me, even my soul companion finds it hard to look at me at times. I am a disappointment to them all, a burden they could do without; my other, dear children keep their distance from me and laugh behind my back. I hear them in the next room but as soon as I enter the room to see what they are up to, silence descends and their eyes are diverted from me. The doctor called after his surgery closed last night. He found me in the garden. I am convinced that he too is laughing at me, having taken great delight at pointing out that most of the vegetables were last year's and the beans had died through the winter. I was shocked to see that he spoke the truth. Am I losing my mind? I stood in front of him, shaking. Tears rolled down my unwashed cheeks. In front of me was a well-educated, expensively dressed, professional man in his late fifties. It dawned on me in a millisecond: this is why Linda spent so many hours down at his surgery. At times, when I came home unexpectedly, he would be in the house alone with Linda. Pieces were falling into place in my mind. Fear rose within me. All the children respected him; he had known them from birth. Was he hoping to take my place within my family? I am such a fool. This is all too much for me to carry any more.

I have read of a place to the north that has great healing power. I have decided to travel there alone. I spoke to Jonathan at length about it, about Iona. It is a good place to leave this tormented life.

August 1st

It seemed to take forever to reach Iona. I slept last night in a small group of stones. I finished off the last of my sandwiches and climbed to the top of Dun I. While I look out over the blue sea now, sheep gather in the field just

87

below me. To the left sits the great abbey I had heard so much of. I was tempted to visit this morning, but what is the point? It's just a pile of stones, like the ones I slept amongst last night. I know I will never visit such a place again, nor even this island. The pain I feel is just too much to bear. I can shed no more tears or take breaths for much longer. I feel alone, abandoned, by all, even the God I once loved and trusted. I will not lie. I have come here to die. I have pills that I have collected over the past few months – some I took from the pill bottle beside Linda's bed. I love my family, and what I do, I do of my own free will. When I am alone, and darkness falls, I will sleep for the last time.

Linda, I love you with all my heart and soul; you have always been the one true love in my life, you have always been there for me. I am deeply sorry that I have let you down so badly and that is unforgivable. I have come to understand I do not deserve you so I dare to hope that in your heart you might one day forgive me. I wish I could have taken Paul's place and that he was the one still resting in your arms. Goodbye. Please remember me.

My dear children, Sheila and Mary, you both mean so much to me. You are the beat within my heart, the smile upon my face. I am truly and deeply ashamed that I have let you down. I understand why you love me no longer and truly believe that you will be better off without me around. I will always love and cherish the moments we had together. I will always look over you. Please do as your mother asks and take care of her in my absence.

Arthur

Closing the journal, Josh laid with it resting on his chest, his arms folded over it. He fell into a deep sleep.

CHAPTER 7

You Will Never Be The Same Person Who Left That Station

Over the past few months, a lot had happened in Megan's life. It started, if truth be known, from the time she first set foot on Iona. Her first night there she had found herself sitting, lost in her thoughts, totally oblivious to all the conversations going on around her, waiting for her dinner to arrive. A lady named Penelope had appeared and sat next to her, materialised out of thin air, or so it seemed.

"You look lost, my dear," she had said, in an accent from the south of England. She wore clothes from a nearby charity shop on the mainland, Megan was later to discover. "It looks like we are to share the same table, the restaurant is full tonight."

Megan smiled to show that she was happy to share but not that convincingly.

"Are you OK?" Penelope enquired.

"I am fine, really I am." Megan didn't know if she was trying to convince herself or this unwanted intruder.

"Have you ordered already?" Penelope asked without eye contact, while at the same time reading the menu. She motioned to the waitress to come and take her order. "Can you bring both meals out at the same time please, and a bottle of your house red."

Penelope's golden hair rested upon her shoulders and her complexion seemed to indicate that she spent a considerable amount of time out of doors. Megan estimated that she must have been in her late thirties or early forties. She held her hand out taking Megan's and introduced herself. Penelope had something about her that endeared her character and spirit to everyone she met. Megan seemed to relax and resigned herself to the present company. For the first time for as long as she could remember, her personal circumstances left her thoughts. It had been too long since she had talked about clothes, jewellery and hairstyles. Penelope's hair looked naturally wavy. Megan could not see any sign of split ends, the conditioner she used left a warm shine. Was this charismatic lady sitting in front of her trying to give the impression that she liked her hair wild and unkempt? Obviously she paid a great deal of attention to the way she presented herself to the world.

When the meal was over and coffees had been ordered and consumed, Megan surprised herself when she agreed to accompany Pen to the local bar. Her new-found companion had explained over dinner that she like to be called by that name by her friends. Two neat whiskies later, the two ladies were deep in conversation over dress styles.

"In my teens, I liked to wear more colourful, baggy clothes," Megan admitted.

Pen smiled, looking at her own reflection in the mirror near the bar. "You mean hippy clothes!"

Both ladies laughed as if they had been friends since school.

"What made you change the way you dressed if you felt comfortable in them?"

"Mother called me to the kitchen early one morning, waking me just after 8 a.m. – of course, that put me into a bad mood from the start. I had just finished school, I was sixteen and foolish. I had planned to get married in the summer. I was hoping to spend the last few weeks lazing around. 'Megan, my dear,' – she always called me 'dear', it wound me up so much – 'You are getting married in a few weeks and you are looking for a job. So, your father and I had a chat and think that it is time you did something with your hair and stopped wearing those silly clothes. Here, I have bought you some new ones to get on with.' Then, she passed me a bag of new clothes."

"Did she not like the ones you had?"

"No, never. The idea of me, her only daughter, wearing somebody else's clothes from the local charity shop drove her insane."

Pen smiled, ordered two more whiskies from the bar and returned to her seat, but not without first stopping to flirt a while with an older man at the bar. Without hearing what was being said, it crept into Megan's mind that Pen was not new to this establishment.

"You married young," she stated before she had even settled into her seat once more. "Was your mother happy with that?"

Lifting her whisky to her lips, Megan nodded slightly. "Mother married at sixteen and her mother before her."

"Was it a happy marriage for you?"

"What makes you ask that?"

"You only have an engagement ring, not a wedding ring. Couldn't help noticing."

"It wasn't. Well, at first it was, but then when I wanted to return to school with the aim of going to university, Steve changed."

"Steve?"

"My husband, my 'ex', I should say."

"What happened?" Pen was looking down into her half-empty glass while she spoke, not wanting to make Megan feel uneasy.

"He went to my mother and between them they tried to persuade me that I would be better off staying at home and trying for a baby."

"How old was your mother when she had you?"

"Seventeen, the same age her mother had her. Generation following generation. That's how everything had been in my family."

"But why so young?"

"Her mother simply persuaded her that it was the way things should be. Even though I am an only child, my mother and father both came from large families."

"Your parents, are they still married?"

"Yes."

"Happily?"

"They think so."

"But you don't, I take it?"

"Not sure. They don't talk much. My mother has her church, Father lives most of his day in the shed. They were not happy with me divorcing Steve. He turned to them for support; the way they stuck together you would have thought he was their son."

"What happened to Steve? Where is he now?"

"Not sure, we lost contact after he nearly split my parents and me up. I went to night school while we were still married, but after the break up I headed off to university. I could never go home during the holidays because Steve had moved into my old room by this time."

"That would make it difficult for you to move on with your life. Did your parents not see that?"

"Yes, partly, I guess. But you have to understand: in my family, divorce was not an option; to them and to Steve, they were just waiting for me to get it out of my system and settle down again with him; divorce was alien to his family too. But when I finished university and decided to stay in Oxford to work, Mother visited me to ask me why I had not been home in a year, and when was I planning to do so. The conversation did not end well. We didn't speak again for at least six months."

"Do you talk now?"

"We do. She finally came to her senses and asked Steve to leave, but even now, deep down, I think both she and Steve would like me to remarry him. I come from a long line of deeply committed Catholics, you see, who came over from Ireland in the late 1800s looking for work. I think Mother feels a little ashamed of the fact I have broken with family tradition." With those last words Megan looked out of the window; for a time, she sat in silence and simply watched the waves breaking against the rocks on Mull.

Megan had been so lost in her own thoughts that she didn't notice that her new friend had moved to talk again with the man at the bar. Pen finally broke the silence when she returned to her seat.

"Shall we make a move? I have had a long day ahead, and by the sounds of it, so have you."

It was only a short stroll to the hotel by the beach, though they stopped more than once to look at the clear, blue sky. When they reached the faded door they were again lost in deep conversation. A now very quietly spoken Megan described the time she had been with Josh and how he made her feel. That her mother disapproved of him and his faith and how this had been wearing her down. Since Josh walked out, she had come to realise how much she had let others, even her religion, come between them. It was clear to Pen, listening to everything closely, that the shame her mother was feeling from having a divorced daughter had overflowed into Megan's new relationship, even to the point that it had destroyed what they had had. She sensed too that Megan had turned away from her faith.

That night, Pen stood by her window looking out to sea. The very sight of the ocean stirred her soul. She knew that sleep would play games with her that night, for the very reason that her loving spirit could not tolerate how one person's belief could harm another's.

Wanting to catch the first ferry off the island, Megan was up and packed well before breakfast was served. To save time she decided to take her bags down with her so that she would not have to return to the room after eating. Placing her bag next to the door, Megan walked into the restaurant. Pen was already sitting by the window; she excitedly motioned for Megan to join her.

"Have you seen the storm outside?" she said quickly, looking out of the window towards Mull. The waves were at times higher than the cliffs. "I have watched the ferry try to dock at Fionnphort a couple of times now, without much success."

"What does that mean?" Megan asked, while still deciding which chair to sit in.

"If its big claw-gripper thingy cannot take hold of the dock, we will not be leaving until the storm stops."

"Tell me you are kidding, please."

News soon buzzed around the hotel that the new arrivals would not be arriving that morning, and possibly not even that day, which also meant that the old guests, those who had already checked out would likely be checking in again for the night. The beating rain and howling wind kept most people inside all morning and then late into the afternoon. By the time the storm had stomped across the island and out to sea, the two new friends had already made plans to stay another night in the hotel. By 4 p.m. the clouds parted to allow the soft, evening sun through. The two girls, lost in conversation, headed out towards the far side of the island. A single track that led down from the golf course opened up on to a shingle beach. Megan felt a powerful energy about the whole place, one so strong that Pen could feel her spirit begin to fall. They sat in silence looking out towards the north coast of Ireland. What it was about that place that made her feel as she did Megan had no idea. Pen, on the other hand, was beginning to understand.

"What are you going to do when you leave in the morning?"

"Home."

"You think Josh will have returned by the time you arrive back?"

"I am hoping he will have, or at least someone will have some idea where he is."

Pen was beginning to feel an attachment to Megan and was hoping she would feel the same.

"I am planning to travel south in a few days' time to see my folks, plus I have some business to attend to. If you would like, we could travel together?" Pen waited for some minutes before the reply came.

"I am just hoping to head straight home."

"Is there a rush? You can call home to see if Josh is there, or check if he has left a message. We could also look around the town to see if he is still there." While Pen sat waiting once again for a reply, she already knew that Josh would be long gone by now. Upon hearing the description of the person who was with him from the barman, she had a good idea of the direction Josh would have travelled. Pen also had a very good idea of where to find Josh, but knew that it was not wise to share this information with her new companion. Not yet.

That night, Megan called Josh's mobile, a ritual she had performed a thousand times since he had left. She also checked the home answering machine. There were a few silent messages, which were really beginning to bug her, but these were getting fewer as the days went on. The evening that followed took the same course as the one previous. Then, the following morning, the two inseparable friends were the first to disembark from the ferry as it docked in Oban. Having called her boss and described the events that had taken place, he had agreed to her taking her annual holiday. With that in place, Megan was easily persuaded to spend a few days staying at Pen's home, which was just nine miles from Oban.

Set within its own grounds away from the road stood a detached house. A stream ran in front of the main living room. Megan found herself standing, looking out of the kitchen window over a well-kept vegetable garden; just beyond lay the ashes of what must have been a huge fire. Logs were positioned at intervals around its circumference for people to sit and watch the energy of the fire.

While Pen set about preparing supper, Megan was left to explore her new environment. The hallway was covered from ceiling to floor with books. It was not a surprise to find shelves full of literature on Pen's occupation as a self-employed counsellor. What she was not expecting to see, though, were shelves filled with books on Wicca, Druidism and other occult subjects. There were handwritten books as well as printed text. Drawn to the handwritten for reasons Megan didn't stop to consider, only a few were in a language she could read. There was Greek, Latin, Hebrew and several scripts she did not even recognise. Pen called from the kitchen, bringing her back into the present moment. It was then that she started to pay attention to some of the other items within Pen's home: a pentagram, a candle burning next to a statue of some goddess with petals placed at her feet. Entering the kitchen, the table was set for the two of them. Water instead of the wine to which she was becoming accustomed was the set drink that night. During dinner, it began to dawn on Megan that while she had spent hours talking with Pen, really she knew very little about her, yet Pen knew almost all there was to know about her.

"Are you a witch?" Megan blurted out. Looking at Pen, Megan felt a flush move across her face. The look on Pen's face was one of total surprise. "Sorry, I didn't mean it to come out like that. I am so, so sorry, please believe me, I don't know what else to say, I…"

Pen smiled. "It's OK. You can relax and not splutter on." Taking a sip of water, Pen watched her young companion, wondering how much she would understand if she tried to explain to her the path she followed. "What brought that thought into your head?"

"I was browsing your books."

"Did you see the ones on poetry, astrology, mathematics, Shakespeare, Christianity, Tao-te-Ching, or Zen?"

"Not really, but…"

Pen cut Megan off rather abruptly in a tone that made Megan sit up. "You saw all the books but your mind characterised me because of the way I dress."

Megan was not one to sit quietly and be outwitted. "Don't forget the symbols you have around your house, plus the firepit in the garden," she retorted quickly.

Pen roared with laughter, clapping her hands together. "Do you understand the symbols I choose to decorate my home with? Do you know why I have a firepit in my garden?"

"No, I am sorry." Megan retreated and again wished that she had kept her thoughts to herself.

"Don't be. To question is good, but how you ask and the reasons you ask, you need to think through more before you enquire."

Pen left her guest to clear the table and place the dishes in the sink, while she excused herself to catch up on her emails. When Pen had finished, she found Megan sitting at the firepit lost in her own thoughts. As Megan saw her friend approaching finally, she smiled, then began to laugh, as Pen started to move provocatively, precisely where the fire would normally dance and flicker. Grabbing her hand, Pen pulled Megan to her feet and they both danced under the stars for what seemed like hours. Later, the two sat back down and, sipping the two drinks that Pen had brought with her from the kitchen, she explained why she had built the pit in her garden.

"Our ancestors would sit around an open fire sharing stories. When two communities joined together for a celebration, or if travellers passed through, they would be encouraged to gather and tell each other their stories, stories about their lives or the lives of their tribes. Teaching was passed down in this way and kept alive, as well as news being transmitted, and new ideas given birth to. Theology from distant lands was introduced through the telling of stories concerning their gods. The Old Testament started in this very way. The stories were told to successive generations to keep alive the history and development of their tribes. I gather here, or places like it, with my friends to share real, life-changing stories. They could be the ones that have been told through the centuries, or new ones of our own making. It sometimes seems in our world that people would rather sit and watch TV fiction, follow other people's stories, than take note and share their own life stories. Some people have stopped looking or taking any notice of their own life and the events that have formed them as the individuals that they are. I have come across many souls who believe that their time here in the world is not important enough to share their stories, that no one would be interested. In a way, they feel unimportant. But in truth, everyone's story is worth sharing, each one of us is unique and has something to offer to his or her fellow brothers and sisters. This circle around the fire is a place of intimate sharing."

When Megan fell into her bed that night she was so exhausted she could scarcely remember laying her head on the pillow but her dreams were haunted.

Josh stood by a natural fire. Not built by human hands from dead wood but a living brush. Her lover was not alone. She could not count the number of people around him. Yet the number changed as people materialised and vanished at random. Everyone was dressed in white, in the same way her priest at Mass had been when she was young. But unlike her priest, all but Josh wore a headdress. There were only three constant figures: Josh, a person who kept their back to her and then, standing next to Josh, was Pen, saying words she could not understand. His mind was being consumed; flames appeared from where his eyes should be. She called to him from across a ravine. At that moment, a startled Pen looked in her direction before turning and guiding Josh away. Out of desperation Megan ran. Deep within her heart, somehow, she knew this was her last chance to be with her soulmate. Out of sheer desperation, she made a leap of faith. Everything was now moving in slow motion. Just in reach of her fingers lay the other side. The other side of the ravine. Megan, her lips breathing words that she would soon regret, was suspended in mid-air: "Josh I made it; I am coming." Pen glanced in her direction and spoke in an ancient language. The ravine widened just enough to take the edge out of her reach. Falling, she called out his name, just before she hit the bottom and came to consciousness.

A startled Megan sat in the dark looking at a silhouette sitting at the foot of her bed. "Josh?" Megan whispered.

"No," Pen answered gently. "You had bad dream." Megan nodded her head. "You want to talk about it?" Pen had the same look in her eyes as she had done when she turned and looked at her in the dream.

"No."

Pen bought Megan breakfast in the local coffee house, before taking her to the charity shop on the opposite side of the road. Within a few hours, both girls were walking back down the street dressed in a similar fashion. Megan had pushed the dream from her mind and done her best to dismiss the foolish notion that Pen was any kind of witch. Megan was beginning to feel free, but free from what?

A day passed into a week. Over that time, they had spent most of their days looking in Oban for Josh; only Pen knew that it was a waste of time. But eventually, Megan explained that it was time for her to return home and go back to work. Hopefully Josh would be there, she dared to think, though Pen knew that was unlikely. During one of their remaining nights, sitting outside around a small fire that they had built together, Pen had encouraged Megan to share her dream. It was then that she had understood more fully the quest that Megan's soulmate must embark upon.

"Do you understand the dream?" Megan asked, not realising the depths of all that she had disclosed to her new friend.

"Josh was undertaking the path of the Eternal Flame; the people you saw were the ancient ones who would guide him. The man who kept his back to you is the one who travelled with him from Iona."

"Why were you there?" Megan was beginning to feel that there was something more to Pen than she was willing to let on.

"That's something I really have no answer to." Pen was truthful about that, at least. She had not known why she would be involved, but the one thing she did know and understand was that if Josh completed his quest, he would never be the same again. There was a possibility that Megan could lose him forever.

CHAPTER 8

From Where Does Your Saviour Come?

Josh stood in the sanctuary of a small knot of trees, looking in the direction from where his saviour would come. There was only one road running through the small village. With no idea of the time the bus would pass through, Josh was hoping it would be before he was missed. He had woken in the early hours of the morning with a great urge to run, where or why he had no idea. Packing the few belongings he had into his bag and resting it on his shoulder, he quietly opened the door to his room. Knowing precisely which steps on the stairs to avoid so that they wouldn't announce his early departure, Josh then left by the back door, cutting through the bottom of the garden. He stumbled a few times in the dark hours of the early morning. The stars danced overhead.

Seeing the bus he was expecting approach from over the horizon, at first just a faint shadow, Josh stepped out on to the pavement, though not without looking in both directions first. A thankful Josh let out a sigh of relief knowing now that he was the only person waiting for the bus. A smile crossed his face as he imagined Gawain still to be resting. Josh could now make out the number on the approaching bus.

"Leaving without a word?" Josh didn't take his eyes from his vehicular means of escape. "I want to help you, Josh."

Josh turned to see Gawain emerge from the same knot of trees. "No one can." The words that Josh spoke came from a place far away. Gawain saw within his eyes deep pools of pain that could drown the universe.

"For the love and respect for your grandfather, let me try."

The doors of the bus opened to reveal a young, attractive driver, her golden hair resting on a red scarf. Josh looked deep into her eyes, then hung his head; Gawain shook his head.

"Morning, Gawain!" The young driver spoke softly as the doors closed as smoothly as they had opened.

Both student and teacher sat in the place the bus once stood, just at the side of the road. Josh shared with his teacher what the old hermit had said about his cup being full with no room for new ideas, or no room even to hear God trying to communicate with him. Josh finished with the story of the previous day regarding Ian. After a short while, Gawain stood and, taking Josh's bag, walked just a few paces in front, making his way home. Putting the bag down in Josh's room, Gawain opened the window to allow a cool breeze to circulate. A deflated Josh stood by the small desk. Resting in the centre of the oak workplace was the white diary.

"Your grandfather sat at that very same desk and began his journey home. He even slept there on many a night. That oak surface has been washed – indeed saturated – by his deep tears of pain, and varnished with great tears of joy too, of jubilation. Tears of a soul returning home."

"Grandfather stayed in this room?"

"For a while, yes."

Josh moved to open the diary, his fingers running gently over the cover. Feeling the soft leather and looking at Gawain, Josh spoke in a tender voice: "You are younger than my grandfather, plus you said that he found you on Iona. So my question is: how do you know all this?"

"The house once belonged to Morgan, a kind, gentle lady who knew your grandfather very well, let him stay here, and she shared it with me. Morgan left it in her will to Arthur, who in turn left it to me."

"Why you and not his family?"

"Because of what it stands for."

"Which is?" Josh's words hung in the cool, morning air for what seemed like an eternity. Gawain had now turned to look out of the window at the proud oak at the bottom of the garden. Gawain was thinking to himself that one day soon he would share the lesson of the oak with his student, but now was not the right time or place for such teaching; first, the foundation of the mind needed to be laid, stilled like a glass of murky water.

Josh broke the silence with a whisper. "You are not going to tell me."

"No, I will not." Gawain smiled as he turned to leave the room. "You will work it out for yourself in time, and neither will you open the journal on the desk until you're ready."

"And that will be…"

Gawain cut Josh's sentence off before he was finished, as he turned back to look deep into the young man's soul.

"When I say you are ready and not a moment before."

"And if I do?"

"Your journey ends there in those pages and you must leave without it."

A defiant Josh stared back at his teacher and spoke with words that emerged from the darkness deep inside him. "I can take it; it is mine." A sick grin covered half of his young, but torn face.

"The police might not see it that way. Remember, you're the stranger here, not me. Who will they believe? An out-of-work bum who ran away?"

"You said you would help me," Josh called after Gawain, who had already reached the bottom of the stairs.

"I did and I will. Just do as I tell you."

"When?" a voice full of torment, searching for meaning, for help, called back.

Not instantly but the reply did come eventually, leaving Josh hanging for longer than was comfortable: "When you promise to allow me to walk with you on your journey."

"Where?"

"Home – not your physical home, but your spiritual one. And you will not open the book until you are told to."

The table was set for two when Josh finally emerged from his room, though Gawain was nowhere to be seen; calling his name did not bring him out from the shadows cast by the numerous candles that Josh now noticed evenly placed around the room. Pulling a chair from the table, Josh sat staring out of the window. The click of the latch of the front door brought Josh back into the room, though his mind seemed to be full of images, memories that felt like he was looking at a million stars while at the same time trying to work out which one was the first to shine its light in the universe. It was impossible to pick out just one thought. Gawain placed a small green canvas bag behind what could only be described as an altar. To what god Josh did not, could not, know. Three candles sat to one end, a small chalice and paten rested at the centre, with to their left a thurible for incense. To the other side of the room, a white cloth covered the simple wooden table.

"Did you not put the dinner on?" Gawain smiled, making his way across the kitchen.

"Where have you been?"

"Paid Ian a visit."

"Didn't know you were friends."

"We're not."

"So why visit him?"

"Told him to stay out of your way."

"Why?"

"Because he is a fool and fills your mind with untruths."

"Bet he told you where to go."

Gawain couldn't help but let a broad smile escape from within. "No, I just said some words he did not understand." With mischief in his eyes, Gawain carried on explaining his visit. "Then I blew dust at him and sprinkled blood on his face."

Now it was Josh who could not hide his disbelief; his jaw hit the table just moments before he started to laugh, but for the life of him he did not know why.

"What did he do then?"

"He went to speak but no words would come out, so he made the sign of the cross." Gawain moved to put the oven on. "Oh, plus I painted a circle with a cross on his door, and told him that if he mentioned my name to anyone I would return but next time it would be in his nightmares."

"So he was right; you are a pagan."

"If you mean a nonconformist, or village dweller then yes, I suppose I am."

The stillness within the room was deafening. Gawain had by this time taken the three candles from the altar and placed them in the centre of the table. The sweet aroma of incense filled the room. Josh watched his teacher, but all the time was wondering *teacher of what?* However, what was clear to him was that at this moment in time, Josh did not care. Gawain proceeded to light the three candles; in the distance, the sound of the wind chimes in the vegetable garden came alive.

Teacher and student sat opposite each other across the table. Gawain rested his hands either side. "Holy Three, bless this meal. Bless the journey Josh will now embark upon. Clear his mind, open his heart to your spirit, protect and guide him, this I ask. Give me the wisdom and strength to be his guide, the one through whom you work."

They ate their meal in silence; to Josh it felt like it might be his last. It was for that day. Josh was told, as Gawain cleared the table, not to ask any questions for the next seven days, only to do what was asked of him and speak not a word. Josh rose from his seat and slipped from the room, retiring for the night without washing.

Josh was woken just before sunrise and led from the cottage through the woods along paths that at times seemed so unlikely that he himself might soon disappear, only for those who came after to conclude that no one had ever passed that way. Light soon began to penetrate the canopy above them. Shapes appeared, only to vanish and form again within the shadows. When it seemed as if they had been walking for hours – though it was in reality less than one – they left the thin, virtually non-existent path and pushed through bushes, which caught Josh's hands and clothes repeatedly. Standing now in a clearing formed by a circle of trees, Josh could make out to the far side a pond with a small stream feeding it and another allowing the water slowly to trickle out. The water was clear and pure. Gawain went down on one knee, resting his backpack on the grass beside him, which was clearly kept short by wild rabbits (this was evident by the droppings deposited near to his knee). Clasping both hands together, he drank the pure, cool water. He then sat cross-legged on the grass, resting both hands behind him so he could lean back and look up at Josh.

"This is your home for the next seven days. You must not leave here, you must not cross from the grove to the woods, and everything you need is here. You may drink from this pure water but never from the flow that leads away from it. There, in the centre, is a stone that rests just below the surface by a few inches; when it protrudes above the water's surface, you may not drink from the pool. When the water reaches the grass where I am sitting, you must not drink from the pool." Josh was about to speak when Gawain put his finger to his lips, showing him not to speak and gently shook his head.

"Tomorrow, I will ask you what lesson you have learned from this. If you answer correctly I will let you eat, but until then you may not speak."

Josh watched Gawain move back in the direction from which they had both come, never once looking over his shoulder; he broke out through the wall of trees that now enclosed Josh's world. Putting his faded bag on the grass not far from the water, Josh began to explore his home for the next seven days. When he had seen all there was, he returned to his bag and sat, only then noticing the sun now high in the sky. In two weeks it would be May, the days would be getting longer; he hoped it would be dry until then, knowing that there was very little shelter, unless he crawled between the roots of the oak at the very centre of the grove. He watched as the pool began to fill; the water was nearly at the edge of the grass. Quick to investigate, he soon realised that if the water coming into the pool was the same, nothing had changed, so walking to the stream that led from the pool, he noticed that it had stopped flowing. A great realisation came upon him that he had not had anything to drink since the night before. With that knowledge came a great thrust from deep within him. Kneeling down on the grass in the manner he had seen his teacher do, he realised that he was too late. His trousers began to soak up the now sodden grass. Looking around the grove to see if he could see any glimpses of Gawain, he clasped his hands together to bring the water closer to his dry mouth. The cool water dripped through his fingers, only a hair's breadth from his aching lips. He heard a voice from deep within him, from where it came he did not know, but he opened his hands to allow the life-giving force to re-enter the pool, to become one again, with only the ripples telling what had happened. *'Only you will know that you took what was not yours, that through ignorance you cheated, and it matters only to you, so don't do it'*. Josh lay on the grass to watch the sun fly across the sky, heading west, heading home.

Sensing that it was late in the afternoon, Josh stood to brush the dirt from his clothes. His eyes caught movement within the pool and he saw that it had returned to its former level. With lips now so dry they were beginning to crack, he put them to the surface to drink but he was too late. At that very instant, the rock broke the surface. Josh fell back, tears running down his face. It must be a trick, he thought. The sun dropped, and so did the temperature, it came like the darkness, fast and heavy. But before the light failed completely Gawain returned, drew water in his hands to allow Josh to drink.

Josh slept under the stars, curled up as if he had returned to his mother's womb. His thoughts were of his childhood and his dreams of Megan. How his heart ached for the warmth of her skin, the smell of her hair, the sound of her voice. What had gone wrong? He found himself sitting behind her in the church she had grown up in, attended Sunday school, even taught there when she was old enough. Megan turned to look at him but there was no life in her eyes; she smiled and turned away. Josh got to his feet and moved to stand next to her. She was then dressed as a bride of Christ, dressed as the Benedictine sister who had taught in her school.

Megan smiled again, "The church needs me, my love. I'm sorry but please do try and understand." Alone and scared, once again he wanted to die and it felt natural that she should lie next to him, to hold and comfort him in the dark night of the soul.

"The pool is you, in the same way that you are the cup overflowing. The water coming in is the overflowing spirit of the Divine; the water leaving is the past that we must let go of, if we are going to stay fresh, healthy and alive to the call of the Divine. If you do not let go of the past and embrace the future, you will become stagnant or unhealthy and you will stop seeing the Divine and stop growing spiritually. Then you die inwardly. There has to be a natural flow in and out of us; the Divine moves through us, feeding and renewing us all the time. If you are not being renewed by the Divine daily, then you cannot possibly feed or help others on their journey."

That night his lover returned and they lay naked under the stars, never once touching, even though his body ached

111

to feel her warmth, her breath resting on his lips before they embraced. Megan turned, raising herself on one arm, smiled and was gone. Josh came slow into consciousness, shaking on the damp grass, believing in his heart that he had lost her forever.

As the sun rose so did Josh.

CHAPTER 9

Josh's Summer

Gawain sat with Josh while he explained the dream and his understanding of the pool. While they ate, Gawain explained that even though Josh was told not to drink from the pool or from where the water flowed out, he was never told he could not drink from the source.

"There are many people in this world, present and past," Gawain explained, "who will encourage you to drink from their well, their teachings and to follow them. Institutions grow up around the teaching of others. First, you will have a person who is truly inspired by the Divine to the point that they will give their whole life to exploring that relationship and encouraging others to do the same. They will give up everything in the same way as the Master said we should." Gawain recounted how the Master had once told a story of a person who found a great treasure in a field, treasure that set his soul alight. "He reburied it, then went and sold all that he had to purchase it; he must have that treasure at all costs. There are many who will try and steal another's treasure because they can see the pleasure and profit it gives them. At first, they become students and then, over time, they try and replace the teacher. They take the teachings they have received and write them down. They then become experts and make themselves an authority upon those teachings. In this way they can make a living. Yet, if you have to pay for spirituality then you are drinking from someone else's well, and not the Divine."

"Like priests?" Josh asked, already expecting a certain answer, but he was surprised at the response that came.

"Depends on the kind of priest you are talking about. There are and always have been holy people within our communities that we support so that they are free to devote their lives to ministering and building up others; they are the spiritual healers. But there are others who step outside of that to make a name and profit for themselves, men and women who will lead others down a path they don't really understand. The treasure that the Master wants you to find is within you Josh. Do not let others steal it and replace it with their own; once that happens you will always be their disciple. We have but one teacher and that is the Master. No one else. There are many disciples of the Master who will help you reach your full potential upon your spiritual quest but that is not the same as replacing him."

"But you said that you are going to be my teacher," interjected a now confused Josh.

"No, you misunderstood. I said I would walk with you, maybe guide you, but never be your teacher. There is only one."

"Guide, teacher, it's all the same. You are just using them in different ways."

"Yes, you are right. The words can be used in different ways to mean the same, but some believe that they have all the answers and that you must take on what they are saying as the truth. But really they should just be guiding you to find the answers for yourself. Only drink from the Divine, remember; listen to others' journeys and experiences, what they have learned and seen, but only report on your own path, and only drink from the Divine."

Josh stood and walked over to the source of the pool, knelt and drank from it. Deep down he understood what Gawain was saying. Upon returning he lifted his small bag. "Staying here for the week makes no sense."

Gawain smiled, rose, picked up his belongings and walked to the edge of the clearing. "Come, I can see you learn quickly, but you should return here every day to spend time alone with the Creator; sleeping here is not necessary at this stage of your path."

Silence, a companion with many shades to her form, accompanied the two of them while they made their way down the windy paths back to the village. Gawain's mind was still and focused on his environment. Josh's, on the other hand, resembled market day with a hive of activity.

Approaching the front gate, Gawain stopped before opening the latch. "If I asked you to take me back to the clearing, could you?"

"I believe so."

Over the following months Josh started to relax in his new environment, his mind, which was once like a glass of muddy water, began to clear. Gawain encouraged Josh to practise sitting still at least twice a day in silence. At first, Josh could see no point in doing nothing for up to thirty minutes at a time. His body would start to react against his direction, an itch behind the right ear, perhaps, later moving to the middle of his back just out of reach. Gawain showed Josh how to sit on a normal dining room chair. Both feet on the ground, base of the back tucked neatly into the back of the chair, hands resting gently on his knees, the spine straight, relaxed but straight, eyes gently closed.

"Concentrate only on your breathing, balance it the same length in and out. Be mindful of this important but simple activity that your body does from the moment you came into this life and will not cease until you leave. For the first week increase each practice by a minute, starting with five. Still your mind, count slowly up to ten, then from ten to one, thinking of nothing else. If your mind wanders gently come back to your breath. You need to control your own mind or it will control you. Like any other form of exercise, you need to practise, train your mind to be quiet and focused on the present moment."

Two weeks into this simple, but difficult, practice, Josh was so frustrated one morning he snapped at the breakfast table. Holding his black coffee with both hands, he questioned the point of concentrating on just the breath.

"I don't get it. What is so important about it? I sit there and time and time again Megan floats into my thoughts, then Grandfather, my job, my sister. What is so important about bloody breathing?" The last few words Josh shouted, letting the words echo around the room.

Both sat for some moments in the silence, letting it soak in heavily like a sponge in water. Gawain, without moving, started to tell Josh an old story that had been passed down through time.

"Deep in the mountains lay a simple monastery; it did not have the finery of certain other religious houses. A young, novice monk questioned his teacher about the educational techniques that he was using to teach him about the spiritual path. 'Why do we sit, day in, day out, concentrating on breathing? I was in the market buying herbs as you instructed when I came across an old friend from school who is studying with the master in the monastery in the town, the one with gold on the gates. That master has twenty students; my friend started there after me and is now well on his spiritual path; he is using a mantra. He laughed when I told him I was still concentrating just on breathing.' The Master asked the student if breathing was important, to which the reply came that the student did not believe it was of any use. 'No, I don't see the point', were his last words before the Master asked him to accompany him alone into the forest, while he contemplated that last remark. The young student was pleased with himself; for the last two years he had never been out on a journey with the Master alone. After just a short walk they came to a river. The Master knelt down and looked into the river. The young student stood for some time observing the old man, before he could take it no longer. 'What are you looking at?' The words cut through the air like a hot knife through butter. 'Come and see, young one.' The young monk knelt down to see what could possibly be of so much interest to his teacher. 'I cannot see anything.'

"'Look closer. You won't fall, I will hold on to you.'

"The young monk's nose was nearly touching the water when he felt the old man's hand on the back of his head thrusting his face below the water, where it was held for what seemed like an eternity. The young, naïve monk struggled for air and only just in the moment before he lost consciousness, the grip was reversed, pulling the young monk out. Lying there on the grass, gasping for air as his lungs burned, the Master stood smiling at him. 'So breathing is not important,' then turned and walked away. 'To master the basics, you must learn balance before you can walk, or you will fall,' he called out over his shoulder."

The summer came, followed very quickly by autumn and at times Josh was left alone for days – sometimes weeks – at a time. Where Gawain went or what he did he never shared. The first time it happened Josh came down for breakfast to find a note. *'I will be gone for a couple of days, practise your breathing.'* At other times, he just disappeared for a few weeks at a time without a word.

Life was quiet in the small, tranquil village Josh now called home. Not much happened there; there was never any gossip when he visited the local shop. Josh's mind began to settle, and for once, for as long as he could remember, he was beginning to be at peace with himself. He found books to read that Gawain had left lying around the house. He looked forward to his time of meditation at each end of the day. Most days, he visited the clearing where he would sit by the pool reading, contemplating where his life was going. Gawain had persuaded Josh not to read from his grandfather's journal. Yet, while Josh walked through the forest day by day, healing memories from the time he had spent with his grandfather, so many years ago, softly entered his mind. He was beginning to see a difference between the person within the dark journal and the person who had guided him in his early years. It was the middle of October when Gawain walked back in, just as Josh was preparing dinner. Two places were set at the table.

"You expecting company?" Gawain said, nodding towards the table. He placed his bag and walking stick in the corner of the kitchen, washed his hands and stood looking at Josh while he waited for an answer.

"Only you."

"How did you know that I would return today?"

"Not sure."

Gawain smiled as he joined his house guest in preparing the food. A slight smirk crept across Josh's face, which was becoming hard for him to fight. Gawain too began to smile.

"You set it every night, don't you?" The look upon Josh's face told him the answer he needed. The two cooked in an uplifting silence. Josh was relieved to have the old man back. Gawain opened a bottle of Chateauneuf–du-Pape and poured two glasses.

"Josh, it is now time for you to choose a mantra, one that is known only to you and no one else; a simple word to focus your concentration, your breathing. Mine is one that allows me to sit in the presence of the Master, the Great Shepherd. You must choose a word that works for you. Now, at first your mind will be full of all kinds of junk from the past, present and future. The aim is to sit with the Master in your heart, not talk to sheep that will be playing, trying to distract you from just being still in your heart."

"Sheep?"

"Thoughts. Don't sit with them, sit with the Shepherd."

During the following week, Gawain noticed the difference in his house guest. Josh was more relaxed, jovial and open to talking about the past. He sat and listened as Josh began to see the difference between the two images that he had of his grandfather and how he desired to understand more of the changes that must have taken place in his life.

"Grandfather was full of life, love and compassion, not only for those around him but for all creation. *That* was the person I grew up with, not the one in the journal." Josh went on to explain his time spent next to the pool, which, he now understood, lay not simply in a clearing but in an ancient grove. He spoke of how he had been able to let go of the last year, losing his job, his faith, home and partner. For the first time since his parents had died, he came to terms with his own grief. He missed them terribly, but it was time to let them go, he saw that now. He described the letters that he had written to his brother and sister apologising for distancing himself from them over the last couple of years and that he was well and beginning to find peace within himself. A mist of sadness descended upon Gawain's face though, as he was listening to his companion being honest about his relationship with Megan. Josh could see now that Megan did not kick him out or even ask him to leave, but that she was the only one who was there for him, trying to help him sort his life out. In his darkness, he had been unable to see her light shining upon him. "I wrote her a letter explaining how very sorry I am for behaving in the way that I did; of how much I did and still do love her, and that I understand that I had pushed her too far and how I take full responsibility for the break up of our relationship, and that I would like to think we could still be friends." Josh had described in the letter what had happened to him since he had left, but never where he was.

"Did you post it?" Gawain asked, but already knowing the answer. Josh smiled. Not a sad smile, but one full of hope.

"Not yet, but I will when the time is right."

Josh rose from the seat on the porch where they were sitting and entered the house, to return within minutes holding in his hands the dark journal. He sat once again, the journal resting upon his knees.

"It is time to fulfil my grandfather's wishes." Josh, a different Josh from the one Gawain had first met, handed him the journal. "He wanted you to hold on to this, not me."

There was still a slight hesitation in removing his hands as he handed over the book. Gawain waited patiently.

"Have you opened the second journal?"

"No. I wanted to at first, stared at it for hours, but now, now I am not sure."

"Do you no longer want to know what Arthur wrote, what was so important to him that it changed his life?"

"I do. I walked through the forest a few weeks back; a conversation I once had with my grandfather materialised out of nowhere. He told me that I should never try and walk in someone else's shoes – though he used the example 'moccasins' – and never stand in another's shadow, but to follow my own path and only mine. I could feel his energy walking beside me. I could have sworn I heard him speak aloud one of his favourite quotes, *A person that forgets his purpose is a fool.*"

"One of many that he liked to quote. Nietzsche," Gawain said, smiling.

CHAPTER 10

Megan's Summer

The time the lift took to reach the fifth floor felt unending for Megan. The walk down the long hall to her boss's office brought to the surface too many painful memories. Colleagues leaned from their desks to enquire after her health, and if she had been able to find Josh. Gerald, her boss and friend, greeted her at his door, concern covering his face like a blanket of snow, slowly being melted by the emerging summer sun.

"Ken called to say you were on your way up." Ken worked in security and for the last eight years had stood at the front door to greet the staff as they entered the building, barring the way to any unwanted guests. "I asked him to let me know as soon as you walked in." Gerald linked his arm through Megan's, turning her away from his office and leading her down the hall to the canteen. Ordering two coffees and paying for them, he guided Megan to a seat by the window. "You look different."

Gerald had known Megan for over nine years; at first they worked as colleagues, sharing the same sense of humour and taste in music, along with many other interests. Those around believed that they were secretly dating, but then Megan met Josh and she acted as Gerald's 'best woman' when he married Hayley. Later, when Gerald was promoted to head of another department, one of the first things he did was to have Megan transferred. He knew deep down that she was not happy with the job she was in. Gerald had spent too many nights on the phone listening to her go on about her boss and the customers she had to look after. Over the years, Gerald had never seen her at work with her hair down, or without a dark grey suit. Her briefcase was a plain, black leather one. Sitting in front of him now was not the Megan he knew. She wore her hair loose and naturally wavy, not straightened, and woven within it were flashes of red ribbon. Her dress was a light blue, the colour of a hazy sky, and the bag hung over her shoulder golden as a Brazilian summer sun. The Megan he knew would not wear sandals to work. Gerald understandably wondered what had happened to his dear old friend, as he settled into the large, comfortable chair.

"What have you done with my friend?" Gerald tried to smile, but it was not hard to see, even for someone who didn't know him as well as Megan, that it was false and full of deep concern. Megan could just manage a brief smile in return, which vanished as quickly as it arrived. "You have been absent with no word of your whereabouts for months."

"I am sorry. I did send a note from the doctors." Megan's eyes never left Gerald's glare. It was if she was reading his thoughts.

"That ran out weeks ago. Where have you been? I have called you, left messages; I would hate to guess the number of emails I have sent. I have even called at your house a number of times. You can talk to me, you know."

Megan then relayed almost all that had happened to her since she and Gerald had last met. She mentioned Pen, but never that she had stayed at her house or the conversations that they had had about her spirituality. When Megan finally finished her coffee it was long since cold. Placing it on the table in front of her, she passed Gerald the keys to her office and company car.

"You want these, I believe?"

"I am sorry, but the powers above me insisted that you be replaced. We did not know where you were or even if you were intending to return to work at all."

"It's OK." Megan spoke as she began to rise from her seat, Gerald rising at the same time.

"What are you planning on doing?" he asked.

"Travel awhile."

"How will you pay your mortgage?"

"I am renting my house out until I can decide what to do." Megan looked into Gerald's eyes and began suddenly to feel sorry for him. "For the first time in my whole life I feel free; I need to learn just to be for a while."

"And Josh?" Gerald asked.

"I have no idea where he is."

Having taken the lift down together, Gerald then walked his friend to the front door. He was surprised when she stopped and hugged first Ken, and then him, before she turned and was gone from his life.

Pen sat in the cafeteria in the small, almost-deserted train station waiting for her friend. She had been surprised when the call came through late the night before, taking her up on her offer of a room for as long Megan wanted. It had been over a month since the two had spoken in person. The one thing that she was not expecting was the excitement in her friend's voice. Pen almost didn't recognise the young lady who was now stepping down on to the platform. Clothes as bright as her smile flowed with her hair, which was resting on her shoulders. It was not until the stranger removed the dark glasses that it dawned on her that the lady she had been watching with interest was her new house guest. Watching Megan's slender body, as if moving in slow motion, made Pen's heart jump a few beats, while a warm smile formed slowly across her gently tanned complexion. The two embraced and with arms twisted like a Celtic knot, they made their way to the waiting taxi.

The rather talkative taxi driver placed the few bags that Megan had travelled with on to the kitchen floor as Megan stood patiently looking out of the open door towards the firepit. Pen insisted that Megan was her guest and that she should be allowed to pay, but then struggled to find the right amount of money. In the end, she bowed to Megan's persistent demand to take her money.

When the door finally closed to leave them alone, Pen let out a loud, excited, "Look at you!" Taking Megan's hands, she began to pull her around in circles facing each other. "What have you done with my friend, Megan?" she laughed.

Over roasted vegetables, new potatoes and home-made vegetarian sausage pie, washed down with a 2010 Chateauneuf-du-Pape, Megan explained how, once she had crossed the threshold of the home that she had shared with Josh, it hit her so hard that just breathing had become very difficult. Living, or staying just one night there without her soulmate, was too much for her to bear. She had closed the door behind her and called her mother, but hung up before giving the phone chance to ring, a well-practised action that she carried out to an exact timing. That night she spent alone in an out-of-town bed and breakfast. Over the next week, Megan had stayed in the same room, living almost like any nocturnal creature to start with, sleeping by day and watching the moon and stars through much of the night. But a chance meeting on the stairs with Joanna, part-owner of the old farmhouse in which Megan was staying, changed everything. That night, the two sat at the dining table after the other guests had left: a retired general and his third wife, who was rather vocal over the affairs of some remote country, though Megan couldn't have been less bothered to remember which; and a retired teacher and her daughter, who were visiting a sick relative in the next village. When the door had closed, Joanna pulled up a chair beside her. Between them, they then finished off the two half bottles of Chateau de Beaucastel Blanc 2008 that had been left over, before Joanna herself departed the room, but only to return with another full bottle, freshly chilled from the fridge.

Through their conversation, Joanna helped her to see that the most important things in life were the people whom we love and who love us back. Money, position, career were illusions. "It's poison to the soul to try and live up to someone else's expectations," she had said. "To live in someone else's persona means that you will never be yourself in your own life."

Joanna had talked Megan through her genealogy, starting with her mother and her parents before her. Megan had explained how her grandmother had been very dominating, trying to control her every move. Megan had relayed a story her mother had once told her as they sipped Colombian coffee together. Megan had always suspected that all was not as it seemed between her parents but it

126

wasn't until then that pieces began to fall into place. This one morning, her mother talked about her youth and some of the boys she had dated; there was one that put a twinkle her eyes, and when questioned about him, she began to blush. It transpired that Megan's grandmother had disapproved of this one boy to the point that she had demanded Megan's mother not to see him again. He came from a Protestant family, you see. Megan's mother declared any notion of a deeper relationship between her and this boy as nonsense and that she had eyes only for her husband. However, Megan felt this not to be true, due to the pain now evident in her mother's voice. When they were talking about her aunties, the same thing happened: one was now divorced and the other in a very unhappy relationship. They all lived the lives that were demanded by their mother, to the point of the style of clothes that they were expected to wear. And it became clear to her. Megan's grandmother showed the same traits as her mother had, wanting to dominate Megan in all areas of her life, even to the beliefs she was to have. One of the reasons she had not married Josh was because her mother disapproved of him and his faith.

"Is it important to you?" Joanna asked.

"Sorry, I am not sure what you mean."

"I feel you seek your mother's approval, even maybe change your behaviour when she is around."

Megan sat for a while thinking through the comments Joanna had made. She watched as Joanna cleaned the tables, folding the napkins that were not soiled and replacing them ready for breakfast. When her hostess had finished laying the table, it seemed to Megan to be very regimented; not a crease or crumb to be seen, nothing out of place.

"Night," Megan whispered, creeping from the room. She found herself standing within inches of the front door, tempted to sneak out into the night and hide from the looming darkness that was fast approaching.

The next morning, Megan explained, she had had the best night's sleep since Josh lost his job. She woke up knowing that she must differentiate herself, find out what it meant for her to live her life for herself, not for Josh, not for her mother. Renting the house was simple; Joanna's daughter had just graduated from university with a 2:1 in history and was looking for a place to live for a while.

Once she had returned home, packing everything into boxes and placing them in storage took all her strength and determination. Shopping for new clothes in the local charity shops was just the therapy she needed. Losing her job, she felt to be sent from heaven and took away the dilemma of what she should do about her career.

"So, my dear Pen, I thought I would take you up on your kind offer and stay with you for a bit. I hope that is still OK with you."

Pen smiled genially. This was the second time Megan had asked that very same question. "It will be good to have you here as long as you like."

"And will you teach me the path that you walk, please?"

"You know very little about it."

"Seen your books."

"I will teach you a little."

"Ever since we were together, I have been thinking, even dreaming, about becoming a witch."

Pen smiled, a smile that was hard to read. Pen asked herself if Megan had really considered what she was asking.

CHAPTER 11

Keep The Rhythm In Their Dancing

November 3rd. For the last time, Josh left the room that had been his home for the past eight months. Closing the door behind him, he knew he was not the same person who had arrived all broken and lost. Safely tucked within his rucksack was his grandfather's journal. The temptation to open it was no longer there. Gawain had sat with him on the eve of the first day of November. Seated around a newly lit fire in the heart of the grove, they had opened the book together. The first page was enough to make Josh realise that there was going to be a great difference in what was written within the book he now held. Josh now controlled his own mind, as Gawain had taught him, and he would not allow the journal to take him back in time. The very words written in front of him he had heard his grandfather say many times to him. "Josh, you need to know yourself, you need to be master of your own life. You must live your life or your life will enslave you."

'To know others is intelligence,
true wisdom is to know yourself.
Mastering others is strength,
but Mastering your very self is true power.'

(Lao-tzu)

ot surprised when Gawain removed the dark
is shoulder pack and rested it on the ground.

ncestors, this night marked both the end and
the beginning of the year. It is a time to look back over the
previous twelve, to them thirteen, months, bearing in mind
their year was different from ours. It's a time to give thanks and
let go of the past. If you have lost a loved one, this is the time to
let them go; it is time to release them upon their journey and
you on yours. When you embark upon your path during this
coming year you must be free to begin to understand and find
yourself. Free, no ties. Just you and the path."

Josh gazed into the fire for a considerable amount of
time. He had already made his mind up to let his grandfather
go, but in reality it was more difficult than he could have
realised. At times we will hold on to pain as we would any
companion, even if it is only a dark shadow of the person we
have loved, even if it means death to our own soul.

Suddenly lifting the journal with one, complete, smooth
movement and without looking too closely, it left his hands
to be consumed by the waiting fire. Both men watched while
flames danced through the once dark tale of a tormented soul.
As Josh watched his grandfather's words being consumed by
the fire that night, he had very little understanding of just
how symbolic this action was.

Once the fire had died down enough for Gawain to feel
it was safe to let it see the rest of the night out alone, they
drove to Oban. Taking early morning tea in one of the cafés,
they waited for the first ferry going across to Mull, catching
the bus to Fionnphort and another ferry. Stepping on to
Iona brought back feelings Josh had spent months trying to
control. Walking up the small incline from the ferry, a very

tired Josh started to say his chosen mantra. Gawain had taught him to use this to straighten his mind and to keep out thoughts he didn't want. Gawain opened the unlocked door to a small, white cottage, within which an exhausted Josh rested the remainder of the day.

The walk to St Columba's Bay the following morning was not the easiest Josh had ever made. The darkness hung in the air, cold and damp. With his coat high up his neck, hands deep in his pockets, the two set off well before sunrise. Sleep had eluded Josh that night; the old cottage was comfortable but wanting in certain basic needs, and it didn't help that he had slept the entire day before. Gawain assured his young companion that the cottage was the very place his grandfather had stayed on his last few visits to Iona. Josh could feel that old familiar presence somehow, but this time there was something different that he could not define.

Once off the single-track road, the dew from the grass crept over the top of Josh's shoes. The hem of his jeans soaked up the moisture as he struggled to keep up with his guide. He thought more than once that Gawain must have the eyes of an owl. Coming down the steep track, Josh's eyes came to rest on the silver path stretching across the sea to Ireland. Gawain stopped, bent over his small backpack, untied and unrolled two yoga mats on to the pebble beach just a few feet from the sea. Both sat facing the sea, where all life first started. Josh never asked what they were doing or how long they were to sit, but he knew in his heart that this was part of his journey to become one with Christ. He knew, too, that this would not happen that morning, until he had become one with himself. Gawain had pointed that out more than once on their journey to Iona.

131

The silence was broken, with just a few whispered words. "Follow the path, Josh."

In front of Josh, just an arm's length away, was the beginning of the silver path; or was it the end? Josh pondered both. He closed his eyes softly, keeping his spine erect, and began to balance his breathing; the same length in as out, the last words Gawain uttered laying gently in his mind. Over the weeks that had passed Josh had begun to master his mind; no longer was he its slave. Even though his eyes were closed he could still see the silver path lying in front of him, calling his name in the whisper of the soft breeze. When Josh opened his eyes the path was no more. The setting moon had been replaced by the great light. Josh had felt its warmth upon the side of his face well before he had opened his eyes. Gawain was standing high on one of the rocks protruding out into the sea.

"Are you ready?" Gawain didn't divert his eyes from the horizon as he spoke. "Water is fluid, always changing, never the same. Whether a river or the ocean, it is never the same and the chance of you seeing the same drop of water again in your life is incalculable; well, to my mind it is. If you choose to walk your path, you must keep your eyes fixed on the Master and only his teachings."

Josh understood whom he meant by his reference to the Master; it was the same title his grandfather had given to Jesus, along with 'Teacher'. Josh didn't interrupt as Gawain continued to speak. "The Master only points to the kingdom, never himself; the kingdom is within each of us, not out there," he said, pointing to where the silver path once was.

"I don't understand."

"You will, in time."

Gawain leapt from the rocks and began to walk slowly across the beach at a meditative pace, as Josh came alongside him. He explained that the beach they were now standing upon was the very place a wandering young monk first stepped out over fifteen hundred years before. "He came here searching for that for which you too are searching."

"Which is?"

"A deeper relationship with the Divine. Some say he was banished from his own land; others that he was a wandering monk who had the fever that most Celts had – the need to explore. But in truth, he came here to learn."

Gawain started to retrace the path that had brought them to the beach earlier that morning. Josh watched as he began to climb the track that rose from the beach. Knowing that his guide had no intention of stopping or coming back, Josh picked up the yoga mats and quickly caught up. Walking just a few paces behind him, they went on in silence. "Silence is your ally," Gawain had once told Josh. "If your mind is disciplined and focused, you will see and hear what the present moment has to say. Only *now* matters."

Josh had no idea where they were heading – the path twisted first one way then the other and at times he had to leap over small running streams. A loch appeared on his right, and he remembered reading in his hotel room on his first visit that it was from there that the inhabitants of this island first got their domestic water, before they were forced to buy it from the authorities. Over the crest of the hill the view was breathtaking, white golden sand and tropical blue sea basking in the early morning rays of light. Walking over the only golf course on the island Josh recalled that he had never seen anyone play there. They kept left of a small farm and once over a stile they headed towards the centre of Iona leaving the ocean behind them. As they continued across the island, Josh felt more than once that they were lost, but when the question was put to Gawain days later, he assured Josh he was not.

"It's a path I have travelled more than once my young friend," he had answered. Josh was not convinced.

They were standing once again in front of the circular wall of stones that Josh had first visited on his initial encounter with Gawain many months ago. Gawain was already standing in the centre when Josh made to step over the wall and join him.

"The door. You must use the door, Josh." Gawain pointed to the entrance. "Always use the door; never take the shortcut in life. Always start from where you are and go through the correct doors on your path or you will get lost." Josh smiled, knowing that he had made the same mistake the first time.

Josh didn't really understand at this point of his journey what Gawain meant, but just nodded and walked through what had once been the entrance. Gawain sat with his back to the stones, motioning with his hand for Josh to do the same.

"The young monk was making his way here to what was once a Druidic school." He pointed to his left where there rested another group of stones. "The ruins of what was once a place of great learning."

Josh remembered reading a different story about this young traveller but decided to keep silent.

"He was looking for answers, for the truth. The name 'Iona' comes from the meaning 'Isle of the Druids'. They were at that time followers of what we now know as the Way. They knew and followed the teachings of St John; his works were brought here from the East. The learned men whom he found here were dedicated to following the Way, the path to truth, just as their ancestors had. The Latin for Druid is *magi*; they were the ones who were searching for the truth; they were the ones who were following the predictions that the Christ was to be born. It is here we start our journey. Your grandfather sat, where you are now, with his guide as he started his journey, just as many had before him, and just as I have sat with many since. May there always be guides for those souls that want to come home."

Josh, who from the early morning had felt tired and not really wanting to engage, finally asked the question many had asked before him. "Why here, I mean this island, this place?"

"The rock formation here is one of the oldest in the world, and so is its wisdom. It is remote; it is a place that can bring you to know yourself. In your time here you have noticed the power of the elements, the rain, the wind, the sun; each in its own way plays its part in forming that which you see. The power of nature around you is the same within; it will, if you allow it, form you. When the Master started his ministry, his path to the kingdom, he was driven out into the wilderness."

Gawain paused. Looking out of the circle he contemplated what he was going to say next. Was he right in passing this knowledge on? Looking at his young companion, he could see for the first time the eyes of his beloved friend; how he missed his wisdom.

"The wilderness is not an outward, physical desert; it is an inner wilderness, a place where we all have to battle our lower, animal instincts. It is in here that we fight most of our battles. It is not until we have mastered this part of our nature that we can progress along the spiritual path towards union with the Divine. Until we have mastered desires and passions of this stage, all will be in vain and we will go round in an ever-continuing circle. Our lower nature always wants to pull us down."

"How did he, the young monk I mean, know to come here in the first place?"

"He came from a very affluent Christian family, where he was privileged to have had his own personal tutor who just happened to be a Druid. No one quite knows if it was even this tutor who brought him here."

"Are you telling me that these Druids were Christians?"

"In a way, yes, they were, but not in the way most people think of being Christian today. They were children of the light."

"I was taught that Christianity came to these shores in the sixth century. It is well documented that Gregory I took to one side a young Benedictine monk, giving him instructions to travel to England with forty other monks under his authority to convert the people of Britain from their pagan ways to Christianity." Josh relaxed, stretching his legs out in front of him.

"That is true. Gregory did send Augustine and his companions, and when they landed they made their way to Canterbury, but that does not mean that the teaching of the Master was not already well established here. There were many churches already flourishing and interacting with their pagan neighbours."

Josh sat awhile contemplating what Gawain was saying before replying. "Then why send Augustine to convert the people to Christianity if the church was already established here? He was even given special instructions not to pull down the pagan temples they worshipped in, but to destroy their idols."

"Idols," Gawain interjected. "That is a very broad word. An idol is something that takes the place of God in your life. Gregory was no fool. He knew that the places of worship that had been used for generations would have a very strong hold over the inhabitants of any land. In the same way church buildings have a very strong-rooted hold over the people today, even if they don't go to church or share the beliefs. I know a true story of a new priest who wanted to remove the rotten pews from his church and was run out of town by non-church people, simply because when they went to weddings and funerals or Christmas services they liked the place to stay just as it was when they grew up. They wanted to sit in the seats that their parents and grandparents sat in. We all have a tendency to follow the rituals of our parents and grandparents. Gregory knew that by using the buildings and incorporating the people's religion into the Church's practice, this would not only further the Church's mission, but also gain control of the people. If you can control anyone's faith and feed them what you want them to believe, you can enslave them to your will."

"Enslave?"

Gawain smiled, letting out a short, low chuckle. "Maybe a little strong, I grant you. Augustine, being a Benedictine, made the vow to be open to daily conversion within his faith. It is a vow we should all bear in mind, to be able to see our relationship with the Master in a new light each day and be ready to follow him. Gregory and Augustine would have seen glimpses of the light in the religions they came across. That is why Christianity today has within it many pagan rituals and

I use the word 'pagan' to mean simply 'nonconformist', those who will not bow to the will of another."

Gawain watched Josh for some time while his young companion sifted through what he had just told him. Before Josh could respond, as if Gawain anticipated what he was about to say, he filled the silence.

"You read theology so you will be familiar with Nostra Aetate." Josh looked hard at Gawain as if he was trying to look through him for the answer. "Second Vatican Council, Nostra Aetate, Latin for 'In Our Age'?" At this Josh nodded, showing that he understood the paper Gawain was talking about, but still his eyes showed he was uncomfortable talking about mainstream religion.

"Within the paper it describes the origin and unity of humanity and that we all return to the one God. It talks about the truths that can be found in all religions. This is not a new teaching: our ancestors, the Druids, taught this thousands of years ago – that the true light that enlightens all of humanity can be found in all faiths and that we must respect each other's path." While Gawain spoke, Josh let his eyes fall to the ground. "In Canterbury Cathedral, on the floor, is what is called the Compass Rose. This is meant to be a symbol of the worldwide Anglican communion. Upon it is a quotation written in Greek from Saint John's Gospel, chapter 8, verse 32. THE TRUTH WILL SET YOU FREE. When John wrote this, he was living in Ephesus, now modern-day Turkey, which at the time was part of the Greek world. This quote was written deep within a pagan culture. In his writings, John tried to show that the old religions were given a new birth within the new faith, that transformation could be had within the teachings of the Master, who is the Christ. Not far from where John stayed was a temple dedicated to the god Dionysus, god of the grape harvest; he was one of the twelve Olympians, the last god to be accepted into Mount Olympus and the only one to have a mortal mother. He was also renowned for changing water into wine. When John writes of the wedding feast that the Master attended with his mother, where under her persistence he transformed water into wine, he is showing us that the old religions are given a new birth within the Christian faith. Similarly, John's writings are full of images of light and of darkness. For John could see the light of the Master in the old religions, showing that the Divine was at the heart of all faiths and fulfilled within the Master through his teachings. Each one of us needs to find the truth for ourselves. It is through the struggle of the search for the light that we will be set free."

For some time, the two companions sat in complete stillness, though for Josh it was only physical. His mind was struggling against what Gawain had just shared with him. A Buddhist saying came to his mind, a simple sentence that bounced from and to every connectable area of his brain that could be imagined. "It's only the chains of the mind that bind us."

Later that night over dinner Gawain explained that the way of a Druid was a philosophy, the development of the mind, of understanding not only ourselves but also the universe of which we are a part and that to understand one you must understand the other. As Gawain continued to steer the conversation around the development, and place, of this Druidic philosophy within the nature and development of religion, and all of humanity, Josh started to question Gawain's view as overly romantic. Surely,

Druidic philosophy was just a rose-coloured myth that the country loved to court: stories of Merlin and King Arthur, Stonehenge and people dressed in white, Gandalf and wizards. But while Josh was debating in his mind, this same conversation that he had had with his grandfather so many years before started to reawaken, at first in his subconscious, then leaking into his consciousness, where his arguments were beginning to weaken.

"Myths, stories, are the ways in which we see and understand the world," Gawain went on. "We each choose a version that we want to believe so that we can make sense not only of our lives but of the world around us." Gawain was stopped in mid sentence, as Josh's thoughts finally caught up.

"So you're saying that all religions are just myth?"

"It depends on your take on the meaning of myth."

"Are you saying that Christianity is just a myth, that God is just a myth?"

Gawain smiled. "No, but the way in which we try and make sense of it could be. But before you say another word, we will travel this land and unpack some of these ideas."

"Why, when we could save ourselves the trouble and just agree that all faiths are the same, with the same message?"

Gawain finished his tea, replaced the mug next to its companion. He rested his hands on the table as he leaned over to whisper so no one else could hear.

"Not all faiths are the same. Christians hold within them many different religions that have been practised since time began, showing that there may well be many streams flowing from the mountains to the ocean. Their beginnings and endings are the same, but not all religions are the same: some deny the existence of any other faith. Christianity follows a gentle flow that began when humanity first began to contemplate the existence of God."

"I am no fool," retorted Josh. "The first primitive faiths, and even the Druids, held the four elements very highly within their understanding of the gods; it was a key element to their faith, as was astrology, worshipping the sun and moon. I hope I don't offend you, but they were a superstitious bunch; but that is not so with Christianity." Josh smiled as he sat back in his chair, lifting his mug to his lips, not caring if anyone heard him or not.

"We'll see." These were the last words Gawain spoke as he left the restaurant, leaving his companion to make his own way back to the small cottage. Josh finished his drink, but instead of following Gawain he headed towards the ocean. The moon danced among the clouds; at times she appeared to kiss the ocean, lighting it up like a silver sheet where the two of them became one just for a short while, before the moon retired to her dancing partners once again, leaving the ocean in darkness. This image stayed with Josh as eventually he walked back to the room in which his grandfather too had once rested while travelling his own path.

It was a little after 5 a.m. when Gawain stirred from his night dreams into the light, woken by insistent tapping on his door. Before Gawain could say a word Josh was standing beside him. Two cups of coffee on a small tray rested in his hands. From the look on his face Gawain knew something fundamental had changed within Josh. Pulling himself up, Gawain rested his back on the headboard, taking one of the cups from the waiting tray. Gawain was surprised that it had already begun to lose some of its heat. This led him to begin wondering just how long Josh had stood outside his door before he had plucked up the courage to enter.

While Gawain sat sipping his coffee, he listened to Josh explain the images that had come into his mind while he stood on the beach the night before: how it looked like the clouds and moon danced while the sea lay in darkness until the ocean and moon became one. In his dreams, Josh explained, he was once again standing on the beach reliving the night's events when his grandfather came and stood beside him. While they stood motionless, Arthur spoke gently, his arm once again resting upon Josh's shoulder. Josh was only eight years old. His grandfather's old familiar voice stirred his soul once again:

"Josh, the ocean has always been there from the very beginning and so has the moon. They have had a relationship stronger than anyone can see or understand. Their relationship is older than humanity itself, it stretches through time to the beginning of creation. At times it is calm, where the moon and ocean become one, turning everywhere silver and surrounded by silhouettes; a deep darkness that encroaches upon this vital but vulnerable relationship. To a romantic couple, it is the perfect picture. What they do not see is that in the darkness sits a creature waiting patiently to devour their very soul. In the darkness lives the demons of ignorance, the only way to neutralise them is to take the light like a sword to penetrate their hearts. There are other times when the moon and ocean will dance while the wind howls with laugher."

Josh looked into his grandfather's eyes and asked a simple question: "Why does the wind laugh at them?"

"They compete at times to see who is the strongest amongst them, while the moon and ocean dance, causing a raging storm. The moon, she tries to lift her lover into her arms but she can only lift him so far before he crashes, tearing at the rocks and reshaping, reforming the earth."

In the dream, Josh began to notice shadows forming around him, bringing fear to his heart. Behind him loomed a creature, towering over him, arms too many to count, reaching out in the hope of grabbing him. To his left lay another creature – was it moving towards him? He was not sure. Then, out of nowhere, a demon hovered above him. He felt his grandfather's hand tighten upon his shoulder. The clouds began to form. At first they were light grey but soon they became dark like the bowels of the earth. They came between the silver moon and her lover. This angered them. The clouds began to scream out, sending out their own light, trying to seduce the ocean. Within the battle of the elements raged chaos and death. Deep within Arthur came words that Josh did not understand, as his grandfather lifted his arm towards the sky. Josh watched as a blinding light broke from the old man's heart, rising up toward the moon and penetrating the darkness of the clouds, pushing them back. The two lights met in the sky, but to Josh's surprise, it was not the moon he had been watching but the sun; the two lights became one. As this union took place, a deep peace filled the air, the ocean lay silent once again and the earth breathed a sigh of relief. The creature behind Josh returned to being a beautiful willow, to his left the rocks lay on the sand and the demon above him, a cloud, dispersed in the now blinding light.

Arthur looked down at his grandson, his voice soft but focused. "Trust the path." When Josh looked once again at the sea in front of him, he was surprised to see a shimmering path stretching out in front of him across the water.

Gawain placed his cup on the bedside cabinet. "You're familiar with Plato's cave?"

Josh shook his head and made his way to the window to look out at the small garden.

"Plato describes a cave where people have been chained all their lives, facing a wall. They cannot move in any direction except towards the wall. Behind them is a fire and each day, between them and the fire, puppeteers walk over a small bridge carrying cardboard shapes of items that can be found out in the real world: trees, birds, horses, butterflies etc. All that the people who are chained see are the shadows on the wall. To them, it is the only reality they know; to them, the shapes are real. One day, one of the people sitting there was lucky, or unlucky, depending on your view. Their chains fell off, releasing them. After a short while, they turned and tried to make their way out of the cave. At first, even seeing the fire was too much for their eyes and it was hard to focus. But slowly, very slowly, they made their way to the cave entrance and then to the outside world. Of course, initially they were blinded by the brightness of the midday sun, which made them turn away and hide their eyes. Slowly, though, as their eyes adjusted to the light, they began to see the world in its reality, the true beauty of the trees, the magnificent strength of the horse, the tenderness of the butterfly; yet there was so much more even than that to see in the world. There was a great depth of energy and beauty in creation. The person returned to the cave and sat beside the people they had grown up with and explained the reality of the world as they had now experienced it, how their perception of life had changed. They tried to release their companions from their bondage but instead of believing their friend, those in the cave turned

IN HIS GRANDFATHER'S SHADOW

against them, declaring them mad, insane, wanting to banish them from the group."

"What does that have to do with my dream?"

"Yesterday, you questioned the four elements within the development of religion; that Christ could not be found within these faiths, despising them as false."

"That's a bit strong, but not so far from the truth, I suppose."

"Within your dream were the four elements, which – believe it or not – are fundamental to your faith. Sea, moon, wind, rocks, or you could say, water, fire, air and earth."

"Fire? Where do you see fire within that?"

"The light from the moon is a reflection of the one true light, the sun, and even you must know that the sun is a ball of fire. While the moon acted as the light, the four elements tore at each other trying to compete with each other to the point of destroying the very planet that holds them. When the true light came forward, it brought all of the elements into harmony with each other. The four elements are in all religions, but the true light is only within one."

"And Grandfather. Why was he in my dream; why did he act like Gandalf?"

"Are you really sure that it was your grandfather who came and stood beside you? And as for 'Gandalf', that is funny even for you!" Gawain swung his legs from under the covers as he stood up, showing his tartan pyjama bottoms. "The elements have always obeyed the Masters, or chosen ones. The Master himself had complete control over the elements; you must realise that. Did you look up to see if it was your grandfather?"

Josh shrugged his shoulders while Gawain made his way to the door as he carried on speaking. "A lot of people make that mistake when the Master comes to them – they see only what they want to see; the mind has a way of playing tricks upon them. Instead of the Master, they see a loved one to whom they can relate more easily."

Gawain returned to his room with evidence of where he had been, passing Arthur's white journal to Josh. "It's time you started reading this, but not now. You can read it later. For now, pack your things; it's time to start your journey towards the light."

"Where are we going?" Josh queried, as they made their way seemingly towards the hermit cell. While Josh had packed that morning, Gawain had done one of his vanishing tricks, leaving Josh in the end just to wander around the garden alone. When Gawain finally returned he had a look on his face that told the world that he was pleased with himself. Without a word, he picked up his bag and headed out of the door and turned into the path at the end of the garden in such a way as to be a clear sign to Josh that he must follow. Throwing his own bag over his shoulders and locking the door behind him, Josh jogged to catch up.

"Ireland," Gawain called behind him. It was the only explanation Josh knew he would receive. Josh was tempted to say, "I think you are going the wrong way" but deep down he had a sense that this was an important step on his path, so he fell into silence alongside his friend. Instead of going into the cell, Gawain walked over to the ruins of what was once the Druidic school. He stood, looking towards the east, and lifting his hands towards the sky, he asked for the one true, eternal light to guide and protect them upon the quest that they were about to commence. Josh stood beside this eccentric figure who was deep in prayer, listening to a long list of names. Only a few he recognised and remembered: one from his Old Testament studies, Balaam; another from stories of myth, Balthasar; and the other from more recent history, Columba. When Gawain finished, he turned to Josh, revealing his face radiant like the early morning sun. "From this school, your journey commences." Gawain turned; his long coat still undone, a slight breeze raised its back with dramatic import as Gawain stepped out. Josh followed at a steady pace, the path twisting between the hills, not even pausing to cross the many streams appearing from the side of the rocks. More than once Josh nearly lost his footing. Gawain had at first set out heading west with the sun behind him, but now they were definitely heading south.

"If we are going to Ireland, should we not be heading towards the ferry?"

"We are," Gawain called over his shoulder, without slowing the pace. Once out of the hills, they headed across the open golf course towards the single path that Josh knew headed to St Columba's Bay. As they approached the bay, Josh could see a small craft sitting on the shingle beach. Two men stood looking in their direction. Upon seeing their descent, one of the men, who was more mature in age than his companion, waved. Gawain waved back, calling out that he was sorry that they were later than they had agreed.

Once on board the small boat, Gawain explained how the route they were taking had been travelled many times by those looking for the light.

"Remember when we sat on the beach and the silver path reached out in front of you? Well, this is the path, the path that many have travelled before you."

CHAPTER 12

Ireland

Leaving the solitude of Iona behind them, they headed out to sea. Even though Josh could no longer see the silver path that once lay under the craft, in his heart he knew it was still there, hidden from sight just below the surface. Gawain tried to explain, while they headed first for Colonsay before changing course towards the beautiful island of Islay where they would spend the night, that at times the true path we seek and travel can be hidden just below the surface of the mind, demanding at times that we must take steps of faith. The journey took longer than any of the more-experienced men first anticipated due to the adverse weather. It was easy to see that this was the first sea crossing that Josh had made in such a small vessel. The colour deserted his cheeks well before Iona was out of sight. The movement of the craft kept him close to the side, knuckles white from holding so tightly to the now rusty handrail and the second day's sailing was no better. Josh never thought that the land they had first spotted a few hours back would now be close enough for him finally to step out from the boat that could have been his tomb on more than one occasion, when the waves had broken over the bow. Clambering out on to firm ground in

Ballycastle, Josh was tempted to kneel in prayer and kiss the ground right there in front of him. He restrained himself though and simply walked close behind Gawain towards a car hire centre. A small, mobile office was standing just a few feet from the only house on the road, not much more than a poorly lit room where it didn't help that even that light was on the blink. Three chairs, a desk and a filing cabinet in the corner were all there was room for. Gawain greeted the tall, slender lady – perhaps in her mid forties – who was seated at the desk. Her silver hair rested halfway down her back. The older man leaned over to kiss this powerful personality, who would dominate any room she entered, Josh thought to himself. Handing Gawain a set of keys taken from her coat pocket hanging on the back of her chair, the lady's green eyes came to rest upon Josh, making him feel at once uneasy, as if she understood his very thoughts. Gawain thanked her and, after asking about her family, made his way out of the door. The whole encounter took less than a couple of minutes.

"You never signed any forms for this car. Are you sure that you are insured to drive it?" Josh asked as they pulled out on to the main road, leaving the small port behind them.

"I don't need to fill in any forms; it's not a hire car. It belongs to me: it's mine, all mine." Gawain was smiling as he spoke, showing the excitement that was written all across his face.

"You come here a lot then, I take it?"

"No. Only when I am accompanying someone on the journey; the rest of the time my friend drives it around for me." Gawain kept silent for a while as they headed out on to the open road. The clouds that had produced such a stormy crossing still hung overhead, giving the impression that at any moment they might fall to the ground. "Arthur knew her quite well."

"How?"

"Arthur came across Silver on the roof of a multistorey car park. Your grandfather spotted her as he was out shopping with your grandmother. While she was busy looking for a new dress for some special occasion he managed to slip away. It was your grandfather who succeeded in talking her down from the ledge upon which she was so desperately poised and within a few days, Silver was a house guest of mine. Like you, she needed help. Now Silver assists others who are lost in the barren plain that we call life. Over the years, Arthur and Silver grew very close; they had one thing in common, you see."

"Such as?" was Josh's short reply.

"The very reason she climbed up on to the ledge in the first place: the loss of a child."

For some time then, the two companions sat in silence, watching the road disappear beneath them. Gawain had insisted on driving, even though Josh had, on more than one occasion, hinted that he did not mind taking his turn at the wheel. Josh woke finally when the motion of the car ceased. Before the headlights faded Josh had just caught sight of a small cottage a short walk from the car. Once inside, he watched his companion light several candles and three oil lamps, one hanging in the centre of the room where the ceiling rose should have been. From the look of the place, not much had changed in the last hundred years. Passing Josh one of the oil lamps, Gawain led him down a short passage to his room. It surprised Josh on entering that, for the time of year, the room was reasonably warm. Placing the lamp on the table in the centre of the room, it was plain to see that the room had just recently been prepared in expectation for the arrival of its night's guest. The bed had been made and turned down, fresh flowers rested not far from the lamp, their fragrance filling the air. Taking one of the apples from the bowl that was also on the table, he bit into it. With that first bite it came flooding to him how famished he was; he was looking around the room for more food when there came a slight tap on the door. Josh struggled to turn the doorknob, which was rather stiff.

"I could do with something to..." Josh stopped in mid sentence. Expecting Gawain to be standing outside the door, he was taken completely by surprise to see a girl, maybe just a few years younger than himself. Her radiant smile infected Josh's tired face.

"What is it that you would like to do?" she responded with a mischievous smile. Standing five eight, mousy-coloured hair resting past her shoulders, wearing colourful clothes that stood out even in the dimly lit doorway, Josh could see immediately that the person in front of him was full of confidence, full of life. Gawain joined them in the doorway. Standing behind the girl, he rested his hands on her shoulders and smiled at Josh.

"You know it's discourteous to stare, especially with your jaw resting on the floor." Gawain let out a deep laugh that showed that he was both relaxed and in a really excited mood. The laugh echoed around the cottage; Josh wondered if there was any corner of the dwelling that could not hear Gawain laugh. Josh knew his face must have been a picture, as the amazing creature in front of Josh also started to laugh, but hers, unlike Gawain's, was a low chuckle.

When Josh entered the dining room, the well laid out table took him by surprise. The aroma coming down the hall had made his stomach sing and sitting down now to a well-prepared vegetarian roast lifted Josh's spirits.

"Did you prepare this?" Josh asked, looking at the girl, realising that he didn't even know her name.

"Caitlin."

"Sorry?" A worried expression now covered Josh's face.

"You were wondering what my name was. My name is Caitlin."

"How…?"

"Don't ask," Gawain interceded.

"Great! Two bloody people now reading my thoughts," Josh muttered under his breath.

"You should close your mind if you don't want others to know what's going on inside your head." A cheeky grin crept over Caitlin's face as she spoke.

Josh knew instantly that he could not be upset with Caitlin; there was an aura around her that touched his very soul, lifting it up within the universe and holding him there like a merlin hovering in the warm, spring afternoon thermals.

While Josh ate his meal he became lost within his own thoughts, fading in and out of the conversation going on between his two table companions. He was beginning to see a whole new side to his grandfather. Right now, Josh could not decide who was the more mysterious, Gawain or the first teacher he ever had.

"Did grandfather come here?" The question brought the conversation to a sudden halt in mid flow. Caitlin's expression showed she did not know whom Josh was talking about. Gawain explained who Josh's grandfather was, plus some of the detail of how he had come to be travelling with Arthur's grandson.

"Did you know him?" Josh's sudden question, aimed at Caitlin, made her smile once again.

"No, but I feel that I do. Those who had the privilege to spend time with him talk about him often."

"Why?" Josh's tone showed just a hint of jealousy.

"He transformed the lives he touched; he was a very special man."

"We could all do with some sleep. It's been a long day and we have another tomorrow, so it's sleep time for us all." While Gawain was speaking, he rose from his seat, clearing the table of what he could hold, and moved towards the door. Without any further question, Josh followed him from the room.

"I will just finish clearing up the rest then, shall I?" Caitlin called after them, with sarcasm in her voice.

Once alone, Josh knelt in the middle of his room as if to pray, but instead he wept. The one person in his whole life that he thought he knew and wanted to be: he had no idea of who he was. In his mind now, others knew his grandfather better and that was too much to bear.

When Gawain came into the pre-Victorian kitchen the next morning, Josh and Caitlin were already sat on opposite sides of the table in deep conversation. Josh was a little taken aback by the news that Gawain was Caitlin's biological uncle on her mother's side. When he had asked what kind of wreckage they had pulled her from, he was even more surprised to find that she had had a very happy childhood, growing up in a rather normal family, if there were such a thing. Caitlin described her childhood, playing in the fields at the end of her garden; school was in the next village, to where she would walk or catch the bus in the winter. When Josh suggested that she lived in the old museum of a cottage they were now in, her laughter caused the table to tremble under her resting arms, spilling their tea.

"I live five minutes' walk away," she explained. Josh had learnt a lot from her about her uncle by the time Gawain entered the room. The cottage belonged to him, left to him by his grandfather, with whom he had sat while the old man slipped away to the next life. Caitlin laughed as she described her uncle, of whom she was clearly very fond, as rather prudent with his money, to the point he would not spend any on the cottage. Caitlin mimicked Gawain; it showed that she had had years of practice. "It's been like this for a hundred years and never hurt anyone; I like it like this, it's comfortable." Caitlin moved her eyebrows in the same way as her uncle when he was trying to make a point. On a more serious note, she also confided that Gawain was the perfect uncle and friend. "He never lets you down." She spoke with passion as she squeezed Josh's forearm, her voice conveying the love and affection she had for her uncle at every turn.

Gawain pulled out the chair to the table and joined in with the conversation. "Bad news; I have not been able to get us in tomorrow morning." Gawain's face was a true image of disappointment. "This has never happened before; they have always been able to squeeze two, if not three, in before."

Caitlin returned to her seat, passing her uncle a coffee. "What was their reason for saying no?" she asked, placing the mug directly in his hands.

"New manager. Just started last week. Who it is I do not know, and Hill is off sick with some kind of stomach bug."

Caitlin explained to Josh, while Gawain sipped his steaming hot coffee, that Hill had worked at Newgrange ever since it was first opened. Located just a few miles away from where they were staying in the Boyne valley, Newgrange had attracted many visitors to its prehistoric monument and subterranean chamber over the years. She went on to explain how Hill was a great and trusted friend of Gawain's and had always accommodated his requests. Nonetheless, Caitlin didn't share her uncle's disappointment on this occasion; she was certain, deep within her soul, that if Josh was meant to be deep in the womb of the earth, the universe would find a way of making it happen. In her eyes, it always did.

Later that morning, Josh sat watching Gawain from the comfort of the kitchen. His friend had been sitting outside in the freezing cold for well over an hour in complete stillness, mind, body and spirit. With just five days to go before Christmas day, Josh's thoughts were beginning to refocus on Megan; it was, after all, a time of year that they both thoroughly enjoyed together.

When Gawain stood finally, a warm smile radiated from his face. Striding into the kitchen, Josh was surprised to hear Gawain, who was now completely peacefully at ease with the world, say: "We will set out around 1 a.m., it's just a short walk to the womb."

"How will we gain entry if we do not have tickets?"

"Snow. It's going to snow and no one but us will be able to get there – they will all be caught off guard."

"You're mad!" Caitlin laughed over her shoulder, making her way from the room. "Utterly mad, and that's one of the reasons I love you so much."

Josh stood once again gazing out of a bedroom window. A little after eleven, a deep blanket of snow began to cover the earth, at first it started slowly, picking up momentum as time passed. Josh watched as first the path vanished, then the small shrubs. By the time the slight tap came on the old pine door all colour had been removed from the landscape; all was white. Once in the kitchen, Gawain passed Josh a pair of snow boots from the cupboard in the utility room. Caitlin was already standing by the back door, dressed as if she was going on an Antarctic expedition. When the door closed behind them, all three looked as if they were joining Captain Scott on one of his journeys. The cold bit at their skin, walking became arduous through the deep drifts, down into the Boyne valley and across what were once open fields. In the distance they could see the mound that was their destination.

"How did you know it would snow?" Josh asked when they stopped for a short rest, sipping hot nettle tea from the flask that Gawain had packed into his rucksack.

"I saw it in my mediation."

Caitlin smiled, which neither showed that she believed him or not. Josh was beginning to see that it was hard to tell what she was thinking. On one occasion, it even occurred to him that she would be a good poker player.

"How will we get in?" Josh asked when they were getting very close.

"He has his own key."

Gawain stopped and removed snow from a large stone at the foot of the shaft that they were about to enter. "Remember this stone; you will come across it many times."

Josh stood looking at the stone, which was highly decorated with intriguing engravings. "What do they all mean?" Josh asked as he began to follow his two companions down the narrow shaft.

"You must work that out for yourself." Gawain had taken a lighter from his coat pocket to light one of the torches that had been prepared for those lottery winners who each year were lucky enough to be drawn to sit in the Mesolithic tomb that had kept guard over the Light for five thousand two hundred years. Once they had reached the far end of the shaft, Gawain set the flaming torch in the waiting stand. Josh sat on the ground in the precise position that Caitlin motioned him to.

"Josh. Remember Plato's cave?" Gawain whispered. Josh nodded. "When humankind started on their spiritual journey home, it started with the worship of the Sun and Moon; two lights, one that guards the night and the other the day. One light is a reflection of the other. With the Sun, Moon and Earth, you have the trinity, each needing the other. We all spend time in caves during our lifetime; in this cave it is only the chains of the mind that bind us. We each have the capability to release ourselves; we can all set ourselves free if we want to. The Master sees how each one of us binds ourselves or allows others to bind us. In the darkness we are alone and vulnerable. This sacred site is a womb within the earth and the light that will come along that shaft to penetrate the soil gives the waiting seed buried within new life. The Master searches us out as we hide." Josh understood that the faith within him was the seed that Gawain alluded to. While the three sat waiting each became submerged within their own thoughts.

"Joshua." This made Caitlin smile into her coat, which was pulled up to keep out the biting cold. She knew when

Gawain used anyone's full name the journey was about to commence. Caitlin smiled because deep in her heart she knew that walking with another soul setting out on the fire quest gave her uncle purpose. It also brought him closer to his soul friend, whom he missed so deeply, and for whom on the anniversary of his death each year he still lit a candle. Caitlin could sense the emotion hiding within that one word, that name; this was the ultimate journey, the one journey that would fulfil his friend's ministry, the journey that Gawain could not complete himself. The work Arthur had started so many years before, the soil in which the seed had been planted, was ready for the light. Deep in Gawain's heart he wished his beloved friend were here to witness this dawn: the Awakening.

Gawain spoke with a soft voice. "Do you remember when you were young and spent time outdoors with your grandfather?" Josh acknowledged without a word that he was following what was being said. "He spoke about the soil of the mind and heart, told you stories of the Master and his friends."

"Thaddeus."

"Yes, Thaddeus. He was one of your grandfather's favourite disciples. The light that comes here tonight has travelled great distances to greet you; it will search your heart and mind and you will see things differently. Tonight the darkness has prevailed, rising up to meet the light, as it begins its ascent. The stone now beside you has writing upon it, in the form of pictures. As the light hits the stone it will travel across it, hitting only some of the pictures, leaving the others in complete darkness. What the pictures mean is not important. The stone represents your heart. While the light rests within this place, ask yourself if there is any area of your heart that you want to keep the light out of so the rest of creation will not see the darkness within you. Now is the time to let the past recede with the darkness and begin anew. Let the earth rebirth you."

Josh sat for what seemed like an eternity for the light to appear. His whole life seemed to sift through his mind; at times he felt as if the pain from the past would be too much to bear. Where was Megan, how could the most perfect relationship, their love, die? Yet even while he was in pain, his eyes wandered to Caitlin, as something about her stirred his soul and he did not understand why.

Catching Josh unawares the light came and so did peace – at that moment he knew that nothing was hidden from the Master. It was like time itself had been suspended; Josh's early years, the death of his grandfather, meeting and losing Megan, his career, his faith. Then came the parts of his life he wanted no one to see; this was the darkness that would engulf his entire world. The light passed over it, not lingering for a moment; it felt almost as if he was being cleansed. Practically unawares, Josh closed his eyes, as the voice came from within: *'Joshua, you must let the light into even the darkest parts of your life.'* A deep healing came from the centre of his being. When Josh opened his eyes he watched the light pass over the stone, only then understanding its significance. The markings that stayed within the shadows represented that which he would want to hide from the Divine. Yet the voice was clear: if he truly wanted to move forward, nothing should remain in the darkness. The cave was his life, his mind, and the stone his heart. Closing his eyes Josh meditated just as Gawain had instructed him on their walk that night, a discipline he had learnt some months earlier. Setting a circle of light around himself he allowed his mind to sink into the earth, to mould itself within the womb in which they were sitting.

Josh could see the beginning of time, the forming of the universe. At first it was just darkness, a darkness that was so familiar to the human soul. Blackness so heavy there was the great temptation to close his eyes, and yet a voice from deep inside him told him not to. *'You must look for the light, Joshua, even if it hurts to do so.'* He felt a great sleep coming upon him, his eyes began to roll in their sockets, his eyelids were heavy, too heavy and they began to close. *'Joshua, so many have started out on the quest for the answers you seek and yet, from the beginning of time, humankind keeps falling asleep because the truth is too much for them. Not you, too, Joshua. Keep looking for the light.'*

Josh struggled to reopen his eyes; he knew he was deep in his meditation but it was still hard to open his eyes. Even upon opening them, all he could see was darkness, so what was the point opening his eyes if there was nothing to see; why not just give in to the desire to sleep, to rest, to turn away from the quest and follow the way of the world? There must be an easier path than this. Doubt began to creep in that he was wasting his time and he closed his eyes once more, but that same, inner voice became stronger again, a familiar voice now that he had heard in the past, a voice he thought at first to be his grandfather's, but now he was not sure. It was a voice that spoke into his soul bringing solace. Open them he did. Within the darkness, at first like the smallest of seeds, was a speck of white light. Josh knew deep within that he needed to return to the source of the light, that this was about going *back*. But in that same moment, his mind told him that made no sense because he did not remember ever being there. Josh watched as a figure stepped into the darkness causing a great explosion like nothing that had been seen before or would ever be seen again. Within the darkness, more lights began to appear, but these did not move, they just disrupted the blackness, which began to scream and fight back.

Not long after, Josh found himself sitting once again within the womb of the earth, Gawain and Caitlin nowhere to be seen. Seated in front of him was a familiar figure. At first he thought it was his grandfather again. Josh smiled, but then he could see that it was in fact the old hermit whom he had first met on Iona. Cross-legged in front of him, he reached out and took Josh's hands within his.

"Are you the Master?" Josh asked. The hermit smiled and shook his head slightly.

"I come from the Master to guide you in the darkness of your mind. In the beginning of time when the One created all that is, it was in perfect communion with him. All there was was harmony and the great peace. Within that communion, humanity knew the One intimately, but the eyes of humankind became heavy with sin and the darkness crept in to separate them from the light. Darkness goes by many names and cannot always be seen until it is too late. Like the shadow of a tree on a hot summer's day, or the long shadows at dawn or dusk, it can look attractive or enticing. It can creep upon you without notice and enslave the soul."

"How does one know?" Josh asked.

"By the fruits they bear: life, love and peace come from the light; death, hatred and destruction come from the blackness." With these words, a great silence filled the very heart of the womb, until, finally, it was broken: "Blackness of the mind caused by sin brings tension and disharmony within the universe, which is reflected throughout humanity and can be felt within the individual soul."

While Josh listened, his eyes were drawn back to the stone, as not a single carving was left within the dark. It then dawned on Josh that the entire room was filled with light, not a single shadow to be seen.

"The disharmony in the world comes from the darkness that dwells inside us. If you want to bring peace to the world you first have to find peace in your own soul." The old man stood to leave, the wrinkles upon his face moving to form a warm smile. The last words he now spoke filled the room. "The true path home is through love, pure love." With that, Josh found himself alone, deep within the earth. Within him he could feel a deep peace. Then came a small voice from outside him and with that, his meditation came to a sudden halt.

"Sorry, Josh, but we really need to go before we are discovered."

The sky was clear when they re-entered the world. Voices in the distance made the three move quickly for cover; neither one spoke until they were safely within the old cottage and even then Josh was not forthcoming with information. It was not until later that night over dinner, in the light of the roaring fire, that Josh opened up to what had taken place within the womb. Both of his dinner companions listened intently to every word.

When he had finally finished reliving the night's events, Gawain explained that, "What happens within the universe happens inside each and every one of us. The light you saw was the light of faith deep within your heart."

CHAPTER 13

The Divine Uses All Languages

Over the next couple of days Josh began to see the world in a new way. The evening of the 24th arrived and Josh was passed his coat and told that it was tradition to visit the local watering hole. It took less than ten minutes to walk to the centre of the village. The singing could be heard halfway down the street. The Stag's Head was heaving; young and old alike were enjoying the evening's festivities. The two young friends found a couple of seats in the corner that a small group had just vacated, letting the cold air flood into the bar as they stepped out into the night. Caitlin watched through the window while the man in his twenties lit two cigarettes, passing one to a rather older woman.

"You know them?" Josh asked, bring Caitlin back into the room.

"I thought I did."

"In what way?"

"While I was at school I used to hang out with Steve." Caitlin smiled then began to laugh silently. "We were just thirteen and I was more interested in music than boys." Caitlin looked out of the window once more, with a little sadness deep in her eyes. "Steve's mother, without any warning, packed her bag while Steve was at school and her husband was away on business. He has never seen her since. At seventeen he moved in with Helen, twenty years older than him."

"You sound bitter," Josh frowned, while sipping his dark ale.

"I tried to talk sense into him about his relationship; we said words that cannot be taken back and from that time we have not spoken. Silly, really, but that's the way things turn out at times. I did try once to make amends but he cut me dead and walked away."

Caitlin turned, smiled and took Josh by complete surprise. The kiss took less than a second. Josh, on the other hand, seemed to hold his breath for much longer. Through the crowded bar, Gawain looked into the mirror at the right, or wrong, time, depending if it was meant to be a secret or not. Gawain had been standing with one of his oldest friends. Both had been leaning on the bar engaged in animated conversation, but from just one glimpse in the mirror Gawain was now lost in his own thoughts. When he came back to the present moment his friend had stopped talking and was just standing with his glass resting at his lips, a warm smile across his rather worn face, a face that had many distressing stories to tell, if only one had time to listen.

"Not sure you were meant to see that." As the words drifted away, Gawain nodded, showing his friend he agreed. Gawain's eyes moved from the familiar face to rest upon the white dog collar, almost hidden beneath his scarf. For a moment the two stood in silence.

"Gawain, I still believe deeply that you should rethink what Bishop William requested of you."

"Yes, Father," Gawain retorted with a mischievous grin moving like the morning mist across his face. Every time Joe tried to talk about the bishop's request, that he finish his training and accept ordination into the Anglican Church, Gawain would deflect the seriousness of the conversation with the title 'Father', which would somehow stop the conversation dead in the water.

"Not tonight, my old friend; tonight you will talk about it." Joe watched as once again his friend looked deeply into the mirror at his niece and student. They were now locked in deep conversation. Josh's arm rested softly upon her shoulders, while they held hands under the table. Josh must have said something that amused his niece. She smiled in a way Gawain had not seen for a long time, ever since his sister had passed away. Josh kissed her head as she rested it on him.

Gawain turned, looking all of a sudden more centred; Joe knew something had just shifted within him.

"Both you and William know that I have chosen the path I walk. It is not much different from yours; both our paths have been given to us by the Master and I will not be hoodwinked into giving it up for some romantic idea I once had."

"No, not romantic, Gawain, there is nothing romantic about the path I walk."

"I didn't mean you."

"Gawain, William called in when he was this way during the week; he knew you would be home this year – not sure how he knew but he did. He wants you seriously to consider his request."

"I truly believe that the path I walk is the right path and you know it is, too; so does William. Why can you both not just accept that, once and for all?"

Joe smiled, knowing that it was a futile conversation. Deep down he knew and understood the path and the reason Gawain walked it. He stood looking at his old friend while Gawain once again returned to the mirror. He could see the same aura that he once saw around Arthur; the two could be one, he realised. Knowing that the conversation about the bishop's request was over and that he had fulfilled his obligation to William, Joe placed his glass on the bar and leaned close so that only Gawain could hear him.

"Don't be late for Mass, you're reading the first and second lesson tonight." Before Gawain could give an answer, Joe turned and walked through the crowded bar towards the door, not once turning round to look to see if Gawain was trying to wriggle out of reading. He did glance in Josh and Caitlin's direction, though, wondering what his friend was going to do to keep Josh on the right path without any distractions.

Others who craved his attention and advice soon joined Gawain; he had a reputation in the area for being a wise person who followed the old ways, and there were always those who just 'wanted a word'.

Caitlin brushed by Gawain on her way back from the ladies; grasping her arm gently, he pulled her close to him. "Mass is at 11 tonight and you're reading the second reading."

"Nice try, but I am sure Father Joe would much prefer you to read the lesson, but don't worry, we will be there to listen to you, and so you can keep an eye on us to make sure we behave." She smiled and disappeared into the sea of people.

When Caitlin stood to put on her khaki jacket, Josh was taken a little by surprise, but not as much as when she mentioned they were going to Mass. Josh followed Caitlin as she made her way through the maze of people, their fingers interlocked with each other. Once outside, Josh quickly pulled the zipper up on his coat, fighting to keep the chill of the night out, not once questioning where or why Caitlin was taking him. Once they were at the end of the path leading on to the road, Caitlin linked her arm through his. To Josh it felt as natural as breathing as they walked through the village together. St Cuthbert's was nearly full when the two walked through the 8th century oak door. Quickly scanning for the right place for two of them to sit, Josh was dumbfounded to see Gawain already there sitting near the front of the church, saving two seats. Gawain stood and motioned for them to join him. A bell rang to indicate the start of the service and almost immediately the organ struck up with the first notes of 'Once in Royal David's City'. Just the sound of the first few notes took Josh on a journey through time and space. He found himself sitting with Megan in the past at their first and only Midnight Mass. They had just bought their first house with each other in the last week of November, moving in mid December together. They were both excited about celebrating their first Christmas in their own home, but Megan's mother soon put the dampers on it. He was beginning to wonder what his lost soul friend was doing, and whom she was with. Was she too in church or in the arms of a new lover this holy night? Closing his eyes and clearing his mind in the way that Gawain had shown him, Josh began to concentrate on his lost love.

Josh soon found himself standing outside in the cool night air. In front of him he could feel the warmth of a raging fire. Fear gripped him as he searched the flames for his friend. He tried to call out her name but only the crackling of the fire could be heard. Moving forward towards the fire he had to raise his hands to defend the flesh upon his face from the attack of the heat. For a moment, Josh thought that this was Megan's house and that she was trapped deep within. Voices led him, he looked behind him and his fears melted away within the flames of the fire now biting into his back. There in front of him, sitting amongst people he didn't know, sat Megan, but something was different, she looked changed but he could not understand what it was or why. Josh began to move forward, trying to call out her name, but no words would come from his mouth. Standing only a few feet in front of her, he could not understand why she had not noticed him. Megan was deep in conversation with a dark-haired girl just a few years older than herself. A startled Josh turned as he felt someone grab his arm, swinging him around. He now stood a short distance from a blonde-haired hippy – that was the only way he could describe her. Her eyes pierced the night air.

"You should not be here," the hippy announced sternly. "Megan is with me now; go back to your new path!" she snapped. Josh tried to turn his head to look in the direction of his friend, only to feel the hippy's hand grasp his jaw, turning him once again to look in her direction. Her eyes were deep and wild, sending a chill down his spine. "Leave!" she whispered, then blew upon his face. Her breath was ice cold. Before Josh could respond, he found himself once again standing next to Caitlin.

Josh looked deep into Caitlin's eyes; she smiled and reached out to take his hand in hers. Josh didn't have to look in Gawain's direction to feel his eyes fixed upon him. Caitlin, singing at full voice with the entire congregation, at that moment in time was content. Josh assumed the priest must have been well into his fifties, with a full head of grey hair. When Gawain moved forward to read the lesson from the Old Testament, Josh noticed that the priest acknowledged him with a slight movement of the head. Gawain read from the prophet, Isaiah. Then, once back in his seat, Gawain leaned in front of Josh and whispered to his niece in a language he could not understand. Believing she was being reprimanded for holding his hand, he tried to release it. Caitlin's grip tightened as she leaned closer, almost resting her chin upon his shoulder while she spoke.

"Uncle was just reminding me that I am supposed to be reading the second lesson; he was not telling us off." She smiled as she rose from her seat. Her voice was soft and soothing and Josh could not understand a single word, but still he was mesmerised. When she returned to her seat, Gawain smiled as Caitlin spoke.

"You never said which language I was to use." Even Father Joe was trying hard to keep a straight face. "I have told you before, you should always ask well in advance if you want me to fill in for you."

Caitlin let go of Josh's hand when he would not follow her to receive communion, but once back in her seat she wrapped her arm through his and cuddled up to him. A great urge filled Josh to kiss her on the top of her head as it rested on his arm, stopping just inches from her hair. The scent stirred his manly emotions. Taking hold of her hand he linked his fingers through hers, as they stayed for the remainder of the service.

Embracing Joe at the door, Gawain spoke tenderly, "It's good to see you, old friend." The priest spoke softly enough for them to hear, just.

"When I heard that you were home for Christmas, I knew you would want to read the lesson."

Gawain laughed. "You just wanted me here at Mass and telling me at the last minute that I was down to read gave me little choice! You will never change." As Gawain passed through the door, the priest called out to say that he would be visiting Christmas afternoon. He then returned to greeting the congregation as they passed him.

Gawain walked briskly ahead, leaving his house guests to walk slowly, arms wrapped around each other. They walked as one as they stumbled through the door, giggling like teenage children. Gawain watched the pair make their way into the kitchen, and hearing the kettle being placed on the stove, he tried to listen in to their conversation. Their giggling muffled the words coming into the room. In the early hours of that most holy night, Gawain lay awake in his room listening for two bedroom doors to close; he heard only one.

CHAPTER 14

He Never Told Me

When Pen pulled back the curtains to flood the room with light, it was a little after midday. The aroma of black coffee placed on the bedside table, made from freshly ground Columbian beans, filled the room. Standing with her back to the bed and staring out of the window, still holding a curtain in each hand, Pen began to question her still very sleepy friend.

"Did Josh enter your mind last night?"

"Once or twice, why?"

"No reason." There was a long, pregnant pause that filled the room, making Megan sit up in bed to look at her friend, who seemed content to stare out of the window.

"The fire is still smouldering." When Pen finally gave birth to conversation the words that came into being were not the ones Megan was expecting.

Megan was beginning to get used to the way Pen tried to extract information from her, so she knew that something or someone must have disturbed her friend and that she should now be on her guard. Sitting up, holding the mug of coffee between her hands, she watched her friend as she took her first sips.

"Did you enjoy last night? I saw that you made a few friends."

"Yes, I did thank you. It was a very pleasant evening. I really liked Jane; she was funny."

"In what way was she funny?" Pen's tone made it seem as if she was a little annoyed with Megan for enjoying Jane's company. She remembered at some point during the evening seeing Pen out of the corner of her eye watching both her and Jane enjoying themselves. She thought that it was strange at the time. Pen had stood with her back to the fire, as if she was in deep conversation with someone, but she was alone.

"What was funny?" Pen asked again, this time her tone showed how much she needed an answer.

"You know she has just broken up with her partner?"

"I do."

"Well, she was just telling me all about it, but she made it sound hilarious."

Pen began to laugh. Letting go of the curtains she turned and crossed the room to sit on the bed next to Megan.

"I have heard those stories too. And listening to them made you think of Josh?"

"Not really."

"Then what did?"

"For a brief moment I felt his strong presence within the group, as if he were there too."

"When?"

"At the same time you started talking to yourself." Megan began to laugh.

"What's so funny, my friend?" As Pen was speaking, she could not help but notice how beautiful Megan was, sitting up in bed with the quilt pulled up to cover her warm, soft, naked body hiding within its depths.

"I know you weren't talking to yourself."

Pen's expression changed and, yet again, so did her tone. "Then who was I talking to?" Pen seemed anxious for her reply.

"I think you must have been high."

"I don't do drugs, you know that and I certainly would not allow them at a gathering to celebrate the one true light. It would dishonour our femininity to the Master."

"You mean the goddess?"

"You may call her what you like, I suppose, but why choose that title?"

"I overheard others talking about her last night."

Pen made no comment on what Megan was suggesting nor was she going to be drawn into an earlier conversation to which she had not been party.

"Do you miss him?"

"I do, very much; he was part of my life and a big part of my future plans. We thought we would be together for all eternity."

"When was the last time you heard from him?"

"You know the answer to that." Megan looked away to try and hide the tears fighting their way to the surface. Her voice could not hide the pain. "The day he walked out."

"Drink up your coffee before it goes cold and then come downstairs; we have guests coming soon for dinner."

"Who?" Megan asked, feeling startled at the suggestion that the tranquility of the day was to be broken.

"Friends I would like you to meet." With those last words, Pen was gone, closing the door behind her. Megan was beginning to feel that Pen was jealous of Josh, but for the life of her she could not understand why.

Dressed in her new, second-hand dress from the local charity shop, Megan made her way into the lounge. Pen's promised guests had already arrived and were sitting next to the open fire with drinks neatly resting in their hands. They both rose from their seats and admired her pale green dress as it flowed freely with the movement of her curved body, showing more cleavage than even Pen was used to her displaying.

"Darcy." The first to speak, the first to move in Megan's direction, was a rather tall, dark, dashing gentlemen in his late forties. Holding his hand out to greet her, Megan took it in hers, noticing the smooth softness of the palm of his hand that showed he was not the kind of man who engaged in manual labour.

"Darcy," Megan repeated, while trying not to show her surprise at the sound of his name.

"His mother just fell in love with the name the very first time she heard it." Darcy's companion was now standing beside Megan. The tightness of her clothes showed off the slenderness of her body and the fullness of her breasts. She moved closer to stand by Darcy, linking her arm through his, making sure Darcy could feel the closeness of her body. Her aim was clear; to remove his eyes from the low cut of Megan's dress.

Megan didn't need it explaining to her why Darcy had made the first move to introduce himself; he must have been used to being in the background when together with his companion. Standing a slender five eleven, curved in the right places, silver wavy hair, it was her green eyes that caught everyone's attention. If Darcy had not moved first, Megan was not sure if she would have even noticed him. Everything about Silver filled the room.

Megan joined Pen in the kitchen to help finish off the winter feast, the name Pen had given to it.

"This meal is older than Christianity, my young friend," Pen had explained, a few days before. Pen had described how in the early days of humanity the different tribes would gather in the main dwelling, which fulfilled the role of a common meeting area. It would be dark, cold and very dangerous outside at that time of year. People came together for safety, plus there was not much else that they could do. The food that had been harvested needed eating, animals slaughtered could not be kept through until spring. The wine and ale that was made in the summer was now ready to drink. So you could say, as Pen had explained it, "everything was ready for a party". The cause for celebration was that the god of light had just done battle with the god of darkness, defeating him once more, banishing the dark, frozen days like demons that did his bidding so that the lighter days, like angels, would return, bringing with them the warmth of the great light in the sky and fruit from the earth. The winter feast, Pen had added, continued to be celebrated in nearly every home in the land.

When Megan had tried to argue that most people were celebrating Christmas and that it was really Christmas dinner they were sitting down to before they opened their presents in the afternoon, Pen's argument had been that most people were not celebrating the birth of Christ; they had not gathered to worship or offer any other devotions that would be required in most faiths. Most people just saw it as a holiday. Her own voice had changed when she'd stressed that people must be believers

175

and to be a believer they should gather with other disciples in worshipping the creator and in celebrating the birth of his Son, the redeemer of all creation. People could not be Christians and not fulfil the commands of the Master.

Pen, without raising her voice, had been quite forceful.

"The teaching of the church is very clear about participation and church attendance, and that not going is simply not an option. To be a Christian, our Lord was clear, you have to work alongside other Christians. It is not a solo faith of one member; it's a body of people each called into discipleship. If you are not going to participate in the sacrifice of the last supper, if you are not willing to put yourself out and state what you believe with your sisters and brothers, then it's just a winter feast and you are back in the Dark Ages, believing what you want to believe to bring comfort to your own little world and not seeing the Master at work."

"Pen." Megan spoke her friend's name, but then stopped herself from asking the question that perched frozen on the tip of her tongue, remembering the conversation from a few days earlier, a little uncertain of the ramifications if it leaped into the physical world to nail its true colours to the mast.

After a few moments, Pen turned, but not before she had placed the utensils that she had been using on the worktop. "Cat got your tongue, my friend?" Pen's smile was a warm peace that just radiated from her, putting Megan at ease deep within herself.

"You called this a winter feast a couple of days ago and I understand your reasoning." Megan stopped so that she had time to consider the next sentence before it came into being. "Last night, when we gathered around the open fire, at times it felt like we were worshipping Christ."

"Expand on your reasoning."

" 'Lord of light, the one true light.' Then someone mentioned him by name, not (I would say) in the way that I am used to but his name was honoured all the same. We even passed the bread and wine around the fire."

Pen was smiling from deep within herself. "What were you expecting, my dear, witches dancing around the flames?"

"But that is what you are, is it not?"

"I have never told you that I was. I have never spoken about it in any way." Pen went silent to see what kind of response Megan was going to give, but then decided to turn back to the task in hand. Picking up the utensils once more, she added, "What is stirring within you, Megan?"

"I need answers." As Megan spoke, tears streamed down her face, and her raw emotion could be heard within the silence of the room. Pen turned to see her friend distraught to the point of breaking apart. Crossing the room, Pen's arms enfolded her weeping friend.

"What's going on?" Pen asked again.

"Last night, I felt close to God, closer than I have for a very long time, but I am a Christian, or at least I like to think so, and last night of all nights I should have been in church to make my communion." Not knowing the reaction she would receive from the next few words, Megan braced herself. Pen, in turn, could feel the tension building up inside her friend and began to wonder what was coming.

"I miss Josh."

The words came like an arrow into darkness, striking not Pen but Megan's heart. It was then that she knew she needed to find her soulmate at whatever cost. "I want to find him," she whispered.

"Then you will, if it is willed by the universe."

Pen let go of Megan when Silver called through from the lounge. "Pen, your other guest is here."

Pen moved towards the door, then vanished from the kitchen, giving Megan time to compose herself to meet the new arrival. Megan decided to stay awhile in the kitchen, away from the guests. She could always reason that she stayed to finish off what Pen had started.

When they were finally introduced, Megan was quite taken by the new visitor. She was in her late twenties, with short, dark hair and very petite. Her clothes were colourful, matching her personality. Gina was invited to pray over the gathering, which took Megan, but seemingly not the others, by complete surprise. The conversation around the table was light and at times witty. It was obvious that everyone, except Megan, were good friends.

"This pie is excellent, Pen." Gina complimented Pen by raising her glass.

"Vegetarian pie and vegetables from your garden, I take it." Silver too raised her glass.

Megan began to fade from the chatter around the table, her thoughts flickering between Josh and her parents, all mixed up in the previous evening around the fire.

"Megan." Pen had to repeat her name several times before Megan responded, during which time the conversation came to a standstill, all eyes were fixed upon the youngest member at the table.

Silver asked politely, but firmly, "Please inform us where you just were."

"Sorry, I don't understand."

"Your thoughts had taken you from this gathering to somewhere else."

Megan felt propelled to tell everything, as if she had been drugged with a truth serum. "I was just thinking about a good friend, my parents and the events of last night."

"I hear it was a good gathering, nearly a full house," Darcy remarked and seemed pleased with his contribution considering the amount of wine he had consumed.

"I hear you had an unexpected visitor," Gina added.

Pen tried to change the subject, but was stumped by Silver's inquisitive mind. "Please share, this sounds interesting."

"It was nothing," Pen said, standing to clear the table and giving Silver a look that screamed that she wanted the conversation to go no further.

Silver smiled and changed the subject by asking Gina when she was intending to move to the south of England to take up her new post. When Megan enquired what the new post would entail she was taken aback by the news that Gina was an ordained priest. For one, she did not look or act like one and secondly, for the life of her, she could not understand why a priest would be sitting here at the winter feast, as Pen would call it, with a group of witches.

During the late afternoon, as the light outside was slowly fading, Pen slipped out into the cool evening air to walk through the small woods joining her garden. Feeling Silver's presence approaching from behind, she never even broke step as Silver linked arms with her. They walked in silence, each waiting for the other to share what was on their mind. The moon came out to light the path in front of them.

"Have you seen Gawain?" Pen asked finally.

"I did and he was in good spirits."

"I take it he was not alone?"

"He was travelling with a young man."

"Good, I hope he can help him." There was distance within Pen's words.

"Is it he that troubles you?"

"I have been asked to help Megan and I am becoming fond of her."

Silver stopped and turned to her friend, holding her hands. "What do you mean, 'fond'?"

"She reminds me of someone I knew once and I am lying to her. When she talks about finding Josh, my heart wants to take her to him." Pen looked towards the house where she could see Megan talking to Darcy through the kitchen window; they were laughing together.

"We both know that it's not possible for them to meet at this time, and we also know he will not be the same person she knew when they were last together." Silver looked towards the house too, watching Megan and Darcy laughing. "He's such a flirt and very harmless – totally devoted to me."

"You hope," Pen laughed.

"Megan, I believe, is changing from the description you first gave me; she now looks like your sister." Silver watched the words melt upon the now distraught face of her closest friend.

"I still miss her. If only I had known what she was going through, the struggles life was throwing in her direction, she might be here now."

"Pen, you also know deep within you, she learnt what she came to learn and her path was complete."

Pen's face began to show the pain which had formed her. "She was nineteen, she was young."

"She is eternal; her spirit is still evolving."

"I know. It's hard sometimes to believe in this life when there are so many souls in torment. Why is Gawain's seeker more important than mine, that I cannot take her to him?"

"Gawain's not told you?"

"Told me what?"

"His seeker is Arthur's grandson."

Pen nodded and began to walk back to the house. "No, he never told me, and that now makes it all the harder."

CHAPTER 15

This Above All:
To Your Own Self Be True

The house was illuminated only by dancing candlelight; the table was set for three. Gawain made sure that Caitlin would sit next to him, leaving Josh facing the two of them. The tree in the corner of the room was also lit by candles, their flames moving in the draft of the old cottage. In front of Josh sat the white journal, opened on the first page to reveal a sketch that Josh recognised as being by his grandfather's hand. A woman whom he knew to be the Virgin Mary with a child sitting upon her knee. Underneath was the word 'Theotokos', which he knew meant 'God bearer'. To the left of the drawing were the words:

It started with a single thought; nothing in this world starts in any other form. In the beginning was the Word. This is the beginning of the human journey. Out of the darkness came the light, the light of all knowledge. It is to the darkness that we return to be reborn once again, not a physical birth, but a spiritual one. Nicodemus came in the darkness; Elijah hid in the darkness of the cave. Both heard the voice of the Master calling them into the light and countless others have heard the same voice, but few have responded. The cave that most are trapped in is the cave of the mind, bound by their own chains. In the darkness they hide from the Master. All enquirers searching after the truth will first stand at the gate perplexed. In front of the genuine seeker there are many sacred writings stretching back through time, tracing the spiritual development of nations, tribes, individuals. Only the pure, intuitive soul who is embarked upon the path can see the Divine's hand at work, weaving its golden thread through all creation. Within all sacred scriptures, they will see the one true lord of light. But be wary. Only a fool will look outside their own culture for the one true path for them. One's roots are deep within the soil of their own spiritual paths, the paths that have fed and formed the culture in which they are born, both physically and spiritually.

Josh looked up from the pages of the journal set in front of him, his eyes searching deep within the faces of his table companions.

"I know these are my grandfather's words. Is he saying that I must look within the pagan religions for answers to my questions? Was he a pagan?" When Josh stopped speaking, his eyes once again traced the same page. Josh read and reread the words.

"Your grandfather followed the spirituality of this land and you must do the same if you want to find the answers to your soul's desire," Gawain explained as many had done before and would do after him. They would stand at the gate and not understand the path set in front of them. The problem, Gawain went on, was that there were more teachers out there who tried to encourage less-developed minds to believe that they, and only they, had the map to the promised land and that the Divine spoke only through them. There were very few souls who were strong enough and brave enough to blaze their own path home to the Divine. These masters took on disciples to try to help them understand that the power to return home lay within. Sadly, in many cases, when the master died, the disciples, instead of carrying on the work of teaching others to find the power within themselves, took their master's teaching and taught only that which they had been taught, never daring to build upon it. They became authorities upon that which had been passed down to them. They then made others bow to them, to jump through the hoops that they set, the standards that they required.

While Gawain was talking Josh's eyes fell upon a text he was familiar with:

But you are not to be called rabbi, for you have one teacher; and you are all students. Matthew 23:8

"This was one of Grandfather's favourite verses; he would quote it to me many times during our walks in the forest. He was insistent that I follow only the Master. I can't believe I had forgotten that important teaching." Josh looked again into the eyes of Gawain. "You are going to tell me that it applies to following my grandfather too."

Gawain leaned forward and turned over the page. He pointed to a short sentence at the top of the left-hand page.

Follow only the light within, the Master. Follow no one, not even me, for once you follow another teacher you take your eyes off the Ancient One and you will be lost in another's world.

Josh started to turn the pages, not stopping to read the contents. More than halfway through the journal, Josh stopped turning and reflected upon the words written once again below a picture of a young woman holding a small child. He had seen the picture before but could not recollect where. The words at the bottom made Josh sit back in his chair; he felt excitement and disappointment at the same time. Dare he turn the pages and keep reading or not? Somehow, out of respect for his grandfather, he closed the journal and pushed it across the table, the words he had read last still filling his mind.

These next few pages are a reflection upon my own understanding of my journey through this world, how I see and make sense of the Divine in my life and in those around me. You are free to read on, but first I ask that you make your own journey upon your path to understand the Master and the work he is involved in. If you do not, then my words will overshadow yours forever. Be careful upon the road before you.

"Why did you push the journal away? Are you not interested in its contents, do you not want to understand your grandfather, do you not desire to be like him?" Gawain's words were true: Josh did want to understand his grandfather, but to be like him? The answer was both yes and no. A comment Arthur once made while they were walking through the forest echoed though his mind.

"When you stand in front of the Master he will never ask you why you were not more like Abraham, Moses, or even me, your grandfather. He will look deep into your soul and ask you very seriously why you were not Joshua, the person He called you to be."

Josh explained how he so much wanted to be like his grandfather, a man of great faith, a man who understood his own path and had a real relationship with the Master, and he could no longer do that by trying to walk in his grandfather's footsteps.

"What I am beginning to remember and hear from you two, is that Arthur was a true seeker and teacher of the way."

"Guide, not teacher," Gawain corrected Josh.

"Yes, sorry, that I understand."

"I have asked Caitlin to work on your meditation; my young niece has asked if I minded if she accompanied us a while longer." Gawain looked at the very image of his sister sitting next to him. "She might as well make herself useful."

Pushing the journal back towards Josh, he rose from his seat.

"You will need this. That which is written at the beginning is what we give to all those seeking the truth; it is only the memories of Arthur that are kept private; not even Caitlin has read them."

Gawain left to build a fire in the 'drawing room', as he liked to call it. Caitlin and Josh cleared the table and decided to wash the pots before they would join him by the fire. Josh enquired how his new companion was going to help him improve his meditation practice. Caitlin simply smiled, leaned into Josh and rested her soft, moist lips upon his. The sensation stopped his thought process, he turned from the sink, hands dripping soapy water first over the floor and then penetrating her warm top, as he wrapped his arms around her, holding her tightly as the passion rose within him, expressing itself deeply within their embrace.

When they had finished putting the kitchen back to how Gawain insisted it was kept they went together into the drawing room. Caitlin let go of Josh's hand just as she walked through the door. Her uncle was sitting on the floor, cross-legged, next to the unlit fire. Caitlin motioned to Josh to sit next to him in the same manner. Watching Caitlin remove her shoes, placing them next to Gawain's, Josh followed, placing his next to the others. The three sat motionless in identical positions. Silence filled the room for well over an hour.

"The path in front of you is a sacred path only you can travel, no one can come with you and no one can do it on your behalf. We take our shoes off each time we come into the presence of the Master. When Moses approached the burning bush he was told to remove his sandals because he was going to be standing on holy ground; this was his Bethlehem. From that time forward, even though he was reluctant at first to listen to the Divine, he started out on the path that only he could walk; it was a lonely path that cost him dearly.

"Since the beginning, fire has played a central part in humankind's development, not only spiritually but also socially. There is an ancient story. While mankind was still living in the darkness of the cave, a great storm arose, ripping up the surrounding environment, from the sky downwards, striking trees and rocks alike. A young girl was left outside, alone, abandoned in the panic of her tribe to find shelter in the safety of the cave. When she came out of hiding the landscape had been changed forever. As she wandered through the chaos trying desperately to find her way home she came across the sacred grove where her people would gather to worship the two lights that govern the day and protect them through the night; at the centre stood the king of the forest, a great majestic oak. Standing in awe of the sight before her, she fixed her gaze on a branch that had been struck by lightning, fallen to the ground and was now ablaze with the light, from the great light in the sky. When it had hit the ground, smaller branches broke away. The young girl's curiosity got the better of her and, with great courage, she moved forward, barefooted through the burning embers on the nearby ground. Taking hold of the lower part of a branch she lifted the fire above her head. With great fear and reverence she carried it back to her tribe. Upon seeing the fire within the hand of one of their own they fled deeper into the darkness and safety of their cave.

"The elder, who led through his sheer size and power, moved forward when he saw that the young girl was not being harmed in any way. Within the cave there was straw and other combustible material that was soon given to feeding the flame. The warmth from the fire aroused a desire deep within him and he took the girl into his arms and made love to her in the light of the fire. From that time forward, the fire was honoured and kept alight by the women of the tribe, a practice that is still kept by them to this day. Within each of us there is the cave of the mind, a place of safety, refuge, a place to which, whenever we are challenged, we can escape. It can be a cave just like Plato's cave, but the chains are the ones we inflict upon ourselves.

"The reason some seekers give for setting out on the path is that deep within them is a great need to change. If you want to change then the first thing you have to come to terms with is that you must change your understanding of the world around you. The fire we light tonight is a symbol of inner transformation. Within the power of the fire there is active, eternal energy that reaches back through time to the beginning of the universe, energy that will travel on into eternity. Within its power, it is capable of bringing new beginnings, cleansing and purifying, giving new birth to your soul."

For some time after Gawain stopped speaking, only the sound of the fire filled the room, filling the silence with its erratic crackles. Josh could feel the warmth of it brushing over the surface of his skin. His mind was reflecting on the story Gawain had just shared about the young girl. Within the flames he found himself deep in the very same cave. Naked in front of him lay Megan curled up with her back to him. Inside his soul burned a desire to lay with his friend, to hold and devour her. Josh heard Caitlin's soft voice calling him deep into the fire, a call he could not resist. Josh knew that if he really wanted to move on in his life he had to let go of Megan; he knew she was happier without him. He also knew he had to let go of the fire that burned deep in his loins.

"Josh, I believe that you are familiar with the works of Freud and Jung. Jung wrote that it was wiser for those born and nurtured in the West to keep their roots deep within their own spiritual traditions. Did you read the first line in the journal?"

Josh nodded and reopened the front cover to expose the words Gawain referred to. Looking into the crackling fire, Josh spoke the words from memory. In the dancing flames Josh was once more remembering other words his grandfather had told him to learn and always hold on to, words from William Shakespeare:

"This above all: to thine own self be true."

"The line that follows…" Gawain too looked into the only light in the room as he spoke. Without taking his eyes from the naked flames the words flowed from Josh's lips:

"And it must follow, as the night the day, Thou canst not then be false to any man."

"Thomas Merton once wrote in his book, *New Seeds of Contemplation*: 'How do you expect to arrive at the end of your own journey if you take the road to another man's city?' "

"I remember," Josh spoke as his mind was overwhelmed by memories, "once sitting in Grandfather's living room staring into a similar fire and telling him how much I wanted to be just like him when I grew up. He turned and held my face in his big, gentle hands. With love, he reached into my soul and spoke words I had forgotten until now, but he also referenced the next sentence that Merton wrote, the one that is not on the front page. "*Young Joshua, you cannot really expect to reach your own perfection as a child of the Ancient by leading somebody else's life, not even mine. The Sacredness inside you will never be yours; 'you must have the humility to work out your own salvation in the darkness where you are absolutely alone.'* "

Gawain rose in the orange light and made his way from the room, leaving Josh to sit pondering the words laid out on the pages resting on his crossed legs.

If you are to make sense of your path through this world,
you must take all that you have read and learned and make

it your own. Believe only that which you can make sense of,
only report on your path and not the path of another. The
gate is narrow, room enough for only one on each path.

Josh could feel the softness of Caitlin's eyes resting upon
him. For some time they both sat in the light of the fire. Josh
allowed his thoughts to alight upon a conversation he once
had with his grandfather though it was really hard for him to
bring to mind every word that was spoken. He remembered
sitting in the fading sunlight under the weeping willow set
in the old garden; Arthur had just returned from a journey
that had taken him away from the family for some weeks.
Still dressed in his shirt and waistcoat, Josh saw the silver
cufflinks for the very first time. A circle with a cross in the
centre, which he came to know as a Celtic weave, a symbol
that made both circle and cross one and the same. Within the
weave there was just one strand. Josh's smile caught Caitlin's
eye. On the top left-hand side of the front cover, Josh could
now see the very same design imprinted into the white
leather. With his fingers he traced the pattern. Josh's smile
deepened to a grin, before a chuckle broke from his lips.

"What's so funny?" enquired Caitlin.

"On the first journal that I had there was a Celtic circle
imprinted into the leather, in the top left-hand corner. I would
trace my finger round it for hours wondering what had led
Arthur into the darkness. At times I thought he was telling me
that he had found an alternative path to the conventional one
that the rest of humanity followed, or at least most of them."

"Such as?" Caitlin's voice was soft and at the same time
warm, like it had ridden on the back of the dancing flames to
bring magic into the room.

191

"Some 'pagan path' I suppose. And with all that Gawain has introduced me to, it has only reinforced that belief."

"Such as?"

"Sorry?" Josh lifted his eyes from the pages resting on his lap and rested them on Caitlin's half-lit face, with the other half hiding in the shadows. Something about her made the blood pump faster through his veins.

"You said, 'all that Gawain has introduced me to'. All I want to know is what he has shown you that is pagan."

Josh's eyes returned to the journal and the comfort of its text. Silence once again descended within the room, leaving only the odd spark leaping into the air from the fire on to the hearth, where it glowed for just a short time before it was no more. Josh began to realise, as he contemplated all that had happened during his time with Gawain, that there was not one occasion that could lead him to the conclusion he had expressed just moments earlier. It was the words of others that had coloured his mind, leaving him to think that Gawain was some mysterious Druid.

"Gandalf." The name materialised from nowhere to trickle into the night air and, no sooner had the word escaped, Josh wished he had kept his lips tighter; he bit his lip till he could taste blood.

"Merlin, actually!"

"Merlin?" Josh repeated.

"In many ways, Gawain represents Merlin."

With half of her face still hiding deep in the shadows it was hard to really know if Caitlin was making fun of him or not, nor would she tell him by the tone of her voice. Caitlin followed the characteristics of her uncle in many ways. She stood and moved towards the door, sharing her thoughts as she went.

"Pagan means 'nonconformist' or 'village dweller', so really in some way or other, we are all pagans." With the last word came the click of the door. Once again Josh was alone with his thoughts.

He drifted back in time to yet another conversation he had had with his grandfather, this time while they laid on the wet autumn grass, set within a clearing in some woods not far from Arthur's home, both resting their head on the palm of their hands.

"Grandfather, why did we have to walk so far to see the stars; we could have quite easily lain in your garden?"

"Sometimes, Josh, to see the light from the heavens we have to retreat from the world."

"Why?"

"There are times when the lights all around you can stop you from seeing the one true light." Arthur's words hung in darkness of the room now just as they had done in the night sky when first they were spoken.

Josh now understood what his grandfather was trying to teach him, that there would come a time when you had to retreat from the world and the lights of others if you wanted to experience the one true light. He sat in semi-darkness for the rest of the night. The sound of footsteps outside the room brought him back to consciousness. Still sitting in the half lotus position, he tried to stand, only to fall backwards. His mind was awake but his legs were most definitely not. The sensation of blood being allowed once again to move freely through his legs made Josh call out in pain.

CHAPTER 16

Light Is Knowledge, Light Is Freedom

The decision to leave before lunch was Gawain's.

"We can eat on the way or when we arrive there," he said. Neither Josh nor Caitlin could think of a good enough reason to object, except that they had very little time to pack their rucksacks. Caitlin finished her coffee and left the cottage before her companions had finished their breakfast. Shortly before, Gawain had placed home-made bread on the table just out of the oven. When Gawain had not heard Josh leave the living room at the same time as his niece the previous night, he found it hard to sleep so had spent the night making bread. After first packing his bag, he had headed to the kitchen and decided to bake. Caitlin was now leaving by the back door, doing her coat up as she walked hastily through the gate, turned left and headed for her home. In less than a couple of minutes she was pulling her bag from under her bed. The Kiki backpack had seen better days. Caitlin and her bag had been companions from her early teens, when she had travelled around Europe with her uncle during the long school breaks. On her twentieth birthday she had packed her bag and journeyed solo around most of South America. Not one person had known where she had gone, which made it all the more strange when, one morning over breakfast, Gawain sat beside her in a backstreet café. He had never explained or answered any of her direct questions as to how he had found her. What drove her to near despair at the time was his unwillingness to leave her side until they were back in Ireland.

Sitting on her bed now, Caitlin wondered when she would next sleep between those sheets again. Before she finally closed her bedroom door, she stopped to pick up the only picture she had of her mother and herself. She smiled, kissed her mother's image and returned it to its resting place. Making sure the heating was on auto, she closed the back door. When she re-entered Gawain's kitchen, her companions were dressed and waiting.

"Someone please remind me why we are walking for five hours when we have access to a perfectly good vehicle," Josh asked, leaning against the wall.

"It's the physical part of the journey and a pilgrimage needs to be both physical and spiritual."

Caitlin smiled and added to Gawain's comment – doing this always gave her great pleasure. "You must never forget the mental side of the journey too. On any pilgrimage there must be the meeting of all three within the heart." While she spoke, Caitlin pointed to her heart with her right hand. "Upon the journey, all three must and will be tested; if one fails the whole fails. Within every seeker there will be a great battle, one that they must overcome."

Gawain put his arms on Caitlin's shoulders. "You have heard that speech before." He spoke so that only his niece could hear.

So it was that, a little before nine, a tired Josh followed Caitlin and Gawain out into the cold, January air. Heading

195

south away from the village, Josh was finding it hard to keep to the rhythm Gawain was setting. A couple of times Josh had to jog to catch up.

"Have you any idea where we are heading?" Caitlin asked when she finally got beside him.

"The Hill of Tara." Josh felt pleased with himself, which was quite obvious as it was written all across his face.

"That is correct, but first, the Hill of Slane."

"Ah, the home of St Patrick."

"In a way, yes." With those words, Caitlin pushed ahead and was soon twenty-five steps or more in front of Josh. The three wanderers kept to the fields and overgrown footpaths. Gawain walked at a steady pace. The walk reminded Josh of the walk to the clearing by the pool where he had spent many days learning how to meditate. It was late morning when the three rested on the side of a small wood. The temperature had risen a little; it was no longer below freezing at least. Josh cradled his hands around the hot tea Caitlin poured from the purple flask she carried.

"Another hour and we will stop for bite to eat," Caitlin explained reassuringly while at the same time replacing the lid on her flask and placing it back in her backpack.

"You know a nice restaurant out here?" The words Josh spoke could be seen evaporating into the cold air.

"As a matter of fact, young traveller, I do." Caitlin smiled warmly as she answered him.

"You have been this way before?" Josh was hoping to catch Caitlin out and could not help the smile that crept across his face.

"More times than I can remember; in fact, I first made this journey with Arthur when I was very young."

"I don't believe you. When I asked you if you knew him, you said no."

"That's true, but just because you spend some time with someone does not mean you know them. I was young and, sadly, I didn't know who he was at that time. I had pleaded with my uncle to take me along with him on one of his trips. There were a few others on that one occasion.

"How many of you walked this way with him?" A tone of jealousy was beginning to raise its ugly head. Josh still didn't like the idea of sharing his grandfather with anyone else.

"Just a couple, two young women, Pen and the other I believe you met – tall, slim with silver hair, goes by the same name." When she had spoken the last word, she looked into her uncle's eyes. Through the whole conversation to this point, he had just sat watching the two lovers lock horns. Now, Gawain's eyes showed his deep disappointment in his niece, his eyes cutting deep into the wound Caitlin caused by her own words. In her soul's depths, she knew what she had been taught: never to play with another's mind once they had started out on the fire quest. She had failed. Standing up faster than melting snow on an open fire, the young traveller now swung her backpack over her right shoulder and stepped out on to the path once again. She didn't look back for well over an hour. The three walked on, each in their own world, lost in their own thoughts.

A little before one in the afternoon they were walking along an abandoned road, with moss and grass covering the centre of the tarmac making it appear like the track of a railway. They turned up a long drive with a row of beech trees neatly spaced out on either side. At the bottom, hidden from the road, was an old cottage that had seen many summers, but was well kept. Before they reached the bottom of the three steps, the door opened to reveal a woman in her late sixties, perhaps early seventies. Her grey hair was tidily fastened in a bun, over her blue dress a white pinny was tied neatly around her waist. The aromas coming from inside gave away the many hours that she had clearly spent preparing for their arrival.

"Boots off before you come in, young man." Her accent was not local. Josh did not hesitate to do as he was commanded. Gawain and Caitlin had already started to remove their footwear, a drill they had done many times in the past.

"Over near the fire." As each succession of words were spoken, Josh carried out the lady's instructions.

"Pam, this is Josh, Arthur's grandson." Gawain felt it time to introduce the stranger in her home.

"Arthur's grandson. Now, that's an honour to have you eating at my table. I can see, looking at you now, a slight resemblance in the eyes."

"You knew him?" Josh felt stupid asking such a silly question.

"Knew him very well. He was my cousin on his father's side, so that makes us family." Pam smiled and before Josh could react she covered the short distance between them and wrapped her arms around him. "Family, my boy." With those words, she kissed him just below his fringe. Josh was too taken aback – not to mention too tired and hungry – even to start thinking about how this old lady, who lived in Ireland but came from who knows where, fitted into his family history.

After lunch, which was more like a feast, the four sat in front of an open fire. The old clock sitting on the mantel struck two.

"We have just under three miles to go 'til we reach the Hill of Slane, but looking at the weather it might be better if we stay here tonight and go on in the morning, if you are OK with that, Pam?" Gawain asked.

"You can stay here as long as you like, I could do with the company. I don't see many folk this time of the year."

That night, they gathered around the open fire; a tired Josh sat in awe of the old lady perched on her three-legged stool. He was spellbound listening to the stories she retold of her time with Arthur, as they had played in the streets not far from their families' respective homes, stories that just came to life in her telling of them. Arthur in his youth sounded like any other boy growing up in the overcrowded city. She laughed out loud when she told how his grandfather had got given detention for not doing his homework and then argued with the head teacher that once he was out of school he would not and should not be told what to do. He was amazed at the length his grandfather would go to so that he did not have to go to detention.

"One night, the head caught him climbing out of the toilet window; caught by his ear, he was led off to the headmaster's office yet again."

Josh was disappointed to find out that in Pam's early twenties she had moved away to live in the north of England, just south of the Scottish border. She lost contact with Arthur until one day, out of the blue, he knocked on her door. It was during one of his many trips to Iona. When Josh enquired what the purpose of the visit was, Pam smiled and politely said that it was between her and Arthur.

"After that first visit, he would frequently call in unannounced; when Pap died and I was all alone, it was

Arthur who took me on the same walk that you are embarked upon. Arthur was not well, but he had promised that he would take me and he did. I fell in love with this place." As she spoke, Pam let her eyes trace the room. Her face was one of perfect peace and contentment. "This house was empty at the time, so he persuaded me to move here. The rent on my old house was going through the roof; I think the landlord wanted me out after Pap died. So I came here and my only rent is to welcome guests on the fire quest." With a deep sigh, Pam rose from her resting place, excused herself and retired for the evening. For some time the three sat in silence, watching for the second day running how pure energy could devour an old log that Pam had placed on the fire before she'd left the room. Caitlin smiled when she heard the small mutterings of an old prayer come forth from the old lady's lips, a ritual she always performed. Caitlin had always wanted to ask Pam what the words were that she said, but never felt that it was appropriate just after she had said them. She promised herself to enquire the next morning, which of course always slipped her mind.

The next morning there was a deep, pure white blanket covering the whole landscape. The snow never let up all of that day nor the rest of the week. Five whole days had passed since the three had arrived only planning to spend the one night but, as it turned out, staying twelve nights in all. In that time, Josh had memorised the first four pages of the journal. The words from Merton and Freud were beginning to churn over in his mind. Josh spent hours talking to Pam about Arthur and the rest of his family. Gawain spent hours in meditation, as did Caitlin. At first, Josh made excuses not to join them but by the end of their time there, he too joined his companions in meditation. Pam joined them once or twice, but mainly she preferred to sit alone in silence.

Finally, the wintry conditions relented. With snow still on the ground and a little before 10 a.m., the three travellers set out to cover the last few miles to the Hill of Slane. Josh stopped to view St Patrick's Church from a distance, allowing his companions to go on without him. When he arrived back alongside them, Caitlin and Gawain stood looking over at the Hill of Tara. Josh stood next to Caitlin. Without either one consciously thinking about it, their hands interlocked.

"Josh, how much did you read of your grandfather's time here and his love for the place?" Gawain asked.

"Nothing. It was very clear, and you reinforced it enough times, that I must not read another's account without first experiencing it for myself." Caitlin squeezed Josh's hand slightly as he spoke, reassuring him that he had answered correctly.

"And why would that be?"

"My mind could be coloured by another's experience."

"This is one of the places where the old ways clashed with the new. Over on Tara stood the King of kings. In this area, centuries ago, there were many smaller kings; the King of them all lived over there. It was on that hill that the King would decide when the great fire of Beltane was to be lit. Once the fire of Tara was ablaze, others would spread out across the darkened landscape like stars in the sky. Around 450 CE, on Holy Saturday night, Patrick, when darkness descended upon the world, lit the holy fire in celebration of the resurrection of our Lord, re-enacting the battle between dark and light, which had been at loggerheads since time began. When the Master walked out of the tomb, darkness was defeated once and for all, for those who accepted his teachings and walked in his footsteps."

"And for those who don't?" Josh interrupted, intrigued to understand the answer to a question that had plagued him and Megan for a long time.

"They sit in darkness." Caitlin spoke just as Gawain was getting ready to answer.

"Light is knowledge, light is freedom. The true light brings transformation and healing for those who let it in," Gawain added. Silence stood among them for a short while before Josh dispelled it once again with a simple question.

"What happened with Patrick?"

"He was taken to the Hill of Tara, to face the King of kings; it was there that he bent down to take a shamrock from the grass in front of him to explain the Trinity of God."

"Why?" Josh asked in almost a whisper.

"You remember sitting in the womb at Newgrange. At the very end it is shaped just like a shamrock. Patrick was explaining that Christianity was not a new religion to these isles, but the revelation of the old, a continuation, a development within the life and understanding of the native people. The people of those times, and some still today, believed there to be a spirit that covers and is woven throughout all creation, like a golden thread holding all together. Our ancestors saw it hovering in the sky or racing across the landscape in the form of a sage, always protecting those in its care. Patrick chose the simple shamrock because people felt close to nature; their simple spiritual paths were one with the elements. Over these islands, there are places where the veil between worlds is very frail, almost invisible. There are more sacred places than people recognise: most of the Christian churches are built upon holy ground, in these thin places, places that link humanity with the Divine. At one time, people were more in tune with the land around them and the cycle of nature. You remember the pool of eternal youth on Dun I? Like the pool, Brigid is also associated with Tara. Here, she is the guardian of the holy flame, the perpetual sacred flame. Not far from where you are standing, nuns dedicated their lives to tending the sacred flame in her honour. Within many churches, the sacred flame still burns at the side of Our Lord's Mother, or next to the Holy Sacrament, the presence of the Master himself. Patrick, in his own way, was making the connections between the new, Christian practices and the ancient ways."

The view from Tara was breathtaking. The cold breeze bit deep into their faces. Josh sat as Gawain instructed, eyes closed. Setting up a circle of light around him, as if he was sitting within the sacred flame, Josh's thoughts, his intention, was to let go of the past, to allow the flame to devour all that held him back from the path ahead. To allow himself to be led in the same way as the Israelites were led out of slavery to freedom. Floating in the back of Josh's mind was another conversation he once had with his grandfather. It was so long ago it was hard to remember the exact context. He remembered sitting next to a roaring fire. They had both spent the late afternoon gathering twigs and then lit the fire at the bottom of the garden. Two baked potatoes wrapped in tinfoil lay at its heart.

"Josh, the hardest thing to let go of is the past: assumptions, preconceived ideas, teachings that no longer apply, past wrongs and broken hearts. But to be free we have to live only in the present. Let go of the past or it will hold you back, stop you from being free, stop you from being who you are and, most of all, it will stop you from true transformation."

These were the thoughts that filled Josh's intentions in that precious moment on the Hill of Tara.

As is so often the case when travelling, the walk back to the small cottage that had been their home took no time at all. Josh felt tired both physically and mentally. The cold had penetrated to his very core. The meditation had taken three hours, during which Caitlin and Gawain had sat watching his every move. Tired though he was, Josh felt clean within his soul for the first time in as long as he could remember. He sensed that he had been with the Ancient One, that things, indeed, would now be different for him.

They spent a further two days at Pam's. Josh was under the impression that they would see the week out in the cottage, but the next morning something happened to make Gawain change his mind. The phone had rung, which in a way was unusual. Pam answered and passed it to Gawain. Within half an hour they were all packed up and headed for the coast on foot.

CHAPTER 17

Allow Her To Heal You

A startled Pen woke in the pure, white light streaming through the window. Lying there she knew deep in her soul that it was time to help Megan come to terms with the loss of Josh. The time had come for her to walk with Megan on her own path. It was late morning when Pen mentioned to Megan that the hour to leave had arrived; they were going to visit friends in Ireland.

"Silver leaves today and we are travelling with her on the ferry."

Both Megan and Silver looked surprised, but for different reasons. For Megan, it was the first time a visit to Ireland had been mentioned and for Silver, she was convinced that Pen's intentions were to catch up with Gawain and Josh. Pen refused to look away when she met Silver's stare, nor would she share her thoughts or plans when they were alone, perhaps because Pen herself was not sure what she would do if she sensed they were near Gawain.

The ferry left not a minute early or a minute late. The crossing was not kind to Megan, who spent most of her time below deck. Once the ferry had docked safely, Silver and Darcy parted from Pen's company without any acknowledgement that they even knew each other. It was just a short drive to their overnight accommodation, where they were welcomed by an attentive hostess. Megan took to Pam instantly, as she noticed the sound of the washing machine humming in the background.

"Have you had other guests?" Megan asked over a cup of nettle tea, a flavour she had never tried until she'd met Pen.

"Yes, they left a few hours before you arrived." While Pam spoke, she watched Pen out of the corner of her eye. She sensed that there was something deep down inside her friend that troubled her. It was unlike Pen to break the code. Pam also knew it was unwise to question her on the topic.

For over a week that they stayed at the cottage, both Pen and Megan walked in the surrounding countryside. For Megan it was time to explore her new habitat, if only for the next few weeks; for Pen it was a time of healing. She had watched her young companion grow over the time they had spent with each other, and she sensed that Megan had been in her cocoon for far too long; now, as spring approached, it was time for this butterfly to emerge. Watching Megan, and knowing of the deep love she held for a young man who had run off at the first obstacle, she was not sure deep down if she ever wanted to meet him. Walking to the window and watching fresh snow settle on the ground, she tried to remember the last winter that they had had so much snow. Megan got to her feet from her place in front of the fire, while unknown to her, Pen watched her reflection in the window. Megan straightened her dress that was fitted to her slender body revealing all the right curves, as she moved elegantly towards the kitchen, Pen still watching her every move. Memories of her late sister flooded her mind. Pen was never one to bring boys home; she enjoyed her studies too much. Her mother would even joke that she would marry her books one day. Her sister, on the other hand, brought three, maybe four, boys for dinner over the short time she could. One, a tall, thin boy who looked like he could do with a good hot meal, came round most nights for nearly a year. Pen remembered walking past her sister's room late one night after returning from the library and hearing her sobbing her heart out. They sat that night, locked in each other's arms, until the sun climbed once again into the sky. The shaggy boy, and for the life of Pen she could not now recall his name, had been spotted out with a girl from the same school. When questioned, Shaggy shrugged his shoulders, turned round and walked out of her life. For weeks her sister would sit in her room hoping to catch a small glimpse of him as he walked by to school. It disturbed Pen to see her sister become a recluse like that. Shaggy was the last boy she ever dated, maybe even spoke to. Pen's thoughts came back into the present as she overheard Megan ask, "Do you want any help, Pam?"

Pen was determined to help Megan move on from Josh. She turned from the window and looked back into the room; she could sense Gawain's presence within those four walls. Knowing that Josh was on the path and would not be the same once Gawain had woven his magic upon his soul, she swore to herself that she too would help the lost soul in her care and help her to find the inner transformation enabling her to move on in her life.

◆ ◆ ◆

The weeks passed swiftly. The snow finally departed, giving permission for colour to return to the landscape. On the hilltops, snowdrops were appearing, forming clusters and blankets wherever they ventured – the first sign of new life. Imbolc was fast approaching and with it, signs of transformation. Standing on top of the Hill of Tara in the mid-afternoon sun, Pen explained to Megan that the hill was once the home to the King of kings, and that it was here that St Patrick first spoke to the king of Tara about the Master, the true King of kings.

"Megan," Pen's voice was soft and peaceful, a voice full of love, "it's time to ask yourself who the king is in your life."

Without moving her eyes from the breathtaking view that stretched out in front of her, Megan answered, "I don't believe in the Christian faith; that's why I asked you to teach me your path."

"I follow the path set before me by the Master, I follow his teachings."

"Not true. I have seen what you read; I have sat around your fire with your friends." Megan turned, looking deep into her guide's eyes, as her voice wavered. "You do not act or dress like a Christian, so don't play with me."

Pen placed her arms around the waist of the young woman in her care and guided her down the path that led away from Tara.

"Around the fire, did you not receive the sacraments in bread and wine?"

"Are you telling me that was the Lord's Supper?"

"My young friend, if you had not be so absorbed in conversation with those around you, and paid attention, you would have seen and heard the priest blessing the bread and wine."

"I have been to many services and they were not like that one."

"Not all dresses look the same, but they are dresses. One might be formal, the other informal; never judge with your eyes, only your heart."

Megan pulled away, walking just a few steps in front; she was soon lost in another world, a world full of Josh.

◆ ◆ ◆

"In a few days' time, it will be 1st February, a day dedicated to St Bridget, or Mary of the Gael, as she is sometimes known; she is one of the patron saints of Ireland."

"Thought Patrick was," Megan replied to Pen without taking her eyes from her breakfast resting on the table in front of her.

"True, he is, but so is Bridget. Not far from here in Kildare there is an abbey of hers." Pen paused, which to Megan seemed ages but in reality was only some thirty seconds. "There are many things I could share with you about Bridget, but to start with we will go with only three, the midwife, the blacksmith and, most of all, her healing."

"And this is going to help in…?" Megan was cut short by the wave of Pen's hand.

"You want to know about my path, so we start with Bridget. Bridget is the keeper of the Eternal Flame." Pen spoke slowly, pausing as if she was searching for the next few words, almost as if she was trying to pluck them out of the air. "The blacksmith works in metal, and he works with it deep within the fire, shaping and reshaping his work until he finds the shape he is looking for. Fire is one of the four elements, the one that can bring about true transformation. If we allow him, the Master can transform his true disciple if only they would surrender completely to the fire of his love."

Later that morning, while Pen and Megan walked, Pen explained the transformation that she saw taking place within Megan, that she was no longer the person she had first met so many months ago. The conversation moved on to the desires and aspirations that Megan once had. As the mid-morning sun grew stronger, Pen began her magic and helped those same desires to begin to be rekindled.

"Now is the time to let go of the past, of all that holds you back. See the snowdrops? They are a sign that spring is here, a time when the earth is reborn. Bridget, if you allow her, will be your midwife and help you give birth to the new you. If you work with her and allow her to heal you, she will bring you transformation."

CHAPTER 18

Lindisfarne, A Place To Be Reborn

Caitlin could be stubborn, a trait that ran through the family. Gawain insisted they walk back to his cottage where they could spend the night, before he and Josh headed back to Iona. Caitlin laughed as she pointed out that they had already agreed she could accompany them upon Josh's path. Josh retired to his room and left uncle and niece in deep discussion on the reasons Gawain now thought it best that she stay behind. Lying on his bed he could still hear them reasoning out the two different points of view. Turning over, Josh wondered who would win; his heart hoped for Caitlin to triumph, but he knew why Gawain had decided otherwise. It was strange being back at the cottage, after he had believed he would never see it again. It was not hard, of course, for anyone to see that Caitlin and he were more than fond of each other. Both Caitlin and Josh believed in their hearts that that was the reason for Gawain's change of mind in letting them walk the path together. Neither one put it down to the phone call that Gawain had taken just moments before he announced their departure, nor did they hear the voice on the phone warning Gawain that others had decided to bring Megan to the cottage. It was clear that Gawain had not been himself since the call, but for Caitlin and Josh they could not see past the growing feelings that they had for each other. Romance can do strange things to the human mind, taking us into a world no one else can follow, a world made for two where nothing else matters. The dream can last for eternity or it can be shattered in the blink of an eye.

Caitlin was furious at having to return home so soon. She threw herself on her bed and sobbed into her pillow. It had been a long time since she had had feelings for anyone. The last time she let anyone – or should it be said the *only* time she let anyone – remotely close was while she travelled in South America. Danny was five years older than Caitlin, a boy full of confidence, coming across as very mature. Caitlin travelled with him for a few months before she found out that he was lying and stealing from her. When she confronted him the first time, he was so convincing she believed that she had misjudged him, but that night while Caitlin was sleeping, he stole all the money he could get his hands on and slipped away. From that very moment, Caitlin trusted no one, and always listened to the voice inside her. Even though she had only known Danny for such a short time she had fallen for him; it took a long time for the pain to heal. Lying quietly in her room with no light, she knew she didn't want to let Josh slip away, but what could she do?

The next morning, the two travellers left the car sitting in the drive, and headed down the main street. Josh was a little disappointed that Caitlin didn't show before they left; his heart was now torn between his feelings for her and those for Megan.

It took a few days before they reached the coast where the small vessel was once again waiting for them. On their return to the now familiar cottage, and as they only planned to stay for one night, there was no food in the cupboard. Showered and wearing fresh clothes, the two did what anyone in that situation would do – they headed for a pub. Once in the bar, Josh could not believe what he saw. Sitting next to the fire already eating her evening meal was Caitlin.

"What took you so long?" she asked without looking up from her plate.

Pulling up a chair beside her, Gawain made no comment, his expression unchanging. Knowing that it was futile to try and keep his two young companions apart, Gawain refused to look at or commune with either of his dinner companions. The look in their eyes while eating together told him that his task, his promise to Arthur, was now going to be very challenging. He retired early, leaving Caitlin and Josh to walk back to the cottage alone.

It took a good full day to walk the single-track road across Mull, during which time Gawain didn't communicate once. This never stopped Caitlin and Josh, walking a little distance behind him, lightly holding hands, releasing only when they thought 'Grumpy' would turn around. Numerous days' walking lay ahead of them and Caitlin and Josh were going to make the most of their time together.

◆ ◆ ◆

The isle of Lindisfarne surrounded by the sea was a sight for sore eyes and aching legs. Sitting on the beach, waiting for the tide to retreat, provided a welcome rest after so many days walking, mainly staying at B & Bs en route. Josh was amazed to learn that apart from Arthur, Gawain and Pen, no one else up until him had walked the whole of the journey.

When Caitlin shared this with him, she squeezed his hand saying, "We are both walking this together for the first time."

Josh removed the journal from his bag at Gawain's request.

This is my last entry in this, my beloved journal. It is strange how life turns out in the end, the first shall be last and the last shall be first. I am in my last few days within this incarnation; I can feel the life that was once strong now fading. I wrote to Gawain, my true brother in spirit, over two weeks ago while my hand was still firm enough to write, requesting that he visit this day to anoint me and take this small account of my spiritual journey into his care. I trust him above all others to take care of it; only he will know how best to use it. I never shared with Linda details of the work I have been engaged in. Linda is with her sister all day so when Gawain comes I will be alone. He will bring my first journal for me to read, and he will return one week from today to retrieve it and destroy it. It is all arranged. I want no soul to read its contents. The path I have travelled has been a difficult one but rewarding beyond anything I deserve. Gawain has been the perfect student and companion and is now the true owner of this book. I have only one regret and that is that I have had very little time with Joshua, a pure, dear soul. I have enjoyed teaching him and hope one day he will follow in my footsteps. I will ask Gawain to look out for him on my behalf. If anyone does, for some unknown reason, come across this book before you read it, find someone who knows the way of the Master. Books make very poor teachers; you never really know why the author wrote what they did, or even if they changed their mind after they had written it. You cannot debate with the written word, and you cannot debate with the students of the author, because they become authorities on the texts and will imprison the true spirit of their master.

Find a guide of the Eternal Flame, someone trained in helping you come to your own transfiguration experience. Their esoteric teachings are never written down, but passed from disciple to student and each student must become a teacher. This is the way it has always been. This is the way it should be with you. Arthur.

Josh sat for some time, lost in his own thoughts, contemplating the events of the past months, from the very first time Gawain walked into his life and all the conversations they had ever had. Never once had he or Caitlin mentioned that they were teachers of 'the Eternal Flame'. It didn't even cross his mind why he had never seen the inscription on the inside of the front cover before nor had he asked if there were such a thing.

"You never mentioned that you are teachers of the Eternal Flame."

"Guides," Gawain was quick to correct once again.

"Teachers or guides, what's the difference?"

"Teachers teach and a guide guides you; there is a big difference between the two. I don't know why your grandfather wrote those words."

Caitlin gazed out to sea while the conversation went on around her; for her, the penny had dropped. She now understood why her uncle had been insistent upon her staying behind in Ireland. A single tear made its way down her cheek. One of the teachings of the path is not to influence another's path by letting your emotions infect theirs. Her love for Josh had clouded her judgement, and would overshadow her new love's steps on the journey he was now to make. Standing without a word and oblivious to the heated conversation going on between her two companions, she walked down the beach towards the receding water that not long since had hidden the path from view. Not heeding her uncle's warning, she removed her shoes and continued across the sand in the direction of the Holy Island.

That night, Caitlin kept away from her two companions, retiring to bed early. A little after nine her uncle tapped on the door to see if she needed anything. For the next couple of hours, the two talked in her room. A cloud came over Gawain as he listened to his young niece as she described her feelings for Josh, how she missed her mother, and the need she had for someone to hold her. During the unfolding of the conversation, it was becoming evident that Caitlin loved Josh enough to let him go, to be free to walk his path through this world. Gawain, holding his niece's hand, was clear that if they were meant to be together they would find each other at the end of his quest.

"What if he chooses Megan?" Caitlin had asked through her tears.

"It will be his choice, not yours." Gawain hated having to point it out.

Caitlin rose before the great light and wandered the island with the depths of darkness wrapped around her as tight as a baby's blanket. She had admired her uncle since she was a child and always wanted to walk as he walked. She had let everyone down, betrayed all that she had come to hold dear. The betrayal she felt deep within her was too much to bear. Now the darkness had entered her heart and she had betrayed the very light that once saved her life and gave her purpose within this strange and trying incarnation. Sitting on the beach facing east, she closed her eyes and listened to the great ocean cleansing the ground she walked. Relaxing her body and focusing her mind on her sacred word she began her meditation. The discipline allowed her to take what was left of her own mind and let it rest deep within her heart in the very presence of the Eternal Flame. Deep within her heart she sensed the first rays of the great light leap over the horizon like warriors of old racing into battle. The Light was there to save her from the darkness of the pit within her. In slow motion she could see now the golden path racing towards her. The light within her being reached out to welcome the Lord of Light. Standing, she allowed her clothes to fall from her body to rest on the earth beneath her bare feet. Completely naked, dressed only as nature had intended, she felt neither the morning chill nor the temperature of the water. She entered the golden path, gently resting on the still water in front of her until she could be seen no more; the golden path closed above her head as if she had never been. Only her clothes paid tribute to her presence ever being there. The sea even washed away her footprints.

CHAPTER 19

Into The Darkness Came The Light

Josh spent the night reading from the pages of his grandfather's journal. The room on the island was small but comfortable, overlooking the ocean and the rising sun. The question still running through his mind was why he had started reading halfway through his beloved guardian's words. While he contemplated these thoughts, he remembered that he had done the same with the journal he had treasured before he had started on this new adventure. He had never read the dark notebook from the beginning to its end. He had always opened its pages at random. Had he missed anything his grandfather had written? A great fear rose within him. He felt a fool to have lost any opportunity to have known his grandfather better. Gawain had told him you can learn so much about the path a person has walked by understanding the darkness that dwells within them. How much had he missed that was now lost forever?

Josh had promised Gawain, before they'd retired to their separate rooms the previous night, that he would not read past the first few pages until the time was right to do so. Josh promised his grandfather and himself that he would now listen to his guides and pay due attention to their teachings.

For the hundredth time, he read the first entry in the book lying within his hands.

August 3rd

Once the light penetrates the darkness, it's hard to see the world in the same way again. A few days have passed since I wanted to take my own life. I had decided to end it all on Dun I, to die and be no more. In a way I did die, but not physically. When the light came there was no warning, no announcement, it just was. I had put the pills in my hand and placed them upon my lips. When you can only see and feel the darkness, you become the darkness to the point where you can see nothing else in this world. She becomes your mistress, courting you, at first just visiting you in your times of despair. Then the dance begins and you become convinced that you are the one courting her, leading her within the great dance of your life. She will hold you in her arms, resting your head upon her breasts; her sweet enticing voice brings at first peace to your wounded heart, like water from a cool, mountain stream to a scalded hand. The dance begins in light, but her dark soul soon begins to sing to your heart, her steps beginning to lead you gently, slowly at first, but then, when her songs have filled your heart and mind, the dance changes pace. You never see the abyss coming until it is too late. To start with, you stumble and your loved ones try with all their strength and love to hold you and bring you home safely, but by the time of the first noticeable stumble, it is already too late. The ears can only hear the sweet voice of your new love; eyes are clouded with her beauty, transfixed by her smile. The heart is convinced you are at one with the world; your new love is the true path. When the last step has been taken then and only then does the long, painful fall begin. She will keep her promise and lead you home to the darkness where you find yourself totally alone and forsaken.

At first, I felt the soft, warm hand resting upon mine, stopping me from swallowing the pills. An old, grey-haired man in his late seventies sat beside me. Where he came from, how he got there without me noticing him, I have no idea. I cannot describe him, he was dressed in the same way my great-grandfather would dress, dungarees with brown gardening gloves tucked just inside his pocket so that they hung out for all to see. In a way, he reminded me of him. We sat for a while holding hands and that night I slept resting in his arms, safe, at peace. When I woke in the morning I was alone, but not for long. At first, I saw her approaching me slowly. Warm smile, surrounded by beautiful copper hair glittering in the early morning sun. That morning their light was one, rising in my new life. Strong and pure like I had never seen before. Morgan rested beside me; I knew she had found what she was looking for after her short climb. She spoke not a word. Her beautiful green eyes filled at the same time as mine. We both cried in silence. I knew she felt my pain. When she spoke it was with a soft, Irish voice, which can only be described as balm to my broken soul. She picked up the fallen pill bottle and replaced the pills that were now scattered on the wet grass, placing the bottle in her pocket.

"Did you take any?"

I could only shake my head in shame.

Josh ate breakfast alone; there was no sign of his companions. Knocking on their doors, he received no answer; popping his head around the door to Gawain's room showed that he had been disturbed and had left suddenly. He never left his room if anything was out of place. This was not the case, from what Josh could see. Caitlin's room was the complete opposite; it was as if she had never been there; even her bag was gone. Josh's heart sank; he believed that Gawain had persuaded Caitlin to return home to Ireland. Making tea, he retreated to the garden, sitting in the morning sun, oblivious to what those rays had taken from him. Returning to the notebook he was soon dwelling in a different world, totally unaware of the commotion going on elsewhere on the island.

August 6th

It's been a few days since Morgan persuaded me to stay at her home on the island. I am now indebted to her for her kind hospitality. We have spent the last few days talking through how I came to be in such a dark place. She makes me feel like I am the most important person in the world. Morgan is like no other person that I have ever met in my entire life. Her very presence is like the midday sun, renewing and refreshing.

August 8th

Morgan encouraged me to write to Linda to let her know that I was safe and well, I told her I would consider it.

August 12th

I sat in silence, feeling very vulnerable, this morning, watching Morgan reading words I had written in my journal. She read very slowly or was studying every word, contemplating the meaning, the feeling behind each sentence. When she had finished she placed the journal down and smiled, a deep penetrating smile that spoke to my wounds, as if she understood everything I had written. We ate lunch in the small kitchen. The solid-fuel Aga on which she cooked also kept the room warm. Morgan asked about Jonathan and we talked through the subjects he had given me to read. Morgan never once criticised what I had written or what Jonathan had taught me. In my heart, I knew she did not see the world in the same way he did. We talked at some length about my encounter with him. We talked into the evening.

August 28th

My life is beginning to take a new direction. Morgan's teaching is helping me see the world in a different way. Her gentle, warm personality brings peace like balm to my once tormented soul.

It was mid-morning and the sun was hiding behind the maple tree in the corner of the garden. Gawain walked into the kitchen and called to Josh through the window. He had decided not to share the events that had taken place over the last twelve hours with Josh, from the moment he found the small note pushed under his door before he went to bed explaining everything, saying how very sorry she was for interfering with Josh's path and could her uncle find it in his heart to forgive her. Fighting back the tears, he had wished he had gone easier on his young niece. He had forgotten what it was like to be in love. He tried to convince himself after retrieving Caitlin's clothes from the beach that she had done nothing wrong. If only he had realised sooner, he would have been in time to stop her. The second Josh walked in the house, Gawain explained that they would be leaving within the hour.

"Caitlin?"

"What?" Gawain was startled and, for once, it showed in his voice.

"Where is Caitlin, is she coming with us?"

Not wanting to lie, while at the same time conscious that he did not want to push Josh back into the darkness, he told the truth, but not all of it.

"I am afraid she will not be coming with us today."

As the two walked from the house past the small convenience store, Josh overheard people talking about how the ambulance had only just made it to the island that morning.

"I wonder what the ambulance was for?" Josh asked.

"The old lady at number 4 had a bad fall." Gawain was quick to answer, this time with rather less truthfulness.

Heading south, they stopped in local B & Bs most nights, arriving late and leaving early. There was something very different about Gawain; at times he seemed distracted. Before breakfast each morning, they met outside to meditate and again before the sun went down, each time for forty minutes. Josh's mind was becoming focused, sharp. He had never had better concentration in his life. He was beginning to remember all that he read and learnt. Occasionally, bad memories from the past came to the surface, but were soon dealt with by Gawain. At night, Josh would fall asleep reading Arthur's journal. Josh would hover over each word, hearing his grandfather's gruff voice; some nights he would end up dreaming of the days they spent in the forest together. During the day, while the two walked, Gawain shared the path of the Eternal Flame.

One day, as they reached the outskirts of Whitby, Josh was startled by Gawain asking him: "Have you kept your promise and only read the first few pages of the journal?"

"I have."

"What have you read?"

"About my grandfather's time on Iona and his encounter with Morgan." While Josh spoke, Gawain showed his approval. "Did you know her?" Josh added.

"I met her once, just before she died. She had asked to meet me, so Arthur and I travelled to see her at her home, which you have been to." Josh nodded his recognition of that fact.

"You never met my grandmother, though, did you?"

"No."

"Why was that?"

"It's not mine to share."

As they walked Josh took the journal from his bag, opened it and reread pages that were becoming familiar to him. Gawain smiled. It did amuse him to see Josh reading while he walked.

September 1st

A letter came this morning from Linda asking when I was planning to return home. I felt excited and petrified at the same time. I had followed Morgan's advice and told Linda I was well and staying at a friend's home on the island. I am excited to see Linda but petrified that she will not understand why I am staying with Morgan, who was a complete stranger until a short time ago.

September 6th

*I met Linda from the ferry and took her to lunch in the
local pub and then we walked along the beach. We talked
openly, hiding nothing. Linda was different, frank and to
the point, with her soul-searching questions, well thought
out. I told the truth at all times; even of my suspicions of
her affair with the doctor. Morgan had made me promise
to do so this morning, just after our morning meditation
before breakfast. It was only when we reached the summit
of Dun I and were standing in the very spot I had
planned to end my life, did I share with her that deep,
dark moment. Locked within each other's arms our souls
cried out to each other. Linda's emotions got the better of
her. Her body went limp as she collapsed into my arms.
I could hold her no longer so I let her down gently, and
there we remained, sitting in the very spot where Morgan
found us, Linda's head resting upon my lap.*

September 7th

*This afternoon, I learnt that Linda's doctor had been
visiting her every day because she was getting through her
tablets for depression too quickly and he was worried that
she was going to take her own life. I owned up to the fact
that I had been stealing them. Linda smiled, showing that
she now understood that fact. It was late afternoon by the
time we both found Morgan sitting at her small kitchen
table waiting for us to join her for supper. I have no idea
why I was so worried about the two of them meeting.
Linda just fell into her arms and expressed how thankful
she was for her saving me.*

September 9th

Linda and Morgan have spent the last two days walking the island alone while I have been reading the books Morgan insisted I read. I saw the two of them return down the road arm in arm like two old friends. It came to me today that they actually have a lot in common with each other.

September 11th

I have seen a great change within Linda since she arrived. I have very little idea of their conversations, her and Morgan, but they must be doing her good. For the first time since Paul's death, I heard her say his name without breaking down. Over supper, Linda even laughed while she spoke about his early childhood.

September 14th

Morgan accompanied Linda and me to the ferry. I was reluctant at first to leave the island, but Morgan insisted that it was the right time for me to go home and be with my other children. Tears flooded my eyes when the ferry pulled away. I have only known Morgan for such a short time, but already she has become an important part of my life.

Josh was beginning to see his grandfather in a different light; his hero was becoming human. Josh put any thought out of his mind of his grandfather behaving inappropriately; he had always been so dedicated to his wife. The more he read these words, though, the harder it was to keep negative thoughts from his mind. Did he keep secrets? Why had he never told his family about Gawain, or even the work he had been doing? Josh had so many questions about Arthur now forming in his mind that he had never before considered. He had already come to the conclusion that some of the questions would never be answered; his grandfather was becoming as mysterious as his own present companion. Placing the journal safely back into his bag, he walked quietly beside Gawain. It was late afternoon when they arrived at the abbey, once so full of life but now deserted and in ruins. Sitting on what remained of a wall, now no more than a pile of stones, they rested in the sun that had stayed hidden for most of the day, but which now shone gently upon them.

"You familiar with the Synod of Whitby?" Gawain asked, before putting his water bottle to his lips.

"Yes."

"It was here your grandfather would often stay. It is the very place the Anglican Church was born, the meeting place of the Celtic Church, which was the true progression of the spirituality of these lands, with the Roman Church, representing the spirituality of the Roman Empire."

"The Church of England didn't come into being for hundreds of years after the events that took place here."

"Not true. The people of these lands have never wanted to bow to Rome, to an outside power. The Celtic Church came to birth through the Druidic schools. The monks who came here from Iona still had their hair cut in the Druidic style. The teachings of the Master were the fulfilment of all the old religions of this land. The Druids were the learned ones – the teachers, doctors, astrologers, lawyers, counsellors, scientists; they were the backbone of this land, woven into the very structures of society, their knowledge flowing like blood through its veins. The Latin name for

Druid is magi, and you know from your childhood that they went in search of the Messiah, a story that is acted out by children in nearly every country in the world. In the early history of these lands, there were around forty colleges spread across the landscape, as thousands of children were educated in mathematics, geometry, medicine, poetry, astronomy, and philosophy. Nobles from across the Channel even sent their children to these schools, in a similar way to the overseas students who might come to study in Oxford or Cambridge today. There were three main seats where the Archdruids would sit, Caernarvon-on-Usk, York and London. Not much has changed there." Gawain could not help but chuckle to himself. "Druids believed in the one true light, the Ancient One. When Christianity came, it was a natural progression within the development of these lands. From the beginning of the dawn of time, the beginning of creation, spirituality grew and evolved along with the other faculties of humankind. Religion has grown and changed, taking on many disguises, each one best suited to the group, tribe or race at that time in that place. It was what brought balance to our progress and understanding of the Creator and the place that we hold in this world."

Gawain finished speaking for a few moments, rose to his feet and began to walk through the ruins, without waiting for Josh. When Josh finally got the message that he was to follow he caught up with Gawain as he was standing in what he described to be the very place the monks and nuns would translate or copy written manuscripts.

"Once religion, spirituality and their associated teachings were written down, and creeds and doctrines enforced, part of our natural development as human beings was imprisoned. To many now it has become irrelevant. This is why the Druids would never write down their religion and beliefs; once it was written down, they understood that it would be restricted to the past. One aspect of being human is to push our physical bodies to their limits, to discover and explore them so we can best adapt to the ever-changing environment, to live and survive longer. We are encouraged to push the limits of our intellectual abilities and develop our minds, too. Both of these activities are encouraged at school from a very early stage."

Gawain began to chuckle, which made Josh look directly at him. Josh had noticed there was something different about his guide since Caitlin had returned home.

"What's funny?" Josh asked.

"A remark your grandfather would very often come out with. It just came into my mind."

"Are you going to share?"

"If anyone ever said that you have to think outside the box, he would come back with…" Before Gawain could finish his sentence, Josh started to laugh and filled in the last few words.

"…it's a bit late when you are in it!"

"I do miss your grandfather's humour."

Josh nodded, signalling that he too missed that part of his grandfather, and up until that moment had forgotten the humorous side of his personality and their relationship. For too long he had concentrated on the words Arthur had written down and forgotten about the personal relationship that he once shared with his childhood idol.

Gawain began to speak once more. "The spiritual aspect of our being is not encouraged in the same way. We are taught from the written word; we are not allowed to question or disagree in the same way as we can with early scientists. Science moves on, making new discoveries all the time: if someone's theory is disproved, we put it down to the limits of the time and culture they were in. This is not the same with religion and past theologians. To disagree with one of Paul's letters, or a teaching in the Old Testament, that is more specifically related to the development of the group of people at the time of writing, you risk being classed as a heretic. Each civilisation had its own religion that had grown and developed over many hundreds of years and was relevant to them and their specific society and culture. When one civilisation conquers another, they tend to overlay that culture with their own beliefs and gods. Once that group leaves, even after hundreds of years of occupation, the old beliefs will begin to rise up again, but they are never the same because, while the people have moved on in their physical and mental development, the old religion has not."

Later that night, after Josh had retreated to his room and showered, he lay across his bed and began to read. The excitement had stayed with him most of the afternoon, knowing that he was now permitted to read more of the journal. Before Josh opened the book he lay with it resting on his chest, contemplating comments that both Gawain and Caitlin had been making over the last few weeks, made all the more significant in his mind after the conversation that had taken place that day. Josh rested there pondering how the words of one person's mind could influence the life of another, how the thoughts and emotions written down thousands of years ago in a different culture and time, with all its limitations, could alter the flow of another's life, of groups of individuals, or whole nations. Josh was beginning to understand, through his meditations, that the time he had with the Divine was much more real and energising than the words of another. Looking back, he could see now how the words of his grandfather's dark journal had shaped his life, by weaving themselves into his emotions. It was easier to believe the words of someone you looked up to, than to disagree, especially if you needed their approval. But now Josh recognised that even that was dangerous, how easy it was to tap into a person's emotions, into their faith, and control them. It was harder to think and work out for yourself your relationship with the Divine and the world than to listen to others; harder to fight against the herd than to move with it. Jesus paid the cost for doing that. Josh promised never to allow another person into his head again, no matter who they were. The dark journal had come between Megan and himself. It was clear to him now how it had influenced him, taking him into a very dark place, isolating him from those he loved and cared for.

Words that Caitlin once spoke continued to haunt him too: "The Divine does not need the words of another to speak to you; the Divine dwells within you and around you; you only need to listen. There is only one teacher and that is the Master. Each one of us needs guides who have travelled the path and who are more advanced, more experienced than we are, people who will not get in the way but will walk beside you and are able to point and encourage you on your way. Just as the Master walked alongside the disciples on the road to Emmaus. A true guide knows the pitfalls because they have travelled that way before. You will know the path and her guides because, as the Master taught, only he is 'the Way, the Truth and the Life', meaning that we should follow his example and live as he lived. The Master is pure love, his way is love and we show only love. There are only two rules to follow, the Master tells us: Love the Lord your God with all your heart, mind, soul and strength and your brothers and sisters as yourself."

Rolling on to his front, Josh opened the journal at where he had got up to and started to read. As he read, he could hear his grandfather's voice:

February 1st

It was an extremely early start today and I feel tired. I travelled to Scotland, catching the 9.23 a.m. main-line train up the east coast – such wonderful views of the coastline. A change of trains at Haymarket saw me heading west across the country. I then killed some time in Glasgow visiting the library and several bookshops, before I caught the 5.45 p.m. bus to a location Morgan had given me.

Now safely arrived, I will spend this night in the local tavern. It's a nice room, even if it is on the small side and the toilet is down the hall. It was hard saying goodbye to Linda at the station. She had insisted that I join Morgan for the celebration at her home on the mainland tomorrow night though she would not accompany me. She met Morgan only once when she visited her home in Iona, staying several nights, where they became close friends. Linda trusted Morgan like a sister. Since our time at Morgan's home, the relationship between Linda and me has been renewed, strengthened. We are one soul again. There is a peace within our home, in our lives once more.

*My relationship with my children too is stronger than ever;
I can see now that most, though not all, of what affected
the family came from my own grief.*

Josh was beginning to realise how his life had been deeply
affected by his grandfather's thoughts, the depression and
darkness that lay within him while he wrote the first journal.
Now Josh's mind was clear, he could see that the person in
whose company he grew up, who started to guide him on his
spiritual path, was not the one in the book he had treasured.
If he could go back in time, things would be different, he told
himself; he might still be with Megan. Closing his eyes and
relaxing his mind, he revisited some of the most precious
times they had spent together. Had he misread the situation
with Megan, he wondered. Did she really ask him to leave?

February 2nd

*I arrived a little after 2 p.m. at the address Morgan had
sent through, only to find the small cottage bursting with
life. I was a little taken aback, jealous that I was not the
only one that had been invited to celebrate Imbolc. And
yet, Morgan was the true hostess and welcomed me in
with such warmth, introducing me to everyone.*

*By the time I left Morgan's tonight, I had come
to realise that she is not only special and has touched my
life, she has touched and healed many lives and is loved by
everyone she comes alongside. I am looking forward, all
the more now, to the next few weeks that I will spend at
the cottage with her. I will return there tomorrow, around
midday, to say goodbye to her other house guests before
they leave.*

February 6th

Morgan questioned me on the readings she had set me before I left Iona in September. They too were handwritten, just like the ones Jonathan had encouraged me to read. I kept my promise and never made notes or shared them with anyone. The instructions given to me were clear: 'Read and reread until you feel that you understand the message written within and then take only that which fits well with you, believe only that which you can accept, then put the book away and move on in your studies.'

February 7th

Morgan explained that she rarely took on a 'neophyte'. When I questioned her on this, she explained that it was rare to come across a true seeker. There are many lonely souls travelling through this world, all at different levels, as she explained it. Some will dip into the spiritual realm, but only for a while until the next craze comes along. They can leap from one spiritual path to the next, from the feet of one spiritual teacher to the feet of the next in the blink of an eye. Each time feeling, thinking that they are experiencing the Divine, that this is the path they are being guided upon by whichever god they are feeling close to at that moment in time. They follow their own emotions and desires, not the Master; his path is hard but rewarding.

February 8th

It snowed today so we sat by the fire.

February 9th

The walk into town was enjoyable, if a little cold. Back to the fire this evening.

February 10th

We talked today about the meaning of spirituality. To me, it is that which links, or defines, our relationship with the universe, the way in which we see the world. Morgan talked at some length about the flame that burns deep within us. For her, it is how we use our spirit that defines us as spiritual beings. I need to reflect upon this some more.

February 14th

After lunch I felt somewhat downcast as I began to pack my bag, knowing that this was my last day here until the spring. Morgan gave me a pile of notebooks, all handwritten, and the name of a close friend of hers whom I had met on my arrival: Bart, which is short for Bartholomew. He lives just over an hour by bus from my home. Bart is going to be my guide as I undertake my studies. I am a little disappointed it is not to be Morgan, but I understand that I need to see my guide regularly and the distance between Morgan and me is too great.

February 27th

It was good to see Bart again. Like Morgan, he has an air about him that makes him stand out from others. We walked through the forest as we talked through my studies; I sensed that he was trying to get an angle on how much I had learnt so far. I agreed to visit twice a month.

March 2nd

When the post came this morning it brought distressing news. My Great-Uncle Arthur, on my father's side of the family, is terminally ill and requested that I visit him in the next few days. Linda told me that I should leave at once. I packed an overnight bag and caught the midday train to London Paddington, and then the Underground to High Street Kensington. Uncle Arthur was overjoyed to see me arrive so quickly. I was taken aback, however, that his two children were nowhere to be seen. It transpired that there had been an argument over money just before Auntie Maude died; neither one came to the funeral. The day after the funeral, a legal letter had arrived, informing Uncle Arthur that his children were contesting her will. Uncle Arthur had 'married into money' and, having subsequently won the court battle that took all of the last five years, he has not seen or heard from his children since. After dinner, I sat beside his bed holding his hand; he was too weak to get up or even move. 'Boy,' he had not called me that since I was young and bounced upon his leg, 'you visited Iona. Tell me why and what happened to you.' He could tell by the look on my face I was uncomfortable with sharing. 'Boy, I am an old man in the last few days of my life. What you tell me I will surely take to my grave. This I promise.' The last few words melted my heart. 'You remind me of your father. I do miss him,' he added.

I talked late into the night, starting with the loss of Paul — just the mention of his name brought tears to both our eyes. He understood and respected that I could not share the teaching that Morgan and Bart were passing on to me. It was gone 11 p.m. when I left him. By the time I returned to my room, I had a deep feeling that my uncle knew more about my path than he was willing to share.

March 3rd

Uncle Arthur summoned me to his room a little after 8 this morning, where we shared breakfast – the smell of toast coming from the kitchen was just too hard to refuse. 'Boy, I have requested the presence of my solicitor this morning. I would like to leave all my estate to you.' He waved his hand to keep me from talking and carried on as if nothing had happened. 'But I know that my children are waiting in the shadows to pick over my bones and will contest my will in court. I am afraid that they will win this time as the money comes from their mother's side of the family and you are from my side. So I called my solicitor; I spoke at some length with him just after 5 this morning. He was not happy but he knows who puts the clothes on the backs of his children. I explained that I want to set up a charity, a trust fund, to support the work that Morgan and Bart are doing in helping others. In time I hope you will follow in their footsteps. You, along with my solicitor, will be trustees of this charity. There will be strict guidelines set down for its use.'

I didn't know how to respond so I sat like a dummy for a while. All that went through my mind was a conversation that Bart and I had had as we walked through the forest, that the universe had a way of helping us follow our path. What is my path? It had not dawned on me that I would one day want or be able to carry on the work that Morgan and Bart were doing, but then why were they helping me, why was I guided to them and they to me?

Edward, uncle's solicitor, arrived around 11 a.m. with the legal papers ready to be signed. He brought with him two doctors from different practices, a colleague, plus a senior solicitor from a neutral law firm from across the city. Uncle Arthur was taking no risks. I signed where I was told, and was sworn to secrecy. I phoned Linda and told her I was going to be a day late.

March 21st

Bart asked me to accompany him to a gathering in the forest near where he lived. I was surprised to find out that he belonged to a Druidic order. Dressed completely in white gowns, they stood in a circle facing each other. I was too far away to hear the words that were spoken within the circle itself, but came away feeling completely at ease and a deep sense of peace within me.

The spring equinox is an important festival that stretches back through the centuries to a point in time that no one remembers. It marks the final point within the cycle for the resurrection of the Sun, its battle now over with the days being longer than the nights. I came to see the connection with Easter, how both celebrate the resurrection of the true Light.

April 3rd

This coming Sunday is Easter Day. Linda is talking about the whole family attending church for the first time since Paul's funeral. I am not convinced that it would be right for me to go.

April 26th

While standing at the bus stop, I was taken by surprise by a familiar voice coming from behind me. On turning *around, I was shocked to find Jonathan standing there. It was an awkward conversation, really. Jonathan invited me to lunch, and would not take no for an answer. Bart was not too comfortable with the idea of me rekindling the relationship, knowing what it led to the last time, but he did agree that I should visit.*

Josh wandered quietly into the kitchen; the sound of the kettle in the otherwise silent house alarmed him and he hoped it would not wake anyone. Sitting at the table while the water boiled and reading about Jonathan stirred emotions deep in his stomach and he could not understand why. He sipped his tea and continued to read.

May 9th

I reread one of Morgan's notebooks this morning before I left to visit Jonathan, hoping that I might have the chance to look through his extensive library. I found what I was looking for: the Latin name for Druid really is the same translation as the notebook lent to me by Morgan had said – 'Magi'. I noticed how the two books could have been written by the same hand, except for the handwritten date at the top of the first page. Morgan's was four hundred years older and showed signs of having been used extensively. Jonathan assured me that his father had translated the book himself from its original language before he had died. Both books described how the Druids had been awaiting the arrival of the 'anointed one'.

I also found extensive handwritten accounts of Joseph of Arimathea and his travels with a young companion.

May 21st

After my time with Bart, I walked down by the canal, the normal route I would take if I had time to kill. By the third lock along, the strangest thing happened, something that has changed my perspective on all I believe. I was sitting watching the boats passing through, when a dog fell into the lock. Without any hesitation, the dog's owner jumped in to save her. I stood and watched how both went down into the murky water. The gentleman came to the surface with the dog in his arms and swam away from the danger of the boat, which at any moment could have trapped and crushed them both. From the other side of the lock, a man came running and threw himself on the floor. Reaching down, he pulled the dog from the water while at the same time the owner was using all his strength to lift up the now very frightened dog. Once the dog was safe, the stranger reached down a second time and pulled up the drenched owner. From further up the canal, his wife then came running. During the conversation that followed, she explained that her husband had never kept it a secret that if her or their children (who no longer accompanied them) or the dog fell into the water, he wouldn't hesitate to jump in to save them; they were under his care and his responsibility and there was nothing he was not willing to do for them, even if it meant his own life. He had just proved himself.

On the bus journey home, what I had witnessed played and replayed in my mind, disturbing it to its very core, my very soul. The events at the canal brought home a new realisation of the incarnation. The Father looked down and saw humanity drowning in the murkiness of this world. We had got ourselves into a position we could not get ourselves out of on our own. Without hesitation or concern for himself God, in the form of his Son, Jesus Christ, entered the darkness of this world to lift us up and return us to himself. When I closed my eyes, I could see the creator reaching down and the son lifting up not the dog, but me. What Morgan had written about the old myths of Egypt and others from around the world now made sense to me. By the time I stepped from the bus, something deep within me had changed, as if a weight had been lifted from my shoulders. I realised that Christ descended and ascended so that I could ascend with him.

While Josh sat contemplating and rereading this last paragraph, he didn't notice Gawain slip through the door. It wasn't until he moved the chair to sit beside him that Josh realised he was no longer alone. Gawain spoke not a word, but took a sip from Josh's mug, replaced it on the table and sat in silence.

CHAPTER 20

Into The Radiant Light

Megan had grown accustomed to her new environment; she was not looking forward to leaving in the next couple of days. For the first time in her life, she was beginning to feel relaxed and contented. Just before the first light of day, she would sit in silence, waiting; she had begun to control her mind. During the day, she walked the open countryside in deep discussion with Pen. The two had become like soul friends. Pen shared all she knew about the path of the Eternal Flame and the way of the Master. Yet the real transformation for Megan was that she was no longer relying on anyone else to tell her how or what to believe. She dressed in the manner that she wanted. Each day, Josh would come to dwell in her heart. Megan discussed with Pen her behaviour towards Josh in the last few months; she even shared some of the passages that she could remember from the dark journal that she had read with him. It was upon sharing this information that Pen began to see why Gawain had taken the direction he had with the young, lost soul, though she mentioned none of that to Megan. Pen knew, through conversations she had had with him, how deeply it cut his soul that he had not kept his promise to his dear friend and retrieved the dark journal, as it had become known, and destroyed it as Arthur had requested. It was the last promise Gawain had made to the person who saved him. A promise he had broken.

◆ ◆ ◆

Glastonbury was different from how Megan imagined, but then if she was questioned on the subject she would have had to be honest and say she had no idea what to expect, having never been there before. The one thing that struck her was that it was just like any other English village. Wandering down the main street, she paused to scan the windows of some of the New Age shops, moving on quickly if anyone looked in her direction. Lying on the grass in the abbey grounds, it came to her that King Arthur was laid to rest in this same place. The thought of the dead king brought Josh again to mind, Josh and his beloved, bloody book. She longed to know if he was safe and well. Pen later found Megan sitting in the tea shop with a book she had acquired.

"I never knew Joseph came here to this very village and that he brought Jesus with him," Megan remarked without taking her eyes from the book. "Not sure I can believe this," she said as she placed the book on the table, and smiled at Pen.

"Why would you not entertain the possibility that he came here?"

"We all know he lived his life in Palestine."

"Do we? Are you sure of those facts?" Taking a sip from her iced tea, Pen carried on. "From the age of twelve, we have very little information of his life, until he started his ministry at the age of thirty."

"There is no basis for believing he lived anywhere except Palestine and Egypt."

"I wouldn't be so sure. If God was going to take the trouble to come into his creation, why on earth would he stay in just one small part of the world? The Jewish nation was not the only people looking for the coming of the Messiah."

"The Hebrew scriptures speak of him coming."

"So do many others, plus the Hebrew scriptures were known a lot further afield than just Palestine. God created everything and that means every race." Pen paused to order another iced tea from the waitress who had tried to get by unnoticed. "Do you not think he has an interest in every soul?"

Megan and Pen sat in silence for a while, Megan staring out into the clear sky; the waning moon caught her attention and she gazed up at it for quite some time. Was Josh looking at the same moon? Where was he? How could someone so close just vanish without a trace? Would she ever see him again? These thoughts flooded her mind. Making her excuses, Megan stepped quickly out into the open air. Taking her mobile from her coat pocket and turning the caller ID off, she called his mobile; twice she hung up before it could connect. Even though she knew he had left his phone behind, she still called, just in case he had acquired a new one. The third time she waited until it went to voicemail before hanging up, but still without leaving a message. Her palms were sweating and her breathing was irregular.

Pen was sitting in the same position when Megan returned and, placing her phone on silent, she continued drinking her tea. Over the next few days, Pen kept disappearing for a couple of hours at a time, each time on her return divulging no information whatsoever of her whereabouts. Instead, their conversations continued, as they talked now about the practices of neopaganism. Pen explained how Christianity was the natural progression from the pagan understanding of the Divine, in the same way that the Hebrews moved from the worship of many gods before Abraham to believing and worshipping just one. Christ could be seen everywhere and in everything. Many pagans today just did not want to conform so they turned to the old beliefs, believing that you had the right to do and believe in what you liked. However, they soon came to understand that within the different occult groups out there, they had just as much structure and red tape as any of the mainstream religions.

When Megan began to examine her environment more closely, she soon realised that it was only her and Pen left. The waitress stood by the window; it was obvious that she was waiting for someone to meet her from work once everyone had vacated the tea room. Over the next couple of days, Megan found herself at the same table, the only thing that changed besides the conversations with Pen were the different flavoured teas: lemon with honey, mint, green; her favourite was a citrus tea called Blue Lady. While savouring the teas, she travelled back in time to when she and Josh had just started dating. Josh had tried to explain the different teas he had tried from around the world and Blue Lady was one of his favourite ones. While she waited for Pen to join her each time, she allowed her mind to rest on Josh; her heart still ached for him, but the tears had dried up months ago. The small bell above the door rang, bringing Megan back into the present moment. Expecting Pen, she was somewhat disappointed to see a young lady in the most beautiful orange dress, along with matching bag and shoes. The girl greeted the waitress in a rather warm, gentle way, arms around each other, finished off with a small kiss on each cheek. It was obvious that this was a ritual they both shared, showing that she was no stranger to the tea room. Sitting just a few chairs away, she rested her small bag on the table while pulling out a novel; she began to read. When her tea came, for which she thanked the waitress cordially, it was then that Megan sensed that she was Irish, due to her soft, peaceful accent.

The waitress looked around the room making sure no one needed her for a few moments. Sitting opposite this very pleasant girl, they began to share what had happened to each other since they had last met. Megan's heart ached for Josh while the young, Irish girl talked about her time with a young man she had met back in her home country. As she described him, it could have been her Josh she was talking about. Megan tried to hide her smile while the young girl talked about her disapproving uncle who was travelling with the young man. Just as she was about to mention his name, the bell rang above the door to announce the arrival of Pen. Her light blue dress caught the sunlight coming through the window, making it almost see-through. It was not hard to see, either, that the window had not been cleaned in a while, due to smudging from small hands at ground level. Smiling at Pen, she turned her mind back to what was being said on the next table. Megan, to her disappointment, had missed the young man's name. Expecting her friend to walk across the almost empty room, she was taken by surprise when instead Pen called her to the door. As the door closed behind them, Megan looked over her shoulder through the window at the back of the young, Irish girl.

Walking through the abbey grounds, the two inseparable friends linked arms as the sun gently kissed the back of their shoulders with its warmth, only letting go with the passing clouds, leaving a chill in the air each time. For a few weeks now, Megan had been discussing her new path through life. One of her childhood dreams, one that had been frowned upon and squeezed out of her, was the desire to be a writer. Sitting on the grass not far from the old refectory, which was now just a pile of stones, Pen took out of her shoulder bag a national women's magazine. Turning quickly to the third page, she passed it to Megan to read. Her excitement was soon taken over with Megan's shouts of joy.

"I can't believe they printed it." Megan had written a short story, based on her childhood.

"I told you it was good," Pen squealed out.

Even though they had both read through the story a thousand times before, they sat in silence holding hands, reading it once more. Megan was blown away to see her name printed at the bottom. Reaching into the brown envelope that the magazine had come in, she pulled out a letter congratulating Megan on the unique story and enquired if she would like to submit another article for next month. Pen then passed her a cheque that was also in the envelope.

"I can't believe they paid me."

"I told you that if you have faith within yourself you could achieve anything you wanted in life."

Pen watched for a while longer, as her friend read the whole magazine from cover to cover.

"What will you write next?" Pen enquired.

"Another short story, perhaps. Or maybe a novel."

"When we return home, we can find you a nice desk to put in your room."

Two days passed before she saw the young, Irish girl again. This time, she wore a floral green blouse, jeans and sandals. Her hair rested on her shoulders; her walk was of a person who had confidence in herself. Watching from a distance, Megan was surprised when Pen came out of one of the second-hand bookshops carrying her latest purchase and warmly greeted the stranger. It was very clear that they were close. Not wanting to be left out, Megan hastily crossed the road and walked briskly down the street. Seeing her approaching, Pen tried to part company with her long-standing friend and head Megan off, but it was too late.

"Pen, I see you found the book you were talking about." Megan stated the obvious, while looking straight into the eyes of the Irish girl.

"Megan, this is a close friend of mine, Caitlin." Only Pen could see the surprise in Caitlin's eyes at the mention of Megan's name. The description that Josh had given her was perfect.

"Caitlin. That's a beautiful name," Megan commented softly.

"Thank you, it's a family name." Caitlin tried not to be caught by Megan's gaze.

"I saw you the other day – you came into the tea room where I was waiting for Pen."

"Yes, I remember seeing you sitting there, but Pen, I never saw you come in."

"Pen just opened the door and called me out," Megan explained quickly.

Caitlin looked at Pen, knowing that she had seen her that day in the tea shop and knew instantly why she had chosen not to engage with her.

"I hope you don't mind me asking, but you were telling your friend about a young man you had met but I missed his name. It's just that he reminded me of someone I once knew." Before Caitlin could think of a suitable answer, Pen interjected, pointing out that it was rude to listen in on conversations that you were not invited to and even worse then to question people on it. Caitlin knew from Pen's body language that she wanted Caitlin's relationship with Josh kept quiet.

"So, you staying at the Cell?" Pen asked, changing the subject quickly.

"Yes, I just needed some space alone." Caitlin sensed that Pen was fishing to see if Josh and Gawain were nearby.

"I will call by in the morning if that's OK with you?"

"I would like that; it will be good to catch up." Caitlin's smile was genuine, and Pen sensed a deep pain within her close friend.

Wrapping her arms around Caitlin, Pen whispered in her ear for no one else to hear, "I will be there before meditation, say 5.45."

Caitlin nodded as Pen released her grip and she smiled at Megan. "Hope to see you again." With those words her clothes caught the breeze as she turned and walked away briskly to avoid any more questions.

Pen took Megan's arm in hers and turned her to walk in the opposite direction. Megan only looked once over her shoulder to see if Caitlin had changed direction, and then started the interrogation.

"Pen, where do you know her from?" Megan's voice showed a little annoyance that she had greeted Caitlin in such a familiar way.

"We go way back."

"How far?"

"Twenty years, I'd say, maybe more."

"Where did you meet?"

"Dear Megan, my dearest of friends, I was in Ireland visiting a good friend who I am close to."

"Her uncle, by any chance?"

"As a matter of fact it was."

"Your boyfriend?"

Pen laughed, a laugh that was contagious. Megan, realising how she was behaving and the ridiculous line of questioning that was taking place, joined in. A lady in a yellow hat walked by at that moment, giving them both a stern look of disapproval, obviously thinking that they had been drinking. Megan didn't ask any more questions about Caitlin. It might have seemed as if she had forgotten all about the encounter, but that was very far from the truth. Believing Pen would leave after breakfast the next day, she decided she would just tag along.

Not a second before nor a second after 5.45 a.m., Pen walked into where Caitlin was staying; totally centred within, Pen moved with grace and purpose. Her encounter with Caitlin had focused her mind. Realising that all the work she had done with Megan over the months could be brought prematurely to an end and that more serious damage could yet be done, this was no courtesy visit. Megan's friendship and trust had become so very important to her, and losing that was not an option she wanted to consider.

It had been many years since Pen had been to the small cottage. Exactly how many years had passed Pen never stopped to think and it was the last thought on her mind. No one was going to harm Megan, who had become more than a sister to her. Every ounce of her, every atom, showed the magic that dwelt deep within her. Very few people would consider crossing Pen twice when she was in this mood. Pure energy hung in the atmosphere around her and the trail she made in the air behind was like electricity to those who were spirituality alive.

There were only three rooms downstairs (and one of those was the toilet with a small shower cubicle). Upstairs were a further three rooms. Standing alone in two acres of grassland, its views to the west looked up to the tor in the distance and, to the east, a small stone chapel. Calling out, Pen sensed that her young friend had already made her way over to the house of prayer. Walking into the Cell, a name given to the circular room many years before, she lowered her head so she could pass under the low door frame. She never once paused or faltered in her approach. The only furniture in the room was a few benches; the windows were a later addition to the stone walls and curved ceiling. Each window depicted a different stage of the Master's life. One in particular always took her eye: a young teenage boy was walking with his guardian towards a well; in the background, a depiction of the small village from which they were walking was etched into the glass.

Caitlin was sat in the lotus position in the very centre. A sliver of light was already penetrating this holy place; the very tip was now resting in the palms of her hands, in turn resting on the lap of the young girl deep in meditation. Without a word, Pen removed her shoes and sat next to her friend. The sun was well into its ascent, covering the room like a golden blanket with its warmth, before a single word was uttered between them.

Caitlin shared most of what she knew about Josh and the relationship that had grown between him and Gawain. Pen remained seated in the lotus position, eyes softly closed and tilted towards the ground, her breathing remaining balanced while the events of Caitlin's account unfolded. Only when Caitlin's voice changed, when she spoke of her feeling for Josh, did Pen open her eyes to look into the pain deep in her young friend's face. The soft, Irish voice was on the verge of breaking as she described her decision to renew her dedication the path.

"I know Josh was in the place he was because of Megan and the deep love he has for her." While Caitlin revealed her naked feelings, Pen reached out to hold her hand. "He is changing, growing stronger in his mind, and I felt it more helpful for him if I was out of the picture for a while."

Describing the morning when she left everything behind by removing her clothes and entering the golden path, going down into the water, symbolising her death in this world and being reborn, she explained how Gawain was already on the beach that morning, as if he had had some strange, prior knowledge of her intentions. Pen, not wanting to interrupt, kept her thoughts to herself that she believed he knew exactly what was going to happen that day.

"Uncle never said a word, didn't try and stop me." Even though Caitlin was on the verge of tears, she never once let the salt water break from her eyes.

Pen knew of her friend's past, of her time in South America, how her heart had been crushed and how the only option she thought she now had was to try another incarnation. To end it all in some foreign land was the choice Caitlin had made previously and she might have succeeded had Gawain not followed his inner spirit and gone in search of her. Without too much trouble he always could tune into her energy. Caitlin believed, at her very roots, that she owed her uncle everything and Pen sensed this.

"It is important to Gawain that Josh be allowed the opportunity to follow the fire path, to be truly cleansed and renewed."

Pen was beginning to realise the sacrifice her once young student was trying to make. Looking to her left, she contemplated one of the etchings of a mother watching her beloved son ascend into the heavens, knowing that she must let go of the physical if she was to stand any chance of pursuing the spiritual path. Not to let go can hinder, even enslave, an enlightened soul, holding them back from following the golden path. Pen had used this window as a means for contemplation many times in the past. She always wondered if the mother in her early forties knew or understood that one day her close followers would have to let go of her physical body in the same way. It is one of the teachings of any spiritual path that one must move beyond the physical, the material world, if one is aiming to become more enlightened.

Megan lay in the semi-darkness, waiting to hear Pen re-enter the home where they were staying. The click of the kettle stirred her soul to the point she left her room immediately in pursuit of the answers that she knew in her heart she would not find. Two mugs sat on the worktop when she entered the room and Pen sat waiting.

A few days passed without Megan seeing the young, Irish girl again. Pen's unwillingness to talk about her early morning visit, though, had only piqued Megan's curiosity all the more. Sipping green tea in the familiar surroundings of the tea shop, Megan now contemplated why this one person, whom she hardly knew, might have the answers her heart needed to have. Each time the little bell called out that a new person had entered her little oasis, Megan would turn within a blink of an eye. When Caitlin finally entered, Megan's heart fluttered and her adrenaline started to flow; then her heart sank. Behind the one person she had been praying to meet stood Pen. Megan tried not to show her disappointment in the way Pen proceeded to control the conversation.

"I have known Caitlin for more years than I can recall." Pen described their relationship, but something was nagging at the back of Megan's mind that she was not being told the whole story.

"Would you like to walk with me around the abbey later?" Megan refused to look in Pen's direction, making it obvious that she meant just Caitlin.

Caitlin searched Pen's face for the answer to give, but instead Pen smiled and said she thought it would be good for the two to get to know each other. Without giving any warning, she then stood and apologised for having to go early, before leaving the two girls alone. Both could feel the awkwardness in the air. It was not long, though, before they were walking the grounds of the abbey, locked in conversation. After some time, Megan had finished telling her new friend all about Josh and the events that had led her to that very moment. The silence hung between them like a glass wall until Megan shattered it with the question Caitlin was dreading.

"The other day, you were talking of a young man you had just met, and his uncle, was it?"

"It was nothing." Caitlin's reply was measured.

"The way you described him, it made me think of my Josh; what was the boy's name?"

"Megan, what do you know about the path of the Eternal Flame?"

"The soul that walks it must be allowed to do so without any obstacles." Megan paused, turned and looked into Caitlin's eyes. "You are not going to tell me are you?"

"I cannot. It is forbidden."

"That's silly! I don't even know him."

Linking her arm through Megan's, Caitlin put her energy into their walk through the ancient surroundings, her hair bouncing slightly upon her shoulders. Even her voice changed, lifting up the tempo somehow.

"Have you seen the resting place of the greatest warrior that ever walked this magical land?"

"Arthur?" As the words slipped through Megan's moist lips, both girls thought of the same Arthur, but for different reasons and in contrasting ways. To Megan, the thoughts were dark and related to the many nights she and Josh would sit in bed reading together from Arthur's journal. If it wasn't for her deep love for Josh, she would curse the man. Caitlin's thoughts were full of light as she held Arthur in such high esteem. Both longed to share with him the effect he had had on their separate lives. Megan blamed him for the break up of her relationship with her soul friend and for his disappearance; Caitlin was forever grateful to him for guiding and teaching others in the quest for the Eternal Flame, the very path that shaped her life and would do so for her beloved friend. She would thank Arthur for bringing them together. Both girls longed to see Josh; only one knew she had a rival.

During the next few days, Pen allowed the two girls to mould the foundations of their relationship. She knew if they were going to come through the next stage of their journey together they would all need a strong bond that could withstand the earth-shattering revelations of what was to come. There was no other emotion that could destroy or fuse together a relationship more than love.

Megan had, by now, become accustomed to the early mornings. Caitlin had called a little after 5.30, with an ethereal mist still hanging in the cool air. Megan felt the dew penetrating her old boots, which didn't protect her feet one bit from the damp earth. Old, but new to Megan, nearly every stitch of clothing came from a number of second-hand shops she had visited over the last six months. The only new clothes were her underwear: this was where she drew the line, she had reasoned to herself.

It was a magical climb up to the tor. The mist lifted just as they reached the summit, allowing the morning sun to break through and allow the colours of the meadow below them to shine through. The bright flowers were enriched by the sun's presence. In the distance, dedicated dog walkers were weaving through the landscape.

They stood in silence for what seemed a considerable time, but in reality it was less than a couple of minutes. The mind, the waves that carry our every thought, move faster than the speed of light and are never restricted to this time frame. One moment it can be in the past and the very next second, our thoughts can be pushing the boundaries of the future, like scouts mapping out limitless opportunities for us if only we dare act upon them. Seldom does an untrained mind dwell in the present moment. Within less than a minute, Caitlin's mind had retraced the time on Holy Island when she'd stood from her meditation and entered the radiant light, that moment on the beach when she had let go of the past and all that chained her. Her thoughts raced through the time that had passed to the present moment. The two people in her life that she looked up to, the two she admired to the point that she wanted to be like them, the two who had had the most impact upon her life, were Gawain and Pen. How much she wanted what they had and believed the only way she could achieve that was to leave herself behind and surrender to the Master and to her path.

"Megan, you are familiar with the Hebrew scriptures?"

"Living with Josh it was hard not to be." Caitlin thought, as she responded in the affirmative, while keeping her heart's immediate response to herself.

"God heard the people of Israel crying out for help."

"Egypt…" Megan was going to say more but Caitlin was in full teaching mode.

"They were in the misery of slavery when they called out, asking to be set free. How easy it is for the past, most of all bad habits, to hold us in a similar kind of slavery. The Israelites were rescued via the Red Sea (or as it can be known, the radiant sea). So it is that we all have to pass through the sea if we want to be set free, made new, enter the promised land, or as some say, make new beginnings. You too must enter the golden path. In the same way as an alchemist turns iron into gold, so can the Master change our souls into something more pure, more valuable than gold."

"From what I can remember from the story, didn't they want to go back to Egypt?"

"It is hard to break away from our old ways; it is always easier to go backwards than forwards. To step out afresh into uncharted territory is difficult and trying; it's always more convenient to stick with what you know."

"Radiant sea?" Megan asked.

"Pen spoke with you about the path of the Eternal Flame, didn't she?"

"While we were in Ireland we studied it, practised it." Megan paused, while thinking through her next couple of sentences. "I like to believe I walk that path."

Caitlin's smile was warm and reassuring that she approved. "I too follow the path."

"Pen follows, but she tries to convince me that she follows the way of Christ."

"She does."

Those simple words shocked Megan, while at the same time it made sense. Within Megan there was the struggle that takes place inside us all, bringing Christ from the past into the present moment, letting go of what others say about him and knowing him for ourselves. The words Pen had used flowed through Megan's mind: "To know Christ, you must let go of yourself."

◆ ◆ ◆

On the first day of the third week that the three had been together, Pen suggested that it was time for the next stage of Megan's path. The three walked through the fields at the darkest part of the night, or at least it always seemed that way, that short time before the dawn. Pen and Caitlin knew the path very well. The great light broke into the darkened world in the same way it had for billions of years, sharing its life-giving energy. Sitting on pebbles in front of a dark, moving mass, the great light danced across the lake chasing the shadows. It never failed to move Pen when finally she saw the golden path slowly unfolding across the water offering a safe haven for all in need of help. When the path reached the side of the lake where they were sitting, Megan stood, her clothes falling to the ground, and allowed the chill of the morning to caress her pale, naked body. Her once smooth skin was covered in thousands of little bumps. Caitlin did the same. Walking into the water, Caitlin took hold of Megan's hands, smiled, and then both girls submerged their nakedness into the freezing lake. Within seconds, they broke through into the new world, wholly cleansed from the past. As they rose, Pen was taken by the beauty of their bodies against the golden light. She watched as both girls pushed their wet hair back with their hands as the water flowed off their figures. The three ladies were unaware that just a few hundred miles away on the east coast of Britain, a young man with his guide was carrying out the very same ritual in the same golden path.

◆ ◆ ◆

Over the next few weeks, Pen stood at a distance and watched Megan grow under Caitlin's magic. She smiled inwardly. She was proud of what she had achieved in such a short time since she had known Megan. As their lives became evermore entwined, it was only Pen, however, who witnessed the two men stepping down from the bus that day. Her friend had aged since she had last laid eyes on him. Letting her eyes fall upon his much younger companion, Pen saw the remarkable resemblance to Arthur.

CHAPTER 21

Tears Of Joy

As the afternoon wore on, Pen took Caitlin aside to share with her what she had witnessed earlier that day. Pen could tell, and Caitlin didn't even try to hide, that she was not surprised.

"You were expecting them?"

Caitlin, taking hold of Pen's hand and without any expression on her face, looked straight into her eyes as she spoke both calmly and directly.

"We both knew that one day the two of them would arrive here. It's where the first part of the path of the Eternal Flame finishes. So please don't try and make out you didn't know what you were doing when you brought Megan here." Caitlin turned to walk away, but then changed her mind. "What were you thinking bringing Megan here? You were asked to help her and from what I have learnt, you have succeeded in releasing her from those chains that held her back in life. As long as I have known her she has been a very balanced and capable person and now you're about to send her back in time? And have you thought through the effect it will have on Josh?"

"Megan has a right to be here; she has a right to be allowed to grow too."

"And Josh?"

"I am guiding Megan."

"Why here? Why now?" Caitlin was becoming increasingly impatient.

"Your concern: is it for Megan, Josh or yourself?"

"I am not sure I understand what you are implying!"

"Oh, I feel that you do. Megan shared with me the conversation she overheard you and your waitress friend having in the tea room."

"You are right." Caitlin's voice changed and so did her aura. "I got close to him; I let my guard down and started to have feelings for him." Caitlin turned and began to walk away.

"Does he have feelings for you?" Pen called out after her. She received no reply.

On her walk back to the place she had been calling home, Caitlin didn't know how she was going to explain her presence to her uncle. Once he knew she was in Glastonbury, he would not be too happy and knowing that Megan was here too might just blow his mind. It took four times as long as it should have done to reach her destination.

Standing motionless at the door, she felt deep in her heart that she had returned to her spiritual home. Her hand resting on the door handle, her heart beat faster as the handle turned, knowing that it was not she who was turning it. Gawain smiled when their eyes met, his arms folded around her and it felt good, it felt safe. Before the young woman could say a word, her guardian explained how it was right for her to be in Glastonbury. Caitlin pulled away so she could look her uncle in the eyes as she told him about Megan and Pen being there too. But he was not surprised, just as nothing surprised her any more about the father figure in her life.

261

"I know Megan and Pen are here too. I felt their presence at the same time I felt yours. It's what prompted me to bring Josh here so soon." Taking Caitlin's hand, he led her into the kitchen. "Don't worry. Josh is meditating in the Cell."

"Does he know we are all here?"

"Not sure. He has been very quiet since we arrived – I'm not sure if he senses you or Megan, or if it is because he feels he has unsettled me."

"What did he do?"

"Nothing, he is doing very well. The seed that Arthur planted so many years ago has been growing in him for some time; it just needed a little help to find the light again. I helped to remove the weeds that were choking him."

"So why does he feel that he has upset you?"

"Your energy changed when you came here; it always does when Pen is around, and if Pen was near you, so was Megan. Josh and I still had a few weeks' walking before we would arrive and you would have known that. I couldn't take the chance that you would leave and, if you left, so would have Pen. I felt that it is more important for all of your paths to be here at the same time, all three of you."

"Three?"

"Yes, all three of you: Megan, Pen and you all have an important role to play, not only in your own path, but each other's too. It's time for Josh and Megan to spend time with each other; either their path is together or it isn't, plus you need to know where Josh's true feeling lie and if your paths are joined or not."

"And Pen?"

Gawain, taking the only member of his family into the main living area, closed the door behind them. Placing the kettle back on to the stove, he took a match and lit the gas. The aroma of sulphur filled the room. Two backpacks sat on the floor near the window looking toward the hut. Watching Gawain place just two mugs on the rather worn worktop, it showed Caitlin that they were going to be alone for a while. She pulled a chair closer to the table as she waited for her uncle to join her. Within those few short moments her thoughts travelled once more through time and space. Her uncle had been right to assume that she had planned in her heart to leave before the two of them arrived. Her time with Pen and Megan had been difficult and rewarding at the same time. Over the short space of time she had spent with Megan she had become fond of her, to the point that she now had an interest in the development of her path. After giving Gawain time to answer, which did not take too long, she asked once more. "Pen. Why is it important for her to be here?"

Taking a chair across from Caitlin, Gawain raised his cup and started sipping his tea while he watched Caitlin's eyes for some time before any sound left his lips.

"After spending some time with Josh, then speaking with Silver, it was evident that there is one thing in this world that could cloud Pen's judgement: a relationship that would bring to the surface a reminder of what had happened to her sister. From what I hear, Megan could be her twin."

"What happens when Josh finds out what you have done?"

"Please enlighten me on what that would be."

"Lied."

"Have I?"

"You never told him that you knew that Megan was safe and with a good friend of yours. How do you think he will act when he finally finds out?"

263

Gawain described his walk, physical and spiritual, since Caitlin had decided to leave. He spoke of the many hours that he and Josh had spent in discussion about the work Arthur had been involved in and how important it was that it still carried on. For the first time in his life, he shared a little of Arthur's journal. Arthur was quite clear of the importance of keeping a confidence, that there would be times a guide would have to protect, shield, a soul in their care. Caitlin listened to the lessons Josh had learnt, the answers he had given and the depth to which he had grown. Knowing that Josh studied theology, and already had a great depth and understanding of spirituality that was built upon the foundations that his grandfather had started, it was not surprising the ground that he had covered in such a short space of time. Caitlin closed her eyes as she listened to the account of the silver path, of how Josh had entered the water on the east coast, not far from Whitby. In her mind, she could see his naked body walking upon the white sand, entering the silver path. Josh turned, lying back, as if to let his body float while he watched the dawn rise and the golden path replace the silver one. Caitlin knew her uncle would never share with her the lesson that Josh had learnt, but she understood the teaching of the golden light. Gawain was not at all surprised when Caitlin described that Megan too had been learning about the path of the Eternal Flame and her time of entering the golden path, but unlike Josh, she had not walked the way of the moon. The reason for that being that only Gawain knew its teaching.

When Josh left the Cell it was almost dark; he could just make out the tor as he walked prayerfully towards the kitchen door. During his time in the Cell, he had contemplated the drawings on each of the windows. Gawain had told him to find the depiction that spoke to him the most. For a time, he had sat looking at the Ascension, remembering his grandfather's account of his time by the canal, watching the dog fall into the water. He allowed his mind to dwell on the old man whom he had met on Iona before Gawain turned up. In those, his darkest moments, the Master had come to him and stayed until one of his disciples arrived to carry on his work. Josh smiled to think that's exactly what happened two thousand years ago: the Master came and stayed until the disciples were ready to carry on his work. Then he saw a shepherd with a lamb resting across his shoulders; Magi bearing gifts (and he had smiled to himself when he thought one looked like Gawain). The image that drew his attention and held it for longer was of a young boy holding his guardian's hand while walking to a well with a small village in the background. Josh knew this was Jesus with Joseph of Arimathea. Josh stood for a few moments looking through the window, watching Gawain drinking his tea alone. By the time he had reached the kitchen door, the room was empty.

It was late when Caitlin tapped on Tina's door. The waitress from the tea room had been home for hours and was just going to turn the lights out for the night. Tina asked no questions as her friend placed her bags on the floor next to the sink.

"May I use your spare room, just for a few nights?" Caitlin asked.

"Sure, stay as long as you like." Tina smiled, and then started to laugh as she pointed out, "I am not cooking, or making you tea, though – that's not my job here."

Caitlin too began to laugh; she walked to the kettle and started to make them both a drink. She smiled when there was only English breakfast in the cupboard.

"Which window were you drawn to last night?" Gawain sat opposite a very tired young man at the breakfast table. Breakfast was egg on toast with some mushrooms that Gawain had collected from his early morning walk.

"The one of Jesus walking, holding hands with Joseph, towards a well."

"Why that one in particular?"

"It reminded me of my time with my grandfather, and my time with you, leading me to a spiritual well to drink from. It tells the story of all disciples; that we walk not only with the Master but guide others too. It is the true calling to walk hand in hand with others."

Gawain nodded very slightly to show he approved of the reason Josh had given and then added, "If the legend is true, then Joseph would have taken him out into the world, a trait that all true disciples must follow. But before they can do that, they have to know themselves. The 'seed' your grandfather once spoke to you about is not only your faith but your intentions of what to do with that faith. Which path do you want to walk? I have brought you to this mystical place, to Glastonbury, where you need to ask yourself a very important question. Over the next few days, your world will hold many options. Keep focused on the work and growth that you have achieved over the last year. There will be voices hiding in the shadows calling you back into the darkness of your mind. What you have experienced and come to believe and know will be difficult for you to describe to others. Hold in your mind Plato's cave; it is hard, if not impossible, to go back to the place you once held. Remember the Israelites once they had crossed the radiant light and found themselves in the wilderness, wanting to turn back. It was hard to rely on the Creator; it's even harder to change and move forward. So many step out on the road of new beginnings, each year so many people make a New Year's resolution, only to go back to the old ways within a few weeks. The one constant in creation is change: the world, the universe and humanity are changing. They change together because they are all one. Since the beginning of our conception as the human race, called into being in the image of God, the closest reflection we have of the Divine is the life of the Master. Josh, you know your grandfather always told you the truth, but you also know now that he kept certain revelations from you too."

Josh acknowledged that he understood before Gawain proceeded. "I too have kept certain revelations from you while you have walked the path."

Josh knew deep in his soul it was fruitless to ask what the dark secret was that was troubling his friend so. He knew enough by the expression imprinted upon the face in front of him.

"Whatever it is, old friend, I will not let it come between us."

"I wouldn't be so sure about that." With those words Gawain retired for the night.

Josh was left to spend the next day at the Cell contemplating the stories within the windows, not that it was part of Josh's path but Gawain needed to make sure he stayed away from the town until he had had chance to meet with Pen. It wasn't hard to track his friend down. The climb up to the tor was pleasant; the sun, hidden behind low clouds, had not yet reached its peak. Pen sat there, resting on the grass and looking out over fields. Sensing Gawain's approach, she rose to greet him warmly and they stayed embraced in each other's arms for longer than one would expect from just friends.

"It's so good to see you after such a long time," Pen whispered into his ear.

"Too long."

Sitting back down on the grass together, they took it in turns to share the last year, talking about every single moment. It was 3.47 p.m. by the time they walked into the town.

"When are you going to tell Josh about Megan?" Pen enquired.

"Not sure. He has read Arthur's accounts of the work we do."

"Do you think he will understand, then? Will he not think you have been lying to him?"

"I have told him that there are things I have kept from him while we have been together, but how he will react I won't know till the time comes. What are you going to say to Megan?"

"I will tell her the truth."

"When?"

"Tonight."

"Then I will sit Josh down and do the same." With those last words Gawain kissed Pen, turned and walked away.

Once Tina left for work, Caitlin found herself wandering, cleaning and tidying Tina's small house. It didn't take long to make her way through the two rooms downstairs and then her own room and the bathroom, but she hesitated at Tina's bedroom door. When her mother was alive, they would talk for hours if there was ever anything that Caitlin needed to work through. Nowadays, she would clean her house whenever she had an important question on her mind. Should she go and see Josh and tell him about Megan or leave it to her uncle? Her head was clear. It was down to Gawain and she should – at all costs to herself – stay away. Her heart, however, told her that if she didn't tell him she could lose him forever. One of the most important lessons of the path, she knew, was always to listen to the heart; the heart never lies, whereas the mind can deceive or distort its perception of any situation. Caitlin at that moment decided to head straight for the Cell and the arms of Josh.

Megan had never been to the Cell, but had a good idea of its location, and had heard both Pen and Caitlin discussing its windows. When neither one turned up at the tea room, and not having seen Pen all day, Megan finished her drink, picked her shoulder bag from the back of the chair and headed out of the town in the direction she had watched Caitlin take on more than one occasion. After fifteen minutes' walking in the beautiful sunlight, she came across a narrow drive on her right. Following her intuition, she walked briskly away from the road and it wasn't long before the small cottage was in sight. At first, she knocked on the door, and then tried the handle; once inside the kitchen she soon realised that the place was empty. Standing at the kitchen sink, she reached out to feel the kettle. It had boiled in the last hour or so. Two mugs sat in the sink. Out of the window she could see what she understood to be the Cell just a few hundred yards from the house. The grass was longer than it should have been in Megan's mind and she laughed within herself knowing that Josh would never allow the grass in their garden to grow so long. At the Cell door she paused to look up at the tor; she could just make out two lovers walking down the slope but without giving them another thought she pushed the door open.

Caitlin paused before crossing the road and heading up the short lane to let a couple of cyclists pass her as they headed into town. She smiled as she overheard them talking of their forthcoming visit to the local pub. It was the last time Caitlin paused before bursting spontaneously into a sprint. Seeing Megan come out of the cottage and head towards the Cell was not a sight Caitlin was expecting. Moving like a panther after its prey, she knew within her very soul that she would not be in time. *Why had she left it so late to set off?* was the main question flying through her mind, as her legs became tired and her breath bit into her lungs. She was too late and too far away as she watched Megan open the door and step inside.

Pen stopped first at the tea shop and was surprised not to find the girls in there in deep conversation; the rooms where they were staying had not been disturbed for some time either. Looking out of the window towards the tor, Pen's heart stopped at the very moment that her mind realised where her young friend was. Knocking the lamp over in her haste to leave the room, Pen didn't stop to see it smash as it came into contact with the tiled floor, sending debris in all directions. Her only concern was to reach the Cell. It took eight minutes for her to reach the short lane, a record for Pen. Seeing Caitlin in the distance reach the Cell door and begin to open it was not a sight she wanted to see and yet trying to run faster was an impossibility, her legs already felt like dead weights.

Megan was taken by surprise to see a male figure sitting in the corner waiting patiently, his hands resting on his lap. He had a smile that touched her heart. She had no idea who the stranger was, but she knew he meant her no harm. Megan closed the door behind her. The older gentleman stood, while holding out his hand towards her and softly speaking her name. Something deep inside Megan made her realise that it was no coincidence that the stranger was sitting here waiting for her. From the very moment she rose from her bed there had been a deep urge for her to visit this place. Megan could not help but notice how faded his dungarees were and the brown gloves sticking out of his back pocket; she surmised that he was someone who worked with his hands, and yet somehow beyond her reasoning and understanding, she knew that he was more than just a labourer. Very few words were shared between them. For the first time in her life she felt whole. Taking the hand he offered, they walked to the window where there were two seats opposite each other. She sat down with the majestic old gentleman and he spoke to her heart. Megan knew that the words that he spoke she would share with no one. One lonely tear broke free to run down her cheek: it was a tear neither of sadness nor of grief but one of realisation, of joy, understanding and freedom. Megan knew then that before nightfall came she would have the opportunity to speak with her soul friend. She also knew if anyone asked her to explain how she knew this and why she felt so sure in her heart, she would be lost for words. This encounter didn't make any sense, it wasn't logical. But in some inexplicable way, the pure and untainted love that radiated from the person in front of her helped to make sense of all that Pen had been teaching her. The touch of his hands, the softness of his words, were like balm to her. The pain of life's disappointments faded away. The whole encounter, for as long as it continued, seemed to be lasting for a lifetime. When the door opened and Pen and Caitlin entered, she realised it was just a few short moments that she had spent in the presence of the Divine. Turning back to the gentleman

271

in front of her she was not surprised to find that he was no longer there. Her hands could still feel the softness of his touch, her soul the deepest understanding of transformation. Her eyes rested on the window of Christ leaving the tomb. She understood the true meaning of the resurrection in every cell of her being, though if she tried to put it into words she knew she would fail. Standing to face her friends it was hard to understand the look of total bewilderment written across their faces. Both seemed short of breath, both gave the impression that when they opened the door they were expecting something completely different.

Gawain found Josh at the edge of a small stream, sitting with his back rested against some large stones. Sitting himself down softly next to him, Gawain sensed a deep shift within his young charge.

"You want to share your thoughts?"

"I was sitting in the Cell this morning when the old man whom I first met in Iona came and sat beside me. We talked about all that had happened this last year."

"What did he say?"

"That I would see Megan before the day was through."

"Is that why you are hiding out here?"

"In a short answer, yes."

"Do you not want to see her, spend time catching up?"

"I want to see her, to hold her, but…" Josh looked into the distance as if he had seen something of great interest. "I want to finish what I have started too, the path, I mean."

"Whatever you do, it will be your path."

"I love Megan, but I feel that is in the past. I have changed; I am not the same person that she once knew."

"Megan will have changed too."

"You knew she would be coming here, didn't you?"

Silence answered the question.

"How long have you known where Megan was?"

"A while."

"You chose to keep it from me."

"In truth, yes, and the reason, I think you know." Gawain's tone was soft but sharp.

The two walked into town, at a pace that would not break a sweat, as Josh searched the faces of everyone he passed. At each shop he paused slightly to scan, hoping to catch a sight of Megan. There were very few people in the tea room. Taking a table in the corner, Gawain knew he could see the door open and who came in. Each time the bell rang Josh looked. An old lady came in with the aid of a walking frame. It took ages for her to reach the first seat she came to. Looking in Josh's direction she smiled. Josh turned back to his now empty cup, promising himself not to look again. He didn't. The door opened and closed many times but he resisted the temptation to glance across the room. When Gawain rose from his chair Josh just assumed that he was fetching the coffee. When he didn't return, only then did Josh begin to scan the room. Through the very murky window he found his guide deep in conversation with a blonde woman. It was like watching a silent movie; the lady was more animated than Gawain. They were not alone. Josh could not see their faces from where he was sitting, only part of their clothes protruding into sight from the edge of the window. Both Gawain and a now very excited lady looked in his direction, making him feel very uncomfortable, to the point he had to look away.

Outside the tea room, only Caitlin understood the Gaelic, which rendered Megan very confused. To her surprise,

273

Caitlin joined in speaking in the strange language but only briefly, before turning round on her heels and walking away with what Pen would call an attitude.

When the bell of the door rang yet again, Josh didn't move. When the voice from the past came, a cold chill covered his whole being. The chair in front of him moved just enough for one of his soul friends to sit down. Josh never breathed a word; his eyes were finding it hard to take in the beautiful image now seated in front of him. He knew without a doubt it was Megan but she looked so different, so young. Her hair now fell on her shoulders, her clothes were relaxed and not at all businesslike. Resting her hand on his she spoke.

"Josh, it's good to see you."

Josh smiled, held her hands within his. "It's good to see you too. How have you been?"

"Good, thank you, extremely good. And you?"

Josh smiled and nodded his head slightly, while at the same time gently squeezing her hand. "You want to walk?"

During the short walk to the door, both looked at their guides sitting near the window; neither were surprised that they knew each other. Within less than ten minutes they were deep into the countryside. Not knowing what do with their loose hands they both fumbled with their fingers. Time evaporated, minutes into hours, each taking it in turns to describe the path that they had travelled since they last saw each other.

"You still read your grandfather's journal?" Megan half whispered.

"Not the dark journal."

"Dark?" Megan sounded surprised to hear him use the word to describe his once most treasured possession in the world, the same word she had once used to curse it.

"Yes, it was dark and you were right when you tried to point it out to me. Gawain burnt it a few months back." Josh went on to explain the two journals. Megan sat transfixed at the way Josh was describing his grandfather and the work in which he had once been involved. At the same time, at the back of her mind she was beginning to make sense of her own time with Pen. The path of which Josh was speaking was the path she herself now walked.

"Your grandfather stopped believing after he met Jonathan," Megan interrupted.

"In the new writings I have, Grandfather explained all that. He wrote about it and I can now remember him telling me over and over when I was a child: *Be careful on what you feed the mind; its diet will have a great effect upon it.* Through his studies, he found that there were several flaws within Jonathan's journals. One in particular concerned Horus, the story that not only crushed his faith but mine too for a time. Like my grandfather I also spent hours studying, searching for evidence that Horus could be compared with the Master. Believe me, I searched hard because I wanted it to be true. But it is not. It is completely different – an embellishment of the truth to deflect people from their path." As Josh finished, he went silent, while at the same time a smile covered his face.

"I know," Megan blurted out. "I too searched through Pen's extensive library looking for answers, even though Pen pointed out on many occasions that there was not a shred of evidence to link the two together."

Josh went on to explain how Gawain had his own theory of why Jonathan's journals disturbed his grandfather so. "Because his mind was submerged in darkness, he never finished reading the journal; he took what he wanted to believe from the pages to make sense of his own grief and his own beliefs at that time. He was so angry with the Master and with the world and he would have believed anything that disproved the Creator. A bit like yours truly, I guess. If he had carried on studying the pages in front of him and was in the right frame of mind, Gawain thinks he might have come to a different conclusion." The tone of Josh's voice softened: "Arthur met someone who changed his life; he was not the same person whom we saw within the pages of that earlier journal."

"I can see that now." Megan paused, and then took a deep breath before carrying on. "You say he knew Gawain. Did he know Pen too?"

"I believe so, yes."

Megan started to laugh.

"You want to share the joke?"

"I want to be so cross with Pen, but I can't. She might have deceived me, or I might have deceived myself, but I don't care. She is one of the best friends I have ever had."

Entering the outskirts of Glastonbury, Josh stopped and faced Megan. Taking her hands in his he asked her how long she was going to be staying. With the reassurance that she had no immediate plans to leave, he took her in his arms and held her.

Megan once more reached the tea rooms to find that only Pen remained. Placing her book on the table, she motioned with her hand for her young friend to join her.

"Are you going to share?" Pen asked finally.

"We talked through all the events of the last year, if that's what you mean."

"Are you seeing him again?"

"We did talk about where we go from here, but neither one of us had the answer."

"What do you want to do?"

Pen knew the moment the words left her lips; she regretted asking, putting her friend on the spot like that. Deep down within her soul, Pen did not want to lose Megan.

From the upstairs window Gawain watched a confused Josh walk down the lane, making his way to the Cell. Half tempted to divert him, he decided to let him encounter Caitlin, who was already deep in prayer within the walls of the Cell. Mindfully opening the door Josh was lost in thought about the afternoon's walk with his soulmate; after dinner he had planned to walk back into town and find her. Caitlin looked up at the click of the latch to see her lover as if frozen to the spot. Josh's heart was now completely confused. All thoughts of visiting the town later that night vanished.

When Caitlin and Josh both entered the kitchen Gawain had already started preparing dinner. The aroma suddenly reminded Josh that he had not eaten all day. The three sat deep in conversation. Josh was not at all disturbed that Caitlin and Megan had already become acquainted. That night, while Josh struggled to find sleep, he became aware that not once on entering his room had he thought about either Megan or Caitlin. A lot had happened to him, he had changed and was for first time in his life free and excited by his path and the life he could lead with Gawain. The seed that Arthur planted so many years ago was now beginning to blossom. He could see it in himself, feel it.

Josh sat staring out over the rolling hills. The tor was just to his right. The early morning light kissed his face. He had made his decision and was now ready to pay the heavy cost.

A couple of days had passed since he had first laid eyes on Megan, and held Caitlin in his arms. He had spent time alone with each of them but never together. The most rewarding time he had spent in those few days was with Pen. She had requested time alone with him. They talked about Arthur and Josh began to see how many lives his grandfather had touched. At one point he could see her love for Arthur in her eyes and hear it on her lips. She had refused to share any information with him about Megan.

The sound of soft footsteps on the grass behind him, mixed with a waft on the breeze of a familiar perfume, stirred Josh's spirit. There was no need to turn around. He knew that his true soul friend was approaching. She stood behind him and rested her hands on his shoulders.

Leaning forward to kiss the back of his head, she asked, "Josh, may I accompany you on the next step of your path?" Tears ran down his face, not tears of sadness or despair, but of jubilation and pure joy.

"Yes, completely. I would welcome your company, your strength." With those words Josh stood up, taking his soul friend into his arms. Looking into her eyes at that moment, he said with utter conviction, "I have my faith back. I truly believe in the Master."

"That makes two of us. You will never be alone again."

At those words Josh embraced and kissed his companion and they stepped out on to their continuing path together.

ACKNOWLEDGEMENTS

I first encountered Josh in the recesses of my imagination in the summer of 2009. I was on sabbatical from my work as a parish priest and was undertaking my journey of the soul to Iona, Lindisfarne and Whitby. As I began to write Josh's story, the beginnings of In his Grandfather's Shadow were set.

It has been a long time and a steep learning curve for me from those early stages to the book you now hold. From a rough first draft, I am indebted to those trusted friends who were prepared to read Josh's story, see its potential and offer their ongoing encouragement that I should publish it. Notably, I wish to acknowledge the invaluable wisdom and guidance from Bob, Catherine, Jonathan, Joy, Karan and Larry. I have been amazed how each person who has read it so far has taken a different perspective on this tale of Josh and Megan, Gawain and Caitlin, each one finding it speaks to their situation, whatever their spiritual path or none.

I couldn't have got this far without the professionalism, support and insight from everyone at SpiffingCovers, for which I am forever grateful. It is only right that I acknowledge here that some of the chapter headings owe their inspiration from phrases within T.S. Eliot's Four Quartets, but I trust that these homages are sufficiently brief as to be within the permissible use of copyrighted material.

The story is written for all those who have journeyed the ways of this life, anyone seeking a spiritual path of their own. But especially, it is for Matthew and Daniell who never hesitated to back this crazy idea of their Dad's to write and publish a book. And to Monique, for your patience and belief as I have set out on this alternative path. Thank you always.